Born in Newcastle upon Tyne, Danielle gained her BA in History of Modern Art, Design & Film at Northumbria University and MA in Creative Writing at Newcastle University. In 2013 she founded *Riposte*, a bi-annual print publication that offers a diverse and nuanced reflection on the lives of modern women which has attracted a loyal readership and following world-wide. She has written for other publications including *Refinery29*, *Vogue* and *Metro* amongst others. She currently lives in London with her husband and daughter. This is her debut collection of short stories.

Chosen as one of the 'Best New Book Releases'
by *Cosmopolitan*

Chosen as a 'Summer Blockbuster Book'
by *Elle*

Praise for *Watching Women & Girls*:

'Danielle Pender examines the pillars of female life – love, duty, ambition, friendship and sex – from every angle'

Vogue

'Danielle Pender explores that impact on women's exterior and interior lives with brevity, depth and wry humour'

The Face

T0049870

'*Watching Women & Girls* is a searing meditation on the moments that make, and break, us. As canny as they are entertaining, these stories are packed with emotional intelligence, capturing the dark and the light of the female experience in a series of vignettes that every one of us will in some way relate to. I loved it'

CHARLOTTE PHILBY, author of *The Second Woman*

'A page-flipping joy of a read. Pender is a generous writer and observer of society who incisively captures what it is to be a woman in our times'

CHARLOTTE JANSEN, author of *Girl on Girl*

'Smart and astute, funny and wry; a catalogue of the modern conditions of dating, working and being. It encouraged me to pay more attention to the world around me and the secret lives of those in it'

AMELIA ABRAHAM, author of *Queer Intentions*

'A moving collection'   *Grazia*

'To see, be seen and know that you are, always, being watched. That is the experience of being a woman today. This thoughtful, meditative and, at times, absurdly funny collection is a reminder that someone is, always, looking right back'   VICKY SPRATT, author of *Tenants*

'A beautifully written exploration of woman and girlhood, with all of its contradictions and quirks. Danielle is a sharp new talent'   SIRIN KALE

'Vibrant, intense and darkly comic this is a powerful and thoughtful collection told through closely observed, spellbinding characters that stay with you'

ABIGAIL BERGSTROM, author of *What a Shame*

'Pender cleverly picks up on how women subvert this gaze and how the perform for it, internalise it, police themselves and project it'   *The Debut Digest*

Watching Women & Girls

A COLLECTION OF SHORT STORIES

Danielle Pender

4th ESTATE • *London*

4th Estate
An imprint of HarperCollins*Publishers*
1 London Bridge Street
London SE1 9GF

www.4thEstate.co.uk

HarperCollins*Publishers*
Macken House, 39/40 Mayor Street Upper
Dublin 1, D01 C9W8, Ireland

First published in Great Britain in 2022 by 4th Estate
This 4th Estate paperback edition published in 2023

3

ISBN 978-0-00-847250-4

Set in Berling LT Std
Printed and bound in the UK using 100%
renewable electricity at CPI Group (UK) Ltd

MIX
Paper | Supporting
responsible forestry
FSC™ C007454

For Mazzy, Mia and Lola.
Always stare back.

Contents

Window Display

The man on the next table to Laura wasn't saying anything interesting but you wouldn't know that by looking at his lunch date. She was engrossed. Her eyes were locked onto his face, her arm mechanically delivered food to her mouth which she chewed and swallowed without tasting. She took large gulps of her white wine as he got deeper into his story about conference calls, diary clashes and difficult clients. She laughed so hard at one point that Laura couldn't help but stare directly at the couple. The woman's mouth was wide open, her head thrown back in religious rapture, her teeth were full of parsley. She punctuated the performance with a breathless 'Ah, that was so funny' and wiped her eyes with a napkin.

Was it? Laura thought. Was anything ever really that funny? How many times do you laugh so hard that you cry actual tears of joy? Once a week, once a month, once a year? It definitely doesn't happen on a Tuesday lunchtime during a conversation about production schedules. She looked at her own lunch companion. A small, drooling child returned her gaze and dropped a teething toy onto the floor. Laura picked up the wet plastic ring and gave it back to the child without wiping it. Between them, a decaying compost heap of food had been picked at and randomly sucked, but not eaten.

Tuning out of her own lunch situation and back into the couple's next to her she deciphered that they both worked at the same advertising agency and were sleeping together. Based on the man's love of his own mediocre ideas, Laura guessed he was a creative director. His Japanese denim and rare trainers were an attempt to pass for mid-thirties but his receding hairline and sagging jowls placed him nearer fifty. The woman was young. From her plump skin and decision to wear high heels during the day Laura guessed she was mid-twenties. She was very concerned with schedules, a client called Raymond and whether it would rain that weekend. Her patchy make-up gathered in the folds around her nose and her mousy brown hair was cut into a style that made her look like her name was Louise. In the open bag at the young woman's feet, Laura spotted a tester-sized bottle of Tom Ford perfume, a thin dirty purse and a strangled Glossier tube of Cherry Balm Dotcom.

'She's great. Very creative, kind of obscure but you know, I introduced her to all of the references that she used in that campaign,' the man said, pushing his half-eaten dish away from him.

'I saw that spot she made. She's done so well. I didn't know she'd worked in your team.' The young woman tucked her hair behind her ears and decided that she was also done with her starter.

'Yeah. She was straight out of college when she came to us.'

'Oh, right.'

'It was a couple of years ago. She was my protégée … I'm like her Aristotle.' The man grinned animatedly. Having already drained his own glass he reached over to swill the remains of her white wine into his mouth.

The woman balanced her fork very precisely on top of her knife and asked, 'You're her, her what?' Sounding slightly confused.

'I was her teacher.' His response was curt. 'I'm like Aristotle, the teacher, and she's Plato, my famous student.'

'I'm pretty sure it's the other way around, isn't it?' She paused. 'Plato founded the academy that Aristotle attended, but I don't know, maybe I'm wrong.'

He sat back and wiggled a little finger into his dark, gaping ear canal. 'You're definitely wrong. I was listening to a Russell Brand podcast the other day and he referenced the whole lineage between Socrates, Aristotle and Plato.'

'Ah OK. I covered it in my dissertation but maybe I've mixed them up.'

The waiter came in between the two tables to clear the couple's starter plates and Laura missed how the philosophical saga ended. She thought about the similar tables she'd sat at in the past and how she'd diminished herself in ways that she was only just coming to understand. She thought about the opinions she'd suppressed in case older men thought she was silly. She thought about the disgusting food she'd eaten because the man she was with had said it was 'the best thing outside of Tokyo'. It wasn't. She thought about the jokes she'd laughed at that weren't funny and the fact she'd felt it was her failing that she didn't think Mark E. Smith was a genius. She thought about all the ways she'd shrunk or expanded herself depending on the man she was with and then she thought about Tom.

*   *   *

Laura first met Tom when she noticed him staring at her reflection in the large front window of his restaurant. He stood behind her at the bar watching her in the glass as she sat at a table waiting for her friend Emma to come back from the toilet. Instantly irritated that she'd chosen to wear the bra that caused exploratory fat to poke through the back section like stray sausage links, she slowly straightened her body and scanned the menu to look busy, pausing on the steak but deciding on the chopped salad. It was dark outside. Opposite the restaurant the orange street lights bounced off the River Tyne as it crept by silently on its journey out to the North Sea. In the window she could see that her dark, heavy fringe was doing the weird thing it did when it got wet, she pulled the spare black hairband off her wrist and scraped all of her hair into a high top knot.

'The toilets are fucking freezing in here,' Emma said as she took her seat opposite and pulled on a leather jacket that held the stale odour of late nights in the inside lining. 'What you done to your hair?'

'Nothing, why?' Laura replied, holding her hand to where her fringe had just been.

'Nowt, it looks nice.' Emma smiled, surprised Laura was drawing attention to the angular features and high forehead she normally tried to soften or hide.

'It was just getting on me nerves. Here, the waitress is coming, what you getting?'

'Ladies, are you ready to order?' the waitress interrupted, standing alert with her pen and pad at the side of their table.

Still looking over the menu, with her peripheral vision lasered in Tom's direction, Laura listened to Emma order the fish starter and chicken main and wondered if she should wear her hair down again.

Throughout their meal Tom stayed behind the bar. He chatted with friends who dropped in for a drink, he laughed easily with the customers as they came and went, and was kind to the waiting staff. Laura didn't look directly at him but she tracked his every move and clocked how many times he looked at her reflection in the window. As she walked towards the door to leave he said goodnight from behind the bar and held her gaze. She held her breath until the cold air sweeping up the river knocked it out of her.

They started seeing each other almost immediately. She had called into the restaurant later that week under the guise of looking for work. He took her number, they went for a drink, but the job was never mentioned again. After that they saw each other two or three times a week. She'd ring him after she'd been out with friends and he'd come and pick her up or they'd meet at the restaurant at closing time. They went for dinner at places where she couldn't normally afford to eat, he ordered for both of them and he always paid. He was forty-seven and she was twenty-six. The age difference was obvious to everyone else but they never mentioned it. She pretended to know what he was talking about when he referenced things like Spike Island and the

Poll Tax riots. He played obscure new music in his car and he was always first with the latest tech so it never occurred to her that he didn't know what she was talking about when she referenced details of her twenty-six-year-old life.

The first time they slept together he told her that he'd masturbated about her after he'd seen her in the restaurant. She made him describe the scenes he'd fantasised about as they had sex and he had a chaotic orgasm. She faked more orgasms than she experienced real ones. This had always been her experience of sex, she was just pleased that with Tom it wasn't always painful. He bought her outfits he thought were sexy. They were tight, mostly a size too small, but they were expensive. Sometimes they were underwear sets, or something more specific and clichéd. She would look at herself in the bathroom mirror – dressed as a nurse, or a secretary, her long dark hair styled however the outfit demanded, her green eyes skating over the fiddly buttons and fastens – and suspect that she hated them, but she was turned on enough by his desire to feel like she was having a good time. The sight of her in any one of these outfits turned him into a mess, he pawed her, licked her, bit her, his breath touched all parts of her body.

Laura listened to her friends complain about the boys or girls they were seeing, the endless rounds of dating games with no discernible winner, and felt sorry for them. Her arrangement with Tom made her feel sophisticated. He looked after her. He hired vans when she had to move flats, he knew about registering for council tax and which credit cards had the best interest rates. She felt secure. He bought her things. A new bike, a guitar (that she never played), artwork for her room in the flatshare where she lived. He presented these new gifts silently as she came into his house – they only ever slept at his house. She would make a fuss about how kind he was and give him a blow job on the stairs to show her appreciation.

On Tuesday afternoons he picked her up from therapy. Her therapist's house was near his place at the coast, a forty-minute train ride from town. It was his one day off from the restaurant so he said it was 'no bother'. The area confused Laura's senses. On the surface her therapist's street didn't look any different to the suburban warren where she'd grown up twenty miles away but the air felt different. The breeze brought with it a bleakness carried in from the North Sea. A damp, flat atmosphere that congregated in the spaces between houses, punctuated only by the squawks of greedy seagulls flying overhead. After each therapy session, Laura allotted twenty minutes to transform back into a presentable version of herself. Standing in the alley behind her therapist's garden she'd let her body convulse with silent screams for ten minutes then reapply her make-up for the remaining time, practising the deep breathing exercises her therapist was pleased she was using.

After twenty minutes she'd re-emerge onto the pavement and wait patiently for Tom to pick her up. One Tuesday as they were driving to his house he joked that her therapist Diane was a 'pub know-it-all' rather than a trained psychotherapist with a PhD and twenty years of experience.

'I mean, what's it all for?' he asked. 'I'm not sure that all this talking is making you any better.'

'Why does it bother you that I go to therapy?' she replied into her lap.

'It doesn't bother me. I just think therapy can be a bit self-indulgent. What do you say to her that you couldn't say to me?'

Laura opened her mouth but didn't answer. If the conversation stopped there, things wouldn't be totally ruined. If she didn't reply he'd stay quiet too and when she looked back at the mental transcript of that moment it would be short, there wouldn't be a gut-rotting monologue that gave him away. If she could control the situation with her silence she could pretend that everything was fine for just a little bit longer. Pushing her nails into the doughy part of her palms she looked out of the window as they drove past a mob of seagulls fighting over a dropped carton of chips on the seafront and mouthed a silent *thank you* when Tom asked if she was hungry.

Two months later Emma gathered all of their friends at a bar in town to celebrate her twenty-sixth birthday. They hadn't yet reached the age when a birthday was more a source of anxiety than a cause for celebration; for them it was still a reason to drink shots with every round and the motivation to find more drugs when the first stash had been sniffed, swallowed or smoked. The bar was billed as a 'live music venue' which meant that the owners could disregard their responsibility to expend any energy on the décor. Whilst mentally debating what to drink next, Laura stared at a group of older women huddled around a small, sticky table nearby. They could have been thirty-five, forty-five, fifty-five. She couldn't have guessed their age. To Laura, at that stage in her life, all women over the age of thirty looked and felt old. Not older. Old. She examined the women's painful orange skin; their static, brittle hair; their polyester-mix outfits. She contemplated the creamy eyeshadow gathering in their oily, baggy eyelids and shivered. Emma trailed her gaze.

'Look at the state of those lot,' she said.

'I know. Honestly kill me if I end up with one of those leathery faces and over-processed hair.'

'It puts the shits up me seeing women like that, the one in the red top has cellulite on her arms. Like what the actual fuck? How do you even get cellulite on your arms?' Emma asked, pulling down the wide neck of her jersey dress to reveal more of her shoulders and neckline.

'I don't know, from being a greedy bitch?' Laura hugged her arms close to her chest.

'Jesus,' Emma said, chasing the last of her vodka tonic in between the ice cubes at the bottom of her glass. 'Is that Tom with them?' Emma recognised him from the photo they'd used to compare if he looked older or younger than her dad.

Laura tried not to seem shocked. 'Oh yeah.'

'Are you gonna go and say hello?'

'No.'

'You two are weird. I'm gonna get the drinks in, do you want another one?'

'Yeah, gerrus a double vodka and diet coke,' Laura replied smiling, still staring at the woman in the red top. Tom caught her eye and waved, she waved back, but neither strayed into each other's territory.

She hadn't expected to see him there. He said owning a restaurant made you antisocial so they never accidently ran into each other. He only ever came into town for work, preferring to stay at home near the coast, venturing only as far as the beach for a walk when he knew it would be quiet. It was strange to see him with people of his own age. They all looked tired, like they'd rather be somewhere else. The men had grey beards, red faces, and stood around in twos and threes holding pints above protruding guts. Tom was thinner and better dressed but something connected them all. Collectively they had the unhealthy aura of children who had grown up in smoking households. Years of passive smoking turning them grey and sickly. She'd never noticed this about Tom before but now it was all she could see.

At 9.37 p.m. Tom messaged her to say he wanted to fuck her in the toilet. She put her phone back in her bag without replying and took a sip of her drink. For the rest of the night, she kept her stomach muscles pulled in tight and acted out the part of someone having a good time. She didn't notice Tom and his friends leave. At some point after 11 p.m. she looked up from her conversation and saw their tables full of empty glasses and drained bottles of house prosecco. Her stomach muscles relaxed and her shoulders slumped down. She checked her phone.

Get a taxi to mine when you're done. I'll pay.

She had another three drinks, watched a band she'd never heard before and had a line of someone else's coke. In the toilet she ordered a cab, while Emma stood uneasily in front of the mirror wiping sweat and eyeliner from under her eyes.

'I don't know why you're going there again. He'll just make you dress up and jizz in your eye,' Emma said, flicking water from the running tap into Laura's face.

Laura looked at her friend's gurning jaw in the mirror, she could hear someone being sick in one of the cubicles and wiggled her soggy toes, wet from the overflowing, blocked sink.

'What else am I going to do?'

'Erm, hang out with your mates?' Emma replied, using her eyeliner wand as a physical exclamation point, steadying herself on the sink.

'I'm going, my taxi will be here any minute. I'll ring you in the morning,' she said, hugging Emma from behind.

'Aye well, I hope his old grey dick doesn't fall off,' Emma shouted after her as she pushed her way out of the girls' bathroom.

Tom's place was a grand, double-fronted house. A five-bed, three-bath hangover from when rich merchants controlled this part of the north-east. The exterior of the house still held some of its grandeur but inside it was rotten. The doorbell was broken so Laura kicked wildly at the bottom wooden panel of the front door. It opened immediately.

'Alright, alright, you don't have to kick the door in.'

'That was quick,' she said with her arm raised up against the door frame, hoping it would steady her.

'I was just getting a drink from the kitchen,' Tom replied empty-handed. 'Do you want one?'

'Yes please.'

She dumped her bag at the bottom of the stairs. As she turned to face him, he pulled her close and she pressed her face into his chest, contorting her mouth to the side to allow in slivers of air.

'You looked really beautiful tonight,' he said as he kissed her head repeatedly in the same spot and gently smoothed down her coat. She felt stuck to him, stuck to that spot on the hallway floor. Tom's comfort was moreish but it had started to sicken her: she had gorged on his feast of convenience but it had only led to more agitation. They stood silently for a long time before he peeled away to get the drinks and she eased her feet out of her scuffed black ankle boots that desperately needed re-heeling.

In the living room, she sat on the sofa and sank back into the cushions. Her eyes trailed the room, studying the heavy cobwebs in the corners, the black damp that rose up the single-pane window frame. Tom had mocked her flatshare for being 'a studenty shithole', but, looking around now, she wondered why she'd listened to him. At least her flat had double glazing and the boiler always worked.

'Here you go.' He handed her a large glass with a small amount of red wine in it.

'What's the point in these huge glasses if you only ever put a tiny bit of wine in them?' she asked, holding it at eye level.

'It's so that you can smell the aroma of the wine. Swill it around in the glass. You're supposed to enjoy the whole process, smell it, taste it, savour it. It's not just about knocking back as much as possible.'

She replied something inaudible into the bottom of her glass and drained the contents in one gulp.

'Did you have a good night?' Laura asked as he sat at the opposite end of the sofa.

'Yeah, it was alright, you know what I'm like. Standing around in pubs isn't really my thing.'

'Yeah, I was surprised to see you. Who were your friends?'

'Old friends from years back. We used to all go raving together, now it's just birthdays.'

Tom had told her numerous times about the old raves he used to go to in fields and disused warehouses. How it was all love, free parties, good drugs and proper dance music. She wasn't in the mood for another nostalgia trip.

'It'll be funerals soon.'

'Very funny. And where do you know your friends from, the youth club?' he said, punching her leg forcefully as a question mark.

Without flinching she said, 'Yeah some of them.'

They stared at each other. His eyes looked small and strained. His mouth was a half-smirk, stained with red wine at its edges. He reached for her foot and started massaging it, his hand moving higher up her leg towards her thigh with each rotation of his thumb. She knew that they would have sex on the sofa, then probably on the floor and would finish with her bent over the coffee table. She wouldn't come, and halfway through she'd remind herself to go straight to the toilet when they'd finished because she didn't have time to go to the doctors for antibiotics that week if she got cystitis again. After five minutes of fumbling on the sofa, he routinely moved her onto the floor in front of the unlit fire. Maybe he thought it was romantic, a move he'd seen in a sexy thriller from the eighties and that he'd rolled out ever since. But rather than being a turn-on, it was draughty and turned her naked flesh purple. She thought about his bed, about how much more comfortable it would be to do this there. As he bowed his head and dribbled into the well of her neck she realised that for him this was comfortable, this was bliss: her body, her vagina, her silence was exactly what he wanted. He didn't feel the cold. He didn't feel winded by the weight of someone thrusting heavily on top of him. He probably felt weightless and absolutely divine. She tried to get into a comfier position but couldn't move his body enough and the stiff carpet underneath tore strips of skin off her back with every push. He dragged her over the coffee table, pulled her hair back and came manically. Panting heavily he fell on top of her making it impossible to catch a full breath. 'Can you get off me please?' She whispered as a tear fell across her face.

In the shower she let a curtain of wet hair close around her eyes and focused on the water gathering at her feet, the drain blocked with a mass of hair and sludge. To filter out the pain in between her legs and the sting of the raw skin on her back she zoned in to the drumming of the water and tried not to think of anything. She didn't want to think about getting out of the shower, or what she would say in the morning, she just stood perfectly still and watched her feet turn a bright burnt red. The sound of plates and glasses smashing in the kitchen broke her trance and she got out. She dried herself on an already damp towel, ignored the loud music coming from downstairs and got straight into

Tom's bed, wrapping the duvet around her into a protective cocoon.

Lying on her side the next morning, Laura studied Tom's face as he slept. Long hairs on solo missions sprouted from his eyebrows. Grey flecked through his stubble and congregated down his chin like he'd dribbled something and never wiped it away. She touched his beard gently to try and smooth down some of the erratic growth. He opened his eyes with a start and they stared at each other without speaking. His eyes were slightly hooded at the sides, and deep wrinkles splayed out down to his ears. When he yawned, tears traced the ravines of skin onto his pillow and she could see into the back of his mouth; his teeth were black and yellow like rows of rotting mushrooms.

Without a plan for what would come next, she said, 'Why don't you go for women your own age?'

Her question cut his yawn short and he looked up abruptly at the ceiling.

'What?'

'Why have all your girlfriends been much younger? Like, why don't you sleep with women your own age?'

'You're not that much younger than me,' he said, wiping the sleep and tears away from his eyes, scratching around for a cigarette on the bedside table.

'Yes I am. I'm twenty-six and you're forty-seven. That's a twenty-one-year gap. That means you could have been to uni and graduated before I was born. If you'd gone to uni.'

'Yes, I know what it means.'

'Do you though?' she said, folding the pillow over to give her neck more support.

'I just don't think of you as that much younger, you're very mature and our age has never come into it, has it?'

'Mature? Oh my god. What the fuck?'

'Is this about you wanting to get married or something?'

She stared at him blankly. 'I don't want to get married. I'm twenty-six, why would I want to get married?'

Tom didn't answer, assuming the question was rhetorical.

'Why aren't *you* married?' she asked, pulling up the covers and locking her arms by her sides on top of the duvet.

He sat up and lit his cigarette. Smoke from last night still hung in the middle of the room, it mixed with his fresh tar exhalation, creating a swirling pirouette of stale air.

'Sally was seventeen years younger than you,' Laura continued, feeling a twinge of excitement. 'Have you ever gone out with a woman your own age?'

'Of course I have,' Tom half-yawned.

'No, I mean since you've been old.'

'I'm not fucking old you cheeky cunt,' he tried to laugh and propped himself up on his elbow to face her. 'Look, I sleep with women who I connect with. I don't connect with a lot of older women because they're all fucking crazy and they've got too much baggage. I can't deal with them. You'll no doubt be exactly the same. You're fucking crazy now and you're only in your twenties.'

'It's very boring to call people crazy because they don't do what you tell them to.'

'You know what?' He pointed his cigarette at her. 'You've fucking lost it. It's not even eight o'clock in the morning and you've gone mental. I'm gonna have a shower.' Coughing as he got up, he put his cigarette out in the over-crowded ashtray, punishing the butt long after it had gone out.

'You really have fucking lost it,' he repeated as he walked out of the bedroom.

Laura lay in the dark smoky bedroom and listened to Tom pass a long, heavy piss onto the shower cubicle floor. Alone in his bed, she smelt his sheets. They were stale. The bottom sheet was yellow in patches. She'd never noticed how dirty they were. She'd never noticed how dirty and decaying his whole house was, until last night. She'd always been impressed by its size, the random yet apparently styl-ish décor. She thought it was bourgeois, even though she didn't really know what that meant. Taking a mental tour of the house she thought about the sunken bath in the main bathroom, which was surrounded by mouldy grout-ing; the missing spindles on the grand staircase; the wide curtains that were stained brown from all of the trapped cigarette smoke; the art and ornaments sprayed with a thick layer of dust; and the fact that none of the rooms had any doors. She sat up and looked at her reflection in the mirrored wall opposite the bed: matted hair, dark eyes, cracked lips. Her head ached, her mouth was dry and her inner thighs felt raw. She got up, wincing as she bent down to pick up her scattered clothes, and got ready as quickly as she could. She took the rolled-up £20 note poking out the back pocket of Tom's jeans, grabbed the last three cigarettes from the packet at the side of the bed and left.

*

Outside, the coastal wind whipped up the streets and the heavy February sky hung low. It was a long walk to the Metro station, past rows of toytown shops. There was a hair-dressing salon named after the owner, Pamela, which looked like it hadn't been updated since the 1970s. She passed a fish and chip shop that only ever opened on a Friday lunch-time, a bookies and a corner shop that still sold pints of milk in glass bottles. In the past, she had always found solace in the quaintness of these shops. She'd found it reassuring that as everything around her changed so quickly, this stretch of shops operated in its own time zone, at its own pace. It was proof that some corners of life were impervious to change. But on that bleak winter morning, they weren't quaint or stoic, they looked slow and pathetic. The greasy shelves in the corner shop window were filled with faded football annuals from the World Cup three years ago, tubs of grey sweets that were once blue, and bottles of Buckfast with ripped labels that tried not to catch her attention. The poster promoting a travelling circus was over a year old and all but one of the personal ads were for 'special massages'.

Laura stared, morbidly fascinated with how that window display had come to exist. Who had selected those objects and put them together as a display? Had they been inter-rupted mid-flow? Did they mean to finish off the job but something else always came up? Was the window just another storage area despite the fact that it had a daily audience? Perhaps one morning the shop owner would be waiting for the shutters to open and the slow reveal would draw their attention to the state of the window display. They'd open the shutters all the way to the top, take a step back and think: 'Look at the fucking state of that window, who put all that shit in there?' Incredulous that they hadn't noticed the disorganised mess until now, they'd feel a sense of urgency to have a huge clear-out. Still standing staring at the window Laura got out her phone and wrote a text to Tom.

You don't need to pick me up from Diane's next week.
I'll make my own way back to town.

She read it several times before pressing send. Putting the phone back in her pocket, she fastened up her felt pea coat and walked to catch the train home.

*   *   *

Laura thought about how she was slowly but surely nearing the age Tom had been when they first met. She looked at her daughter in the high chair opposite, her chubby arms, her strong legs, the inverted knuckles still hidden under layers of baby fat. She took in everything she could of this beautiful buoyant body, the one her daughter would grow into and struggle to maintain ownership of. The body that men would one day look at so they didn't have to look at themselves.

The advertising couple on the next table were leaving. The older man was already halfway to the door while the young woman fiddled with her waistband and gathered up her bag. Laura's daughter dropped her teething toy near her high-heeled foot.

'Oh sorry about that. These things never stay in one place for long,' Laura tutted.

'That's OK, don't worry about it,' the young woman replied through a white-wine smile. 'She's very good, isn't she? She was quiet all the way through lunch.'

Using the napkin from her table, she picked up the teething toy and placed it on the edge of the table. Laura wanted to tell this woman that she didn't have to apologise when she knew she was right, that she didn't have to wear painful shoes to work to be taken seriously and that being good didn't mean staying quiet. But she didn't know where to start. Instead, Laura looked at her young, flushed face, her generic work clothes from Zara, which masked any evidence of her personality, and said, 'Thanks for that, have a great afternoon.'

'You too,' the young woman replied as she turned to join the older man who was shouting into his phone and vaping on the street outside.

Laura cleaned the teething toy with a wet wipe and gave it to her daughter, holding her chubby hand and stroking it softly. The child let out a high-pitched squeal of delight.

'Good girl,' Laura said.

'All done here?' the waiter interrupted, signalling to the half-eaten garlic bread and dough balls spread out over the table.

'No,' Laura replied. 'We're still going.'

Three Sisters

The rain that had soaked the wedding guests all day as they dashed from cars to venues in vulnerable footwear and expensive outfits had finally stopped, leaving the evening air damp and chewy. Katie sat on her folded jacket rubbing her feet. Getting ready in a rush that morning, she'd forgotten that the shoes she'd chosen to wear tortured her feet. Nine hours later her heels were lacerated and a thick purple indentation fell across her swollen toes where the strap of her left shoe had aggressively asserted itself. On the cold stone bench her body hunched over causing stomach fat to gather in the clunky way that she never normally allowed. Even on her own she held her stomach in. She sat in rigid, upright positions or covered herself in layers of clothes so she couldn't see the rolls that formed matter-of-factly around her trunk. But that night, sat on the dark raised terrace, she pulled down the waistband of her shapewear under her dress and pushed her stomach out to its limit. It groaned. She groaned. Her digestive system, not used to processing such rich food, was attempting to deal with oysters, lobster rolls, diver scallop crudo, Argentinian lamb asado and a selection of deconstructed cheesecakes, pavlovas and macaroons from the dessert table. Her colon was in a bad way.

Apart from her immediate family, she hadn't known many of the other guests at the wedding. She'd drunk more wine than she planned to, her glass never dipping below half-full. Drinking was something to do with her hands when all of the guests were unleashed from the ceremony into the large drawing room to mingle, it gave her the confidence to ask questions that would later make people comment on how strange the bride's family were.

'I can't believe you asked that woman who she was leaving her money to when she dies,' Katie's husband Justin had whispered to her as the microphone was passed in between speeches. She'd shrugged and pulled her face into a crease while filling her glass back up to the top.

Trying to stall the early stages of the hangover that was creeping in she lit her last cigarette and looked out over the pristine grounds of the English country manor that rolled out in front of her. From the safety of the terrace Katie could see some of the younger wedding guests below smoking and sniffing coke from monographed vials. On the lawn, they congregated around an Airstream trailer that served champagne in crystal cut glasses, and a collective cheer of 'Wahey' rang out every time one of the glasses smashed. Katie thought it was funny that this crowd of aviation brokers, bankers and hedge fund managers saw themselves as such civilised beings. From her vantage point they didn't look that different to the stag and hen parties she used to serve in the bars of Magaluf, only the drinks and clothes here were a lot more expensive and the bloodlines a deeper blue. She took the last drag on her cigarette, dropped it onto the uneven flagstones in front of her and watched the glow of the tobacco slowly burn out into a pile of delicate grey ash.

In the lead-up to the wedding her sister Joanna had issued instructions to the family about what they could and could not do; the kind of clothes they could wear, the gifts they could buy, who they could speak to and what subjects they could discuss in certain company. Over a side of beef at their mother's house on Easter Sunday Joanna announced that she wouldn't be inviting certain members of the family. As voices rose and glances were cast Katie slowly and silently loaded up forkfuls of beef with fluffy roast potatoes, sweet carrots, braised cabbage and fiery horseradish that made her sneeze. She mopped up the remaining gravy on her plate with a perfect flannel of Yorkshire pudding as Joanna shouted to no one and everyone.

'I'm not some kind of evil psychopath, I just want a nice wedding.'

Katie pushed her plate away and drank down a large gulp of red wine as Joanna stormed out, their mother silently filled the dishwasher and someone in the next room flicked through the Sunday afternoon TV.

Weeks later Katie and Joanna sat in a pub neither of them had been to, it was part of a promise Katie had made to their mother to smooth things over as the older sister.

'You have to invite Auntie Lil to the wedding, you know that don't you,' she said to Joanna who wouldn't meet her gaze.

'It's my wedding, I can invite or not invite whoever I want. I'll have a lot of people looking at me and I need it to go well.'

The muscles in Joanna's neck had tightened so much they pulled her ears back, momentarily giving her face the appearance of someone calm and serene, as if her favourite flavour of ice cream was slowly sliding down the back of her throat. Breaking the serenity, her mouth turned hostile and her face fell to match the tone of her voice.

'She's just so professionally Northern and tacky like she puts it on to prove a point or something. I'm sure she exaggerates her accent.'

'Of course she doesn't,' Katie laughed, 'she's old now. Phil's family will probably see her like some kind of humorous Alan Bennett character.'

Joanna was sweating. She took a sip of her soda water and removed the pale pink cashmere jumper she was wearing. Her face was masked, covered in a green correcting primer and heavy foundation, but now dressed in only a white vest, Katie could see the red welts of a vicious rosacea all over her chest, and a forest of tiny white scars that ran the length of both arms.

Joanna followed Katie's eyes and said, 'Both dresses have long sleeves.'

'You have two wedding dresses?'

'Of course, that's what you have to do. A day and a night dress.'

Katie nodded and crunched a large ice cube from her gin and tonic between her teeth.

*

The only other time the two sisters had sat in a pub together was when Katie was thirty-two and Joanna was twenty-four. At that point they hadn't seen each other for so long that Katie had struggled to recognise the skinny girl who came to sit at her table. Her greasy hair was tied in a high, tight ponytail to hide the clumps that were missing. Swamped in clothes that Katie was sure weren't hers, her face was covered in scabs she'd unsuccessfully tried to cover with make-up that was three shades too dark for her skin tone. Shaking and jittering, Joanna had spoken at an abrasive rate about how she was in great shape, was really happy and hadn't seen Malcolm for months. Katie didn't speak for thirty-seven minutes, she'd known that because the football match on the large TV screens had kicked off as Joanna sat down and Katie noted the time on the clock when she finally broke for breath and stopped talking.

'What do you want, Joanna?'

'Nothing. Honestly nothing. I just wanted to see you, we haven't seen each other for such a long time and I wanted to know how you're doing. How are you doing?' A smile had twitched across her face before blanking out as quickly as it appeared.

'I'm fine.'

'How's your kid?'

'Kids. They're fine.'

'Great. I forgot you had more than one now. That's great.'

The referee blew his whistle for half-time. The men around them had moved to refill their glasses with more watery lager and relieve themselves of the pints they'd downed in the first half. They shouted 'Two more Stella mate' at the silent barman, and clasped each other's necks, shoulders and bellies in lairy embraces. The movement of bodies released a stale smoky stench that had been held tightly within the fabric of the seats and the wool of the carpet even though the smoking ban had been in place for years. Katie watched the muted football pundits on the TV screen presumably discussing the form of the two teams, the missed opportunities, the shots on target, the tactics of each manager. She'd wondered what her tactic should have been for this meeting, annoyed she hadn't planned something better, a better speech to cover herself – but she'd known that with Joanna it was best to be prepared for the worst.

'Do you want another drink?' Joanna had asked, pointing at Katie's untouched orange juice.

'No thank you,' Katie answered, surfing it towards the middle of the table on a curled beer mat. Joanna had chosen the pub they'd met at, and Katie wondered if it was an attempt to intimidate her, to throw her off. It amused her to think of Joanna plotting and strategising. She was almost impressed that any kind of thought might have gone into this.

'You know Joanna, I appreciate this must be very painful for you to sit here and pretend you don't want something but we both know you do and I have to pick the kids up soon so it's probably best for everyone if you just spit it out.'

Her sister had stared directly into her eyes, her knee hitting the table repeatedly as she bounced her foot on the floor.

'OK, I just need a bit of money to tide me over for a couple of weeks.'

'No Joanna. You know I can't do that.'

Joanna nodded her head and cast her eyes to the sticky carpet under her feet. Her big toe pointed through the front of her trainer like the sole survivor of a ship that had run off course.

'I thought you'd say that. Can I stay at yours then? Just for a couple of nights. You know I'd only ask if I was desperate.'

'Have you spoken to Mum?'

'No,' Joanna had said fiddling with her bottom lip, folding it in and out on itself.

'Well,' Katie had said standing up and putting her coat on. 'I suggest you speak to her and I also suggest you don't call me again until you have sorted your shit out. I went all the way for you, Joanna, twice, and I'm not doing it again.'

Joanna grabbed Katie's wrist, digging her dirty fingernails into Katie's paper-thin flesh. 'You're such a cunt, Katie. You always have been.'

Katie bent down to Joanna's ear and in a low, slow voice had said, 'I know. Now get the fuck off me.' She'd prised open Joanna's grasp as the away fans started a chant at the back of the pub, marking the start of the second half.

On the cool dark terrace of the country estate Katie could hear the end chorus of 'Come On Eileen' wafting out of the open conservatory doors below, she wondered what it was about weddings that made songs like 'Come On Eileen' such crowd-pleasers. It wasn't acceptable to play that song at any other event but at a wedding, even a society wedding like this it was a great leveller. Regardless of social standing, the amount of money in their bank accounts or how refined they thought they were, friends and families from both sides always came together to pogo and shout 'Come on, Eileen, ta-loo-rye-ay' at the top of their lungs as the dance-floor erupted at the fiddle crescendo. Katie almost felt sad to be missing out on the chance to watch grown sweaty men jump around to the eighties classic.

From the corner of her eye, she could see a woman wobbling towards her at the far side of the terrace, threatening to uncover her secluded spot. She squinted to see who it was, hoping it wasn't one of Joanna's friends – a blur of blonde women who Katie had nothing in common with. They were all from criminally wealthy families, with names like Daisy or Pru or Bella or nicknames like Darby or Flops. They were the women that *Tatler* loved to describe as 'effervescent' and 'petite' in society features. She guessed Joanna had met them through Phil relatively recently as Joanna didn't have any female friends of her own, and at her hen party none of them had known she was epileptic.

During the earlier photograph line-up for friends of the bride Katie had struggled to tell them apart. They all looked related. Their hair was a glossy, electric blonde, one girl had gone rogue and kept her mane a natural mousy brown colour, but according to Joanna, she was everyone's least favourite. They'd all had some delicate cosmetic tweaks: teeth whitening; an Invisalign brace between the ages of eleven and fifteen; a slight nose straightening or brow lift; subtle fillers; minimal Botox; or, more recently, platelet-rich plasma injections. Each had a healthy natural tan from their Easter break at the family home in Italy or France. They looked well rested. Limbs were long and muscular from the activities they had taken part in from an early age: lacrosse, horse riding, skiing, tennis and now yoga at an expensive studio in Chelsea, Notting Hill or Hackney, if they'd decided to 'rough it' and move to a £1.5 million house near Victoria Park, which their father had bought as an invest-ment. When Katie spoke to any one of them, they smiled, looked at her intently and said 'Yah' in all the right places to let her know that she had their undivided attention. Their manners were impeccable.

They called themselves the Coven, a name that Bex – Katie and Joanna's younger sister – found amusing.

'It's ironic,' she'd said on first hearing about them, 'because they're all from such old money their families trace back to when women were burned at the stake for practising witchcraft and their ancestors probably all had front row seats at the fire pit.'

The woman walking towards her was too large to be one of the Coven. From the outline of her body Katie knew it was Bex. The blue light from her phone lit up her plump sweaty face, she was wearing a satin slip dress and no bra, her huge breasts struggling to stay in place, her nipples vying to escape with each step. Earlier in the evening Bex had attracted looks of admiration and disgust from guests on either side of the family divide as she'd danced with her cousins, unbothered by how little of her full body her dress covered. Katie had watched with a deep love for the little sister she wished she saw more often.

'Bex!' she shouted.

Bex looked up from her phone, screwing her face up to make out who had called her name.

'Oh, it's you! What the fuck are you doing up here?'

'I'm just having a breather, my feet are killing me. It was too hot down there.'

'They just got the air con working again so it's not too bad now. One less thing for Joanna to have a face on about.'

'Is she still upset about the weather and Phil falling over?'

'Honestly, I couldn't give a fuck. I haven't spoken to her since the speeches but I saw her stress-eating some leftovers in the kitchen about an hour ago.'

'Oh my god. I'll go and find her in a bit when my feet have calmed down,' Katie said, knowing that she wouldn't. 'I wish I'd brought my drink out. Have you got any cigarettes left?'

'No but I've got one of these, do you want some?' Bex held up a freshly rolled, unlit spliff.

'Yes!' Katie opened her jacket out and Bex sat down, half her bum cheek hanging over the jacket.

'Phil's lot are a bit much aren't they?' Bex said, trying to hold the first lungful of smoke for as long as possible.

'Wow, I know,' Katie replied, taking the spliff out of Bex's hand and inhaling a long draw.

'I knew it was going to be full-on but Jesus Christ they're like fucking caricatures of the aristocracy. Why do they all have such red faces and terrible hair?'

'Crazy isn't it? Phil's uncle is a sexual harassment case waiting to happen.'

'The one that gave the cringe speech? He's definitely paid off a few women. Who's that old woman in the mint-green hat and matching outfit? The one who looks like a fairground ghost in *Scooby Doo*.'

'That's Phil's great-aunt.'

'She freaks me right out, I could hear this noise in the service, I looked around and it was her chewing on her false teeth, like pushing them in and out of her mouth,' Bex said, miming the motion.

'Yeah, I heard that,' Katie exhaled smoke, staring at her sister's jerking jawline.

Katie, Joanna and Bex were sisters with the same mother but a variety pack of fathers. Katie was the oldest, born in Derby when their mother was twenty. She was the only one who'd had the dubious honour of meeting all of the men who had played paternal roles in their lives. For eight years it had been Katie and their mother moving from women's refuge to bedsit to the spare rooms of friends, ending up at Auntie Lil's for several years. When Joanna's dad came along things improved slightly – they moved into their own home, things seemed calm, there was moderate financial stability and then Joanna was born. Katie had left for London at sixteen, when she realised that the emotional and physical violence in her family didn't happen in every house on their street. Their mother met David, Bex's father, at a hotel in the Peak District where she'd worked part-time. By the time Katie met Bex, she was four years old, the family were living in the Cotswolds and their mother had transformed herself into a respectable Barbour-and-wellies woman who still kept a packed suitcase at the back of the wardrobe. Prepared to discover her mother had married a rich, smarmy man with soft hands, Katie was disarmed by how much she liked David and how much she'd come to love him over the years. David had made his money in haulage, he hadn't been born into wealth like a lot of the people he was now connected to, and he didn't use it as a weapon. Katie trusted him. He'd taught her to drive, bought her books that became her favourites, talked to her as an adult and listened to her opinions even when he disagreed with them. He'd looked after Joanna as if she was his own daughter, often paying for her numerous rehab visits and bailouts. Watching him with Bex often made Katie's chest ache as she saw the deep affection he had for his own biological daughter, and how much Bex took it for granted.

As they'd all got older Katie found it fascinating to trace how their mother's genes had sculpted themselves across each of her daughter's faces. Katie had her grey, observant eyes, Joanna her straight nose and strong chin, and Bex had her high brow and full mouth. If you blended all of their faces together, you'd get a perfect identikit image of their mother staring back at you with the vacant look of someone who'd forgotten what they were about to say. Their mother had always been passive, letting things happen to her, or to her children, without the will or power to change the course their lives were on. Katie had once asked her why they had to move so often and why she couldn't have her own bedroom. Turning away from her then-six-year-old daughter to look out of the window her mother had said: 'Life is just crueller to some people and there's nothing you can do about it.'

From the outside, their fractured family looked like they'd finally turned out well. There were weekends away, Sunday lunches, birthdays and Christmases spent together. Their mother expertly played the part of the attractive businessman's wife, the middle daughter was marrying into a suitably wealthy family and Katie had produced a healthy brood of children. To onlookers, it seemed like they had come through the worst and outrun the horror of scarcity that had plagued their early years. Katie could almost believe the vision that others saw, as long as she suppressed the molten anger that boiled inside of her. Now, it appeared that Bex was the only anomaly; she was young enough that everyone put her agitator ideas down to the naivety of her youth; her recent arrest at a climate change protest was seen as an amusing dinner party anecdote. Katie thought this as she listened to her monologue about the importance of living as a collective and the dangers of capitalism as they looked out over the rolling hills of the historic stately home where their sister had just married the son of a duke.

'It's easy to be an anarchist when you have no responsibilities,' Katie said flatly in response to Bex's insistence on the need for violent reform, to what she wasn't sure.

'I fucking knew you'd say something like that,' Bex said, pushing Katie off her own jacket.

'Well it is, you've got nothing to lose. Come back to me when you've got kids and responsibilities.'

'Oh my god. That is literally the extent of your imagination, isn't it? I'm not having kids. I'm not doing all of this,' she said swirling the spliff around her head. 'We're not all desperate to get married and have kids. It's a mad old-fashioned tradition that was used to pass on property from one man to another, and now women are the fucking sad losers doing the proposing because we're all so desperate to prove that someone else loves us and can bear to be around us for an extended period of time. Even queer people want to get married now. It's fucking tragic. This whole weekend is fucking tragic. I'm actually embarrassed to even be here.'

'You didn't look embarrassed when you were shovelling a six-course meal into your face.'

'Shut the fuck up,' Bex replied with a smirk of acknowledgement that Katie was right.

'I was surprised you made it to be honest, after what happened at Easter. I thought you'd probably sack it off at the last minute.'

'Can we not go into that again? Fucking weddings. Fucking families,' Bex said to the air in front of her.

Watching Joanna walk down the aisle in front of two hundred people, Katie had thought about the number of hours her sister had put into perfecting that very moment. The searches for the perfect dress, the discussions about and visits to the various venues with the exact setting and space for the number of guests she wanted to invite and impress. Did she have mood boards within mood boards on her desktop? Different flower arrangement options, catering menus, place settings and seating plans? How many times had she visited the hairdressers? How many shades of lipstick and foundation had make-up artists applied to her face? What was the perfect body weight and angle for the photographs? What made this final version the perfect one? Looking at Joanna wearing a smile she'd never seen before Katie realised that the finer details of this vision didn't matter, it was always going to look a certain way regardless of exact minutiae. The artisan flower installation could have featured a different variety of rose, dahlia or hyacinth, the locally sourced menu could have included different dishes, her sister's hair could have fallen in a different direction; whatever the details of this final pageant, they would have all conformed to the narrow expectations of this sector of society. What really mattered to Joanna and now to Katie was that this all marked an end. With this expensive spectacle Joanna was putting a distance between herself and who she'd once been, she was presenting herself and Phil as an acceptable unit within this social circle and she was trying to protect herself from her past, from her family.

Katie thought of her own wedding: the dress she'd bought at Camden Market, how much hair her husband had back then, how young they had been and how much time had passed between then and now. Time, she'd thought, would always stretch out in front of her until she reached the point where she was always meant to be. The place where she was safe and things were ordered and proper. *She* was ordered and proper. Katie hadn't hit that place yet and now she worried that she might never reach it. She wasn't even sure where that place was anymore but she knew she was running out of the time she'd once had on her side.

'Do you know what I heard Mum and Auntie Lil talking about in the toilet?' Bex said, breaking Katie's contemplation of how cruel time could be.

'No, what?'

'Uncle Ron's saggy testicles.'

'Shut the fuck up!' Katie yelped, curling her shoulders up around her ears.

'Seriously. Lil was whispering about how low and long they are and that she has to buy him special underpants to hold them up *or they ache*,' Bex said using the spliff to punctuate each word.

'Oh my god, I feel sick.' Katie put her head between her knees in a mock brace position. 'Joanna would have absolutely lost it if she'd heard them talking like that.'

'I know, isn't it actually fucking rank? Imagine how thin and stringy the skin holding on to his balls must be.' Bex stretched her legs out in front and scissor-kicked as if trying to swim away from the subject of their uncle's sagging balls.

'I'd really rather not think about that stretch of skin at all. Like, ever.'

'Getting old looks really rubbish doesn't it?'

'I don't know. I suppose chewing on your own teeth and having dental floss holding on to your testicles does sound pretty awful, but maybe by then you don't really notice it? It happens over a long period of time, maybe by the time your nipples are down by your belly button you just stop caring.'

Bex held the lighter to the end of the spliff, which had gone out, and blew on it sharply causing large hot rocks to spray off into the air like lava lapping at the mouth of a volcano. Katie didn't move and instead let two angry red lumps burn through her dress onto her thighs. The burning pinch felt intensely satisfying. She hated this dress, this wrap dress that was so age-appropriate, so flattering for a woman who had birthed four children. A woman who was once a girl who lived in squats, worked in bondage clubs, jumped to the screeching noise of hardcore bands in dirty basement clubs and went to bed when most people were going to work. Now her Spotify playlists were populated by *Trolls* songs and the *Frozen* soundtrack. Now her knickers were huge, her clothes were huge and her hair was thin. Her body had been drained by the children she had borne and the effort it took to keep them alive.

Above their heads the sky was a slick of turquoise black, Katie could see hallows of light at the edges of her vision but when she turned her gaze towards them an oily darkness fell in their place. She looked up and allowed herself to be surprised by how big and boastful the stars in the countryside were, compared to the light-polluted sky that hung low over her London home. She let her mind hover over the fact that humans share the same atomic make-up as stars, but a sting of embarrassment pierced her haze as she realised she was on the verge of quoting a Moby song out loud. Bex wouldn't know who Moby was and Katie would have to explain, or maybe play some of his music on her phone, or pull up a Google image of him. On getting to grips with who Moby was, Bex would likely address Katie with an expression of utter contempt and she'd lose her.

She turned to look at her sister's face. Her sister's beautiful face. The more she stared the more it felt like she was watching a deepfake video where Bex's face melded in and out of other people's right before her eyes – it changed from Bex to their mother, to Christina Ricci, to the funny one from *Derry Girls*, to pre-glow-up Kylie Jenner, to Billie Eilish. Katie blinked and widened her eyes to settle comfortably back on Bex's sleepy full face. That night on that damp bumpy stone bench she knew everything about her little sister, the strange girl that no one else could work out. From their first meeting when Bex was four – and

Katie twenty-four – Katie was the only person Bex ever wanted to be with and Katie responded by being there for her little sister in ways that she had never wanted to be for Joanna. In many respects Bex was Katie's first child, she still thought of her like that. As a four-year-old, Bex had unexpectedly yanked Katie out of the walled existence she had built for herself. This small child with her uncomplicated love and simple one-dimensional demands was the jolt that Katie had been looking for ever since she'd been a child herself. Her early relationship with Bex was the purest and most honest form of love she'd ever experienced. She thought the love she felt for Bex was a gateway drug for how it would feel to have her own baby. She was sure a child of her own would thaw the numbness she felt, she couldn't believe it would all be so simple. Only it wasn't.

Looking at Bex on the dark terrace, she could see the blood flowing under her skin, the muscles twitching in her calves, she could hear her thoughts whirring and for a moment she thought that they were communicating telepathically. To test her theory, she mentally sent Bex a message.

Without meaning to she said, 'Did you get it?' out loud.

Bex looked at her suspiciously. 'Did I get what?'

'Nothing,' Katie said shaking her head, wishing she wasn't so stoned.

Leaving a gap from when she last spoke – which could have been anything between ten seconds and ten minutes, she wasn't sure – she tried to speak again.

'You might be embarrassed to be here but I'm glad you made it,' she said, hoping to appear more together.

'You know what, I've actually had a good time and obviously I wanted to see you,' Bex bumped Katie lovingly with her whole body and leant against her. 'I'm not staying for the lunch tomorrow though. Like weddings aren't cringe enough they make people gas them up for a whole weekend.'

Feeling like a conversation about Bex's future could be a good way to straighten her brain Katie kissed the top of Bex's head and asked, 'Are you going to go back to Liverpool? What are you going to do now that you've graduated?'

'I'm not having a career chat with you, here, now.'

'You can come and stay with us if you want.'

'In your house? What, with all of your kids and Justin? Who would that benefit, me or you?'

'Fair point,' Katie laughed.

They sat together in a calm silence. Katie felt her mind being drawn back to the one safe memory of her father that she allowed herself to revisit. He was lying on his stomach on the sofa in one of the houses he'd lived in, Katie could never remember the exact house or how old she was, the details weren't important. She was lying on his back and they were singing along to a song on TV, a theme tune from a show, or a song on *Top of the Pops*. From her position on top of him she could feel the reverberation of her father's voice travelling through her and for that one brief moment in time they were in synch, so in synch they were on the same frequency. Sometimes when she cuddled her own children she would start to hum and try to encourage them to hum along with her, so that she could recreate the physical feeling she had once shared with her father, but they never understood her directions and would end up screaming or shouting instead. A rush of irritation burst through her stoned daze.

She took a draw from the cardboard roach and burned her lips. 'You know, I wake up every morning and I do this thing that all of the self-help books tell you to do. I set an intention for each day.'

'What, like, must not be a cunt today?'

'Yes, kind of. I'll set it when I'm on the toilet on my own. I'll picture my day being calm and enjoyable. I'll send love and light to three people.'

'Who do you send it to?'

'It depends.'

'On what?'

'I don't know, maybe if someone's having a hard time or I haven't seen them for a while, or if I'm specifically grateful for them.'

'Do you send it to me?'

'Yes, sometimes. Anyway, I'll wipe my bum, flush the toilet, feel calm, open the bathroom door and it's absolute carnage out there. The kids are fighting, no one is getting ready, someone is whining about there only being Weetabix for breakfast and I instantly feel my arsehole tighten. It makes me want to run away from it all.'

'Do you ever talk to Justin about that feeling?'

'Yeah sometimes … Sometimes when I'm standing, waiting for one of the kids to catch up and I've got the double buggy and I don't even want to get to where I'm hurrying them to, I wonder what would happen if I just walked away.'

'What just walk away and just leave them on their own?' Bex blinked with intense interest.

'Yeah, in the middle of the street. Just turn around and go.'

'Where would you go?'

'Hmmm, I don't know. Just somewhere I could lie down for a while … But then I'd be in a lot of trouble and it would create such an uproar I'm not really sure if it's such a great idea after all.'

'So, what are you going to do?' Bex asked, her eyes skating over Katie's face.

'What?' Katie replied, surprised at the assumption there was something she could do. 'Nothing. There's nothing *to do*. When you have four kids you can't just disappear or sack it all off because you don't feel like it anymore.'

'I still can't believe you've got so many kids, that was such a bad idea.'

'I know!' Katie exclaimed in a high-pitched voice that took her by surprise.

'But your kids are pretty cute.'

'They are aren't they? The other night, Lily and Freddie were in my bed and I was watching them sleep. They were like these two strange little creatures who had just transplanted themselves from another planet, making strange noises and breathing in synch. Their hair was all soft from having it washed and their skin was so perfectly smooth, I had a feeling in my chest that was so overwhelming I had to look at the news on my phone to make it stop.'

*

Bex kicked her shoes and stood up, barefoot on the wet, mossy flagstones. As she bent down to touch her toes, filthy from being encased in sweaty court shoes all day, her slip rose up over her bum.

'Bex, you could have put some pants on!' Katie squealed.

With her head in between her legs Bex let out a long, drawn, 'Shuuuuuuuuuuut uuuuuuuuuup,' bending and straightening her legs with her hands splayed out in front of her, stretching like an overfed cat. Standing up with her hands on her lower back she pushed her stomach out. In the stained satin of her slip dress her belly looked full, bountiful, just like Katie's had with each pregnancy.

'Does it hurt?' Bex asked, completing full hip rotations.

'Does what hurt?'

'Giving birth.'

'I thought you weren't going to have kids, so why do you care?'

'I'm not, I'm just interested in how much pain women have to go through to keep the human race going.'

'Yes, it's painful, it's the most painful thing you can ever experience. The last time I gave birth I felt like my whole body was being ripped apart and I was just going to burst open and leave blood and guts all over the delivery room and that would be the end of me.'

'Wow. Really?' Bex said, pausing mid-hip rotation.

'Really. But, it's the most alive I've ever felt. The pain is so raw it's almost addictive. Not in like a hippy, orgasmic way, but in a total annihilation-of-the-self kind of way. Like everything about you and what you understand of yourself is totally obliterated and you're just going on instinct and adrenaline, and you're in another realm. I kind of love the violence of it all. It's just a shame the rest of motherhood is so unbelievably boring.'

Still standing, Bex swivelled her hips with one hand on her abdomen and one hand on her lower back. She hummed along to Amy Winehouse's 'Valerie' and with her eyes half-closed said, 'Imagine if you could just give birth to the stuff you really wanted, like a cheese sandwich or a new laptop?'

The agony of Katie's overindulgence had passed and she was starting to feel hungry again.

'Mmmm I could eat a cheese sandwich,' she salivated.

'Isn't there a hog roast coming out at some point?' Bex said, succumbing to her munchies.

'I really hope so. I hope they have crackling and apple sauce and all the extras. I'm actually surprised you're not vegan now.'

'Me too, to be honest, but I couldn't give up Nando's.'

'You're such a fake anarchist, throwing digital bricks at anyone or anything that doesn't meet your idealistic standards while gobbling off chicken wings doused in peri-peri sauce.'

'Gobbling off, who even says that? What does that even mean?'

They both burst into hysterics, unsure if what they were laughing at was actually even funny, but unable to stop. They laughed the kind of howl you only experience as a child, a frenzied energy that fed back and forth between them. Tears streamed down Katie's face but she couldn't work out if she was crying with laughter or whether it had tipped over into crying for real. The sensation flipped back and forth by the millisecond until she couldn't take it

anymore and she put her head between her knees. Bex sat
back down next to her and laid her head on her back. They
stayed like that, collapsed for the length of 'Enjoy Yourself'
by The Specials, another wedding classic, Katie thought.

'What did you say to Joanna that first time that Phil
came for lunch?' Bex asked softly, rubbing the back of her
neck.

'Why?' Katie froze. 'I don't think I said anything. I can't
even remember. What did she say?' She sat up quickly,
taking in deep breaths of air.

'I dunno, Joanna said you showed your true colours that
day and others almost saw it. What did she mean by that?'

Phil had appeared unexpectedly two years ago. No one had
heard that Joanna had a new boyfriend but in early spring
a lunch was organised when the family would all meet this
new man who was apparently very rich and very good for
Joanna. She had been clean and working in PR for five
years. There'd been lots of support, lots of residential rehab
and lots of David's money spent on her recovery. Their
mother was keen that everyone be as supportive as possible
of everything Joanna did that didn't involve drugs, assault,
stealing or getting arrested. Katie had seen Joanna at their
mother's over recent years, nothing from their childhood
was ever discussed, their past didn't exist in this new folly
where their mother and David lived. This house represented respectability. With each architectural concrete
surface or tasteful design decision, their mother had tried
to bury and eradicate the events that dictated the pitch of
her voice and the speed of her walk.

The family was to be there at 1 p.m. and the guests would arrive at 1.30 p.m., Katie had asked why Joanna was considered a guest but their mother chose to ignore the question and disappeared into her larder to get more stuffing mix. Joanna and Phil arrived on time and despite his unnaturally red lips and weak jawline, he was confident and likeable. He'd answered Bex's prying questions about his family inheritance and job as an aviation broker with good humour, he'd asked his own questions and seemed genuinely interested in what others had to say. He played football with Katie's sons in the garden and helped clear the dishes. After lunch Joanna watched him with her family, she seemed happy. When they were alone in the kitchen Katie asked Joanna where they'd met.

'We've known each other for years.'

'Really, where from?'

'Through work. He came to one of the launch events I'd organised for a client and we have some mutual friends.'

'You don't have any friends, Joanna.'

Joanna bit the inside of her cheek and smiled weakly, her eyes skittering around the kitchen floor looking for a safe place to land.

'He's from money, isn't he?' Katie had continued, never taking her eyes off Joanna.

'I don't know.'

'Come on, his dad is a fucking duke.' Katie picked up Joanna's glass, took a sip and said, 'You must really want this one to work out. This could be it for you, couldn't it?'

'He knows. I've already told him everything. So, you can't do anything.'

'He knows everything does he?' Katie had always found it amusing to taunt Joanna. The perverse enjoyment she took from torturing her, it was written all over her face, so much so that she didn't have to shift her expression when they were interrupted by her youngest son who was looking for desserts. She didn't miss a beat as she called 'Puddings all round!' in a jolly voice. The only giveaway, if anyone was looking for one, were the angry red blotches that had appeared across Joanna's chest.

Under the pressure of Bex's questions, Katie's clothes and shapewear suddenly felt tighter and more constricting than they had been all day.

'Urgh these Spanx are so uncomfortable, I can't wait to take them off,' Katie exclaimed, fiddling with the middle section of her dress. 'The person who invented them is evil.'

'It was a woman.'

'I can't breathe.' She stood up, lifting her dress aggressively, and peeled off the beige-coloured shorts that went down to her knees and came up to her breasts.

'Why do you wear them? Why torture yourself? I dare you to go back in without them on.'

'No way.'

'Why not?'

'Because then everyone would see the size of my belly and they'd know I'm fat.'

'So, what? I'm fat and I don't wear them.' Bex pulled them down over Katie's bum and she sat back down with the Spanx around her ankles.

'Yeah but you're all young and plump and beautiful and full of purpose and potential. My fat is just saggy leftovers and stretched skin, the signs of an empty broken woman.' She grabbed at her stomach and waggled it as she spoke.

'Katie, you need to get a grip. Your body has created four children, some women would kill to have your body and your kids.'

'I know. You're right. You're so right, you little Buddha.' Katie stroked the side of Bex's face sloppily and smiled a dopey, cross-eyed smile that straightened itself as she tried to make out the figure walking towards them.

'Shit, is that Joanna?' Katie said sitting as upright as possible.

'Oh fuck, I hope not.'

'I knew I could see someone up here,' Joanna shouted before she'd reached them. 'What are you two doing? Why have you taken your knickers off? You look like you're on the toilet,' she said pointing her champagne glass at the Spanx wrapped around Katie's ankles.

'She's making a statement.'

'I don't care what statement you're trying to make, please don't do it at my wedding. We're cutting the cake now and someone is performing a poetry burning, will you come down?'

Katie and Bex looked at each other with question-mark faces, a sisterly symmetry holding their raised eyebrows in place.

'What. The. Fuck. Is. A. Poetry. Burning?' Bex stuttered out.

'Phil's sister is doing it. I don't know, it's mystical, or something. Just hurry up.' She went to walk back to the wedding party, but then paused. 'What's that smell?'

'Nothing,' Katie said, blowing smoke slowly to the side furthest away from Joanna.

'Is the hog roast coming out soon?' Bex tried to distract her.

'Oh my god. You two are wasted aren't you, stay away from Phil's family and don't make it obvious that you're high.'

'Joanna, it's practically legal. You should see what most of Phil's mates are hoovering up in the toilets.'

'Honestly Katie, you're over forty. When is this going to stop?'

'When will what stop? She doesn't even smoke that much, calm down.'

'She knows what I mean. I just wanted to have you both here on my wedding day and to make everything OK, for once.'

'You're so dramatic, we're literally out of the way,' Bex replied, standing up unsteadily with open arms to draw attention to the empty terrace. 'No one even knows we're here and they wouldn't if you weren't shouting.'

'I'm not shouting,' Joanna shouted. Then pausing to lower her voice she continued, 'I knew you two would be a nightmare today, stay up here out of the way.' Looking at Katie, Joanna's face turned a dull gunmetal. 'I'm not the monster you make me out to be Katie, and you know it.' Joanna put her champagne glass down on the base of a mossy gargoyle sculpture, and picking up the bottom of her dress which was catching on the flagstones she turned back towards the stairs.

With her Spanx still around her ankles Katie watched Joanna walk away. For the first time ever she felt drawn to her. She wanted to help her down the stairs and go back to the wedding Joanna had so wanted to be perfect. She wanted to stand by and watch her middle sister shine in front of the people she thought were so important. If that made her sister happy, then that was what she wanted to do. That's what big sisters were for. But Katie knew that would be expecting too much of herself. She knew she wasn't capable of that.

As Joanna walked away she turned back to face her sisters, possibly to check if they were following her. Her expression melted in disappointment as she saw them, darkened, static statues rooted to the spot. In that look Katie saw a flash of Joanna as an eight-year-old sitting on her bed as she packed her bags to leave home. Katie had been babysitting, she had been responsible for Joanna's wellbeing, her safety. Joanna was holding a hedgehog from her Sylvanian Family collection. She had held it in her delicate hands, repeatedly stroking the smooth fur on the top of its head as more items went into Katie's backpack.

'Where are we going Katie?' Joanna had asked quietly.

'*We* are not going anywhere. *You* are staying here with your mum and your dad.'

'But they're not here,' she'd rubbed one eye with a small fist in confusion.

'That's not my problem, is it?'

'Why can't I come with you?'

'Because you ruin everything. Now get the fuck out of my room.'

Looking towards Joanna at the top of the cold stone stairs Katie could see her face as a small child, burning red and shrinking. She could see her small fingers curling around the bedroom door as Katie pushed her out and forced it shut. She could hear Joanna screaming in the hallway begging to be let back in, telling Katie she was scared, that she'd do whatever Katie told her to. As she left, she couldn't hear the cries and screams that continued from inside of the house because she'd slammed the front door, turned her Discman up to full blast and hadn't looked back. She couldn't see the small face of the little girl looking out of the window, the net curtain draped over her head like a child bride as she watched her big sister walk to the end of the street and disappear.

Several weeks after the wedding, Bex sent Katie an email with the subject heading 'Wahey' and a video attachment titled: Jo_wedding_cut. Katie opened it already knowing what it was. In the video she could see Joanna and Phil standing together next to the towering seven-tiered cake decorated with fresh fruit and edible flowers, hands clasped over the same huge pearl-handled knife ready to cut into tier three as a symbolic marker of the food and life they would share together. Cameras flash, Joanna's face is beaming, she's so happy she's smiling with her gums. Just as the knife punctures the thick icing the sound of one champagne flute falling from the top terrace and smashing into the crowd gathered below can be heard. The camera pans quickly to the doors that open onto the lower terrace. There's screaming and shouting, the crowd parts, one of the Coven can be seen clasping her forehead as blood gushes down her face onto her floral Simone Rocha dress, and the very faintest 'wahey' can be heard off camera.

Bar Italia

The last time I cheated on my husband was with a man I met in Bar Italia.

I'd been sitting on a bench along the mirrored wall, mindlessly watching an Italian talk show on the screen behind me. I'd called in for an americano in an attempt to counteract the cheap post-conference wine I'd drunk while standing in staccato poses as men told me things I already knew. The caffeine shot had been slowly working its way through my body, sharpening my cells to match the hectic comings and goings of the busy Soho café bar, when he sat next to me with his back to the mirror.

He placed his beer between us and faced the TV screen. He could have held his beer, it would have been easier. Instead his right hand reached across his whole body each time he took a sip, pushing the bottle closer and closer towards me until the beads of condensation running down the glass met with the sweat on my bare arm.

*

The toilet cubicle was small and damp, littered with the dirt of one thousand tourists, but none of this blocked the pleasure I took from this man. We used the condom I had in my bag and had sex in positions the tight space allowed. I came quickly and watched his face contort as he reached his orgasm. He had a wide, flat face and heavy forehead with a clean-shaven jaw that gave no resistance as he brushed his mouth over mine. I wondered if he had a wet shave every day or if he walked around talking into his phone as he rushed an electric shaver over his chin. I wasn't sure if men actually used electric shavers anymore or if I was imagining a scene from an old movie. The bottom of his left sideburn ended in a precise angle. I was interested to see if both sides were the same length but I couldn't move his head enough to get a clear view. His eyebrows reached out to meet each other as he grimaced with pleasure; dislodged from their regular positions I could still see they had been delicately plucked and shaped recently. Maybe his barber did it as he straightened off his hairline, or perhaps his wife gave them a once-over when she was tidying her own. His whole head was aggressively well kept.

Waiting for him to pass me the wet paper towels I'd asked for, I was struck by the lack of graffiti inside the cubicle, maybe the men of Bar Italia didn't feel the need to send each other covert messages in toilets because their cues on how to be in the world were readily available above ground. As I read the copy for a prostate cancer advert on the toilet door and thought about what to buy my mother-in-law for her birthday, a wet mass of brown paper towels appeared under the door, followed by 'I'll meet you upstairs.' I stayed put and washed myself as best I could.

Outside the cubicle a man at the urinals surveyed me reapplying my lipstick in the mirror. I stared back at him as I wiped away the stray red smudge from the bottom of my lip line and watched his whole body turn towards me until he was pissing on the floor.

I joined my new friend at a table outside the bar where we drank Camparis and chain-smoked his cigarettes. His name was Tony. He told me about his life and I made up a new version of mine. He was married, he had three children and was the marketing director of a sportswear brand but wouldn't say which one. Maybe he was making it up too. He'd met his wife after university and they'd married young. He'd apparently never done anything like this before.

'It must have been you,' he repeated four times, shaking his head.

As each passing minute took me away from my point of climax, I found him more and more boring.

'So, Soraya, have you done this before?' he asked.

'Really Tony?'

'I know, sorry, I'm just curious. I mean have you had affairs before?'

I looked at this man, this smug, wide-faced man who probably had missionary sex with his wife while he pictured images from the porn he watched on his phone locked in the bathroom, and I knew what he wanted me to say. I knew he wanted to punish me for the guilt that was seeping down into his stomach, crawling all over his skin no matter how many times he scratched his arm.

'Yes Tony, I sleep with people who aren't my husband. Why?'

'Just curious,' he said again, tapping the arm of his metal chair. 'I don't know how you have the energy. One relationship is enough for me to deal with.'

Tony assumed affairs were stressful and difficult to manage because Tony confused affairs with marriages. I didn't want to leave my husband and my family. I wasn't looking to upgrade or replace what I already had but I also didn't buy into the juvenile expectation that one person could be my everything. Affairs, when managed and funded well, are relatively simple and straightforward. You set dates in places where neither of you are well known, you have a good time and dispose of all of the evidence – receipts, messages, emails all have to go. There's no space for sentimentality.

Omar taught me this. He was professional, he liked things clean and manageable. I appreciated that and in return I pegged him with a marble dildo whenever we were in the same city. We had met through work, and saw each other every few months for three years. Omar was straight up from the start about what he was looking for and what he could give in return. I liked him a lot and looked forward to seeing him, but I didn't love him. I didn't pine for him when we weren't together. Affairs require a level of detachment and honesty that you don't find in most marriages, that's why the sex is always better. On our last meeting he told me his firm was moving him and his family from Berlin to Portland, so he wasn't going to be in Europe again for a while. This was going to be the last time we'd see each other. He kissed the top of my head at 5 a.m. as he left my hotel room and I never saw or heard from him again.

*

After four Camparis with Tony I was still bored but turned on enough by thoughts of our toilet sex to invite him back to my hotel room. Away from the excitement of the dirty cubicle, Tony's mediocrity was magnified. He looked drunk and shifted uncomfortably at the doorway of my room. He repeatedly smoothed down his well-trimmed nails as he walked around the hotel suite, commenting on its size, the quality of the sheets and the weight of the smoked tumblers on the bar. He burst open a small packet of peanuts from the minibar without asking and nuzzled the lightweight curtain with his nose to get a better view of the city below.

'Wow, there's a bathtub on the balcony!' he gasped, spraying peanut dust against the windowpane. 'We should get in that.'

'I'm going to have a shower,' I replied, already naked.

I turned on the shower and told him to wait. In the bathroom he stood eagerly at the sink wearing nothing but his socks as I washed my hair. I looked at his naked, odd-shaped body, his clammy grey balls and erect purple penis. He gazed back at me, taking in the body I spent a fortune on, my good strong body.

'Are you going to take your socks off?' I said, my voice magnified in the shower cubicle, which was the size of a family bathroom.

'Oh yes,' he laughed nervously, 'I got distracted.'

Holding the towel rack to steady himself, he burnt his hand and clumsily removed the sports socks, which left angry red rings halfway up his calves.

'Get in,' I ordered.

He screamed like a small pug as he had his second orgasm of the night, and couldn't catch his breath until he lay on the bed in the cool, air-conditioned room.

'Fucking hell, that was incredible,' he said with his arms covering his face, his appalling genitalia splayed out on my hotel bedspread.

Physically he was all over the place but he'd arranged his clothes in a very neat little pile, everything folded professionally as if he'd been in the army or worked in a designer clothes store. His attention to detail and order reminded me of Jacob, who I'd met in a restaurant in Clerkenwell. He was eating £12 cheese on toast and drinking rosé. He said he liked my trousers and we segued into a very specific conversation about the stitching on Margaret Howell coats. We saw each other every few weeks for about six months and I let him tie me up but, in the end, his sharp angles, tonal modular clothing, spotless modernist apartment and successful architecture practice belied his darker side. I wasn't the dedicated sub he was looking for and we went our separate ways when he suggested strangulation.

I don't talk about this part of my life with anyone. Not my sisters, my therapist, my best friend, nor the people I work with who might understand this better than anyone in my *normal* life. Women are supposed to be the ones who uphold the morals of society and we face the harshest judgement when we reject what is apparently good for us. I know that even the women who love me the most wouldn't be able to help themselves from judging my choices harshly. They might sit and listen and try to understand, but at some point, they'll tell parts of my story to someone else with the caveat: 'Don't mention this to anyone but …' or 'I mean, I love her, but …' They'll try and work out what is wrong with me, combing over my childhood, my husband and our relationship for clues as to where it all went awry. When I began to fall apart because there has to be a reason. There has to be something wrong with me, this can't be the way a normal woman lives her life. Maybe they'd conclude that I'm a lost cause, that they felt sorry for my husband and kids but all the while they'd wonder what it was like.

I stood in front of the TV and flicked through the channels looking for something mundane to watch.

'What are we watching?' Tony said from behind.

Pausing on CNN, I looked at him in the mirror, propped up with pillows on my side of the bed, wrapped in my hotel dressing gown, scanning the room service menu, his toes flicking in anticipation. They were huge doughy toes with hairs sprouting below yellow nails, fossilised skin flaking around the edges. His attention to detail apparently stopped at his ankles.

'Does work cover all of your expenses?' he asked. 'Can you get me a club sandwich?' A familiar feeling arose in my chest, the feeling of suffocation I get at home when everyone is asking me for something but no one is listening to my replies.

Turning off the TV I said, 'Listen, I've got an early start at the conference tomorrow but let's meet here afterwards, let's say 1 p.m., my flight isn't until 6 p.m. and I've got a late checkout.'

'Wow, you're kicking me out?' he said, bereft he wasn't going to get a free club sandwich.

'Yes,' I said, throwing his neat pile of clothes at him. 'I'm kicking you out.'

At the door he kissed my closed mouth and waved a quiet *see you tomorrow* with the tips of his fingers as I shut it behind him. I showered again, washing everywhere twice and scrubbing under my fingernails. I used all of the lotion in the hotel miniatures, slathering it over my body in multiple layers. I applied various toners, serums, acids and moisturisers to my face until I looked like a polished kitchen surface. I threw my underwear into the hotel bin and lay on the bed in a different hotel dressing gown to the one that Tony had soiled. Then I called my mum. We chatted about my sisters, their marriages, my cousin's new husband and my grandmother's health. I messaged my husband, ordered some pottery classes for his mum's birthday, caught up on work emails and watched reruns of *Beverly Hills, 90210* until I fell asleep.

In the morning I woke up in damp sheets and turned the TV on. Breakfast show hosts delivered horrific news and expressed sound-bite opinions on things they were ill-equipped to be talking about. *Frasier* was followed by *Everybody Loves Raymond*, kids' cartoons splashed across the screen and the weather looked too hot for the time of year. I thought about the conference I was due to attend that morning. The papers I would have to sit through that catalogued the environmental disasters people in the Global South were currently living through, as if they were hypothetical worst-case scenarios. I thought about the paper I'd given the day before and the questions white-haired men had put to me about my methodology, looking for a way to discredit the findings. During the coffee break an American man had spat flakes of his croissant at me as we discussed my work. We both saw the pastry fly out of his mouth and land on my lapel but he'd chosen not to mention it as I'd tried to wipe it away subtly, taking care not to embarrass him. I'd looked at his face and noticed his lips had completely turned in on themselves. They'd shrunk over the years until his mouth had become a beige sinkhole in the middle of his face out of which he spat patronising sentences and flaky pastry. He wasn't worried about the future, he'd said.

'We shouldn't focus on the apocalyptic scaremongering. We should all be more hopeful. Yes, we just need more hope.'

As if hope was all we needed to get behind.

I messaged my colleague Samira and told her I was sick, that I wasn't going to make the second day and would see her at the airport later in the evening. She messaged back:

Too many cocktails last night?

With an orange cocktail emoji, a cringing face being sick and a face crying with laughter. I sent back a woman with her hands in the air.

*

I showered and ordered room service: granola, scrambled eggs with an extra side of bacon, pastries, coffee and two glasses of orange juice. Tony had been right, work did cover my expenses. I sat back with a full stomach on the bed and drained the last of my orange juice. On TV, one of the international news anchors looked like Rhea. I jolted forward to get a better look and turned up the volume. It wasn't her but my mind was instantly flooded with images of Rhea's face and our time together. Of everyone I'd slept with since I'd been married, she was the person I'd almost allowed myself to have feelings for. There was so much I didn't have to explain; how I wanted to be touched, my longing to reach a physical place beyond language. She understood the push and pull of trying to connect with the part of yourself that terrified you the most. She never questioned the validity of my relationship with my husband and she never made me feel guilty for desiring more space in a life that was taken up by the needs of so many others. With Rhea I gave more of myself than I'd expected to, but, in the end, she met someone who could see her as she'd seen me and we parted ways. I never kept anything from any of my affairs, everything was immediately deleted from my burner phone, but I kept a ticket stub from an exhibition of nudes we'd once gone to see together.

In bed I pictured the paintings we'd looked at; the texture of the paint which made the bodies look like they were breathing, the light that surrounded the figures, their commanding positions, their defiant gaze. When I was younger I used to live in my body. I experienced the world physically. I was hungry for touch, hungry for tastes and smells and sensations. I ran as fast as I could, I danced wildly. I ate to experience new flavours. I had sex to feel good. My body was the conduit through which pleasure came to me and I welcomed it all in. Now my life was measured. My exercise was measured, my food was measured, my schedule was measured, my responses were measured, my pleasure was measured and once I'd had enough, I shouldn't be so greedy as to expect more.

Lying on the bed with my pelvis raised I traced my red glossy nails over my body and dug them into my buttocks. I spent hours maintaining my nails, filing them, shaping them, painting them, filling in breakages so that they were all as equal as each other. They were so perfect they looked like salon acrylics, and it always made me happy when someone asked if they were real.

'Yes, they're all mine,' I'd say, glowing inside, proud of my good, strong fingernails.

In this hotel room their presence mocked me. The energy it took to keep them perfect sapped me. I picked at the corner of my index finger nail, chipping into it like a forester chopping down a diseased tree. The first one came off cleanly and each nail followed obediently until I'd created a collection of red lacquered half-moons on the bedside table. I made a mental note to flush them down the toilet before I left, but forgot. They no doubt lay there until a stressed-out maid wiped them into the bin as she turned over the room in the allotted ten minutes (possibly twenty minutes, given the hotel rating) she had to rid the place of my dirt and mess.

At 12.45 p.m. my phone beeped; it was Tony. He was downstairs but couldn't remember my room number and they didn't have a guest by the name I'd given him. He asked if I could come down to get him or text him the room number. I stared at the raw, exposed skin on my fingertips, soft and sensitive, having always been under the protective hood of my long nails. Tony started writing another message, a tonal blue vibrated over three dots as he composed his next command. He only had an hour so I had to hurry up and text him the room number, or tell the receptionist to let him up.

I looked at myself in the mirror opposite the bed and took off the T-shirt I'd slept in. I spread my legs and arched my back, moving my body into positions I'd never seen myself in. I flexed and relaxed my biceps, let my stomach hang out, inspected my armpits and the hair follicles I'd had lasered. I held my legs in a shoulder-stand pose and pretended to ride a bike in the air, pausing to finger the fleshy scar on the inside of my right thigh. I did star jumps in front of the mirror and watched as everything bounced up and down, up and down. I pulled my bum cheeks apart and took pictures of myself in the mirror, zooming in on the parts of my body that others had seen close up but which I'd never looked at. I'd lived in my body for forty-five years, I'd pretended to be so many people throughout my life, but I'd never paid close attention to who I was when no one else was around.

My phone rang. It was Tony standing in the hotel reception with half an erection in his trousers. I didn't answer. He rang another three times and sent a message calling me a fucking bitch. Making a mental note to pick up a new SIM on the way to the airport I took the old one out of my burner phone, put it on the bedside table next to the pile of dismembered red fingernails and turned the TV up to full volume.

Junction 64

The small staff room smelled like men's supermarket deodorant and stale lager. At the corner of the large table, which dominated the room, sat Jonny, staring at his phone. A pained look of concentration gripped his face. He thought I was posh because I hadn't shortened my name from Deborah to Debbie or Debs. He made this known by sounding out the individual syllables of my name every time he saw me.

'Alreet Deb-or-ah,' he said without lifting his head.

'You'right Jonny?' I responded, opening my locker.

'Aye aye, just a bit battered from last night like.'

'Sound. Did you go anywhere good?'

I immediately regretted trying to take our conversation further than a civilised hello, I knew that whatever I said would be used against me later in the shift. I'd once cut my finger during a shift and made the mistake of asking for a blue 'plahhster' instead of blue 'plastaa'. For the next four hours, he'd shouted 'Gis a PLAAHHSTER!' in his version of a high-pitched 'posh' voice from the back of the fryers every time I put through an order.

We worked together at Burger King at the motorway services near Junction 64 of the A1. My mam had noticed the job in the local *Advertiser*. She was eager for me to apply as I'd deferred my place at university to look after her and one of us needed to be earning. Allowing myself to be swayed by what she thought constituted a good job I went for it because the money was better than working the tills at Asda and it was near home if I needed to get back quickly. Also, the description made it sound like a good place to work: *If you'd love to work in a fast-paced vibrant restaurant, enjoy engaging with different people every day and want to feel like part of a family whilst having fun, then this role is perfect for you!* At the time the thought of feeling like part of a family in a vibrant workplace was just what I was looking for – then I met Jonny.

We both started at the same time and held the same level of responsibility – which is to say that we held no responsibility – but he liked to try and pretend he was a supervisor when Barry the manager was on his break, and took every opportunity to boss me around. He was tall and lanky with deep-set eyes and too many teeth in his mouth. He hated me because when he'd tried to get a loan to go to Cyprus with his friends, I'd questioned whether using high-interest payday finance to go on holiday was a good idea.

'Who the fuck are you like? Martin fucking Lewis?' he had said as we chopped gherkins together in the kitchen. 'Geet as if anyone gives a shit what you think anyway.'

He hated me even more when the loan was denied and all of his friends went to Ayia Napa without him. For the two weeks they were away, he'd sent out wrong orders from my section and claimed I'd put them through. I'd received complaints from customers and then a verbal warning from Barry.

In the staff room, Jonny didn't respond to my question about where he'd been the night before, he just shouted 'Fifteen!' into the middle of the staff room.

'Fifteen what?' I asked.

'A had fifteen drinks last neet, just been rounding up what a had and where. Fifteen, canny good gannin for a Thorsday.'

'Wow, nice one.'

'Fuck off.'

'What? I didn't even …'

'Here man fuck off before ya start. Ya making us feel proper ill.'

He looked at me with the top half of his face screwed up as if he was trying to read something far away, his teeth pushed forward into an exaggerated overbite. I wasn't sure what the right response was to diffuse the situation so I turned around to my locker and started getting ready for my shift. I could feel Jonny's eyes boring into my back but he didn't want to carry on the conversation either and slowly moved his attention back to his phone screen.

I still had twenty minutes before my shift started, so I went to see Sandy, a close friend of my mam's who worked in WH Smith's across the forecourt. She'd worked at the service station since it opened in 1989 and was supposed to retire last year but management hadn't brought it up so neither had she. Sitting at the till on her raised plinth she was a Roman empress in a blue branded tabard. She laughed often and exuded a warmth from her soft round body, which brought a tranquillity to the air around her. She could spot a shoplifter from the moment they walked in and could guess what kind of items they'd steal. A lot of the local kids knew her shift pattern and would come in to steal high-ticket items on her days off. Car accessories, headphones, neck cushions, condoms – until they were moved to behind the counter – and, inexplicably, packets of shortbread were all high on a local shoplifter's inventory.

'Here she is,' Sandy shouted from her throne as I walked into the shop.

'Hiya Sandy. How's it going?'

'Aye, aye, alright pet, ye nar. Kids are doing me head in, husband's doing me head in, customers are doing me head in.' She lowered her voice and whispered, 'Manager's doing me head in,' before carrying on in her normal voice, 'Wait till I tell you what our Gary's done. Honestly, it's too much to go into now but what a carry-on, he's got me ill. Anyway, how's you?'

'I'm alright, I'm in the kitchen today with Jonny and he's hungover.'

'Typical, bloody idiot. Just ignore him. How was your mam this morning?'

'She's alright, they told her yesterday that she's got to do another course of treatment but they don't know when it'll start,' I said, spinning around the display of named keyrings on the cash desk, still looking for Deborah.

'Ah pet, I'll drop in tomorrow after work and sit with her so you can get out and do yer own thing if you want.'

'OK yeah, I might go into town or something.'

'You do that. Listen, come and get me when you're going on your break and I'll take mine with you. Alright?'

Tapping the empty space where the Deborah keyrings should have been I said, 'Alright.'

'Here, there's an open box of Wispas in the stockroom that I haven't put out yet, just on the inside of that door. Get yasel one and I'll write it off as being lifted by one of those little toerags.'

I smiled and mouthed thanks as a family with two loud children came in.

In the kitchen I clocked in and made a black coffee with two sugars. We didn't open for another hour, everything was still and resting. There was a low hum coming from the fridges, fryers and drinks machines, all on standby, ready to spring into action and produce any combination of the high-fat, high-salt, high-sugar, low-nutrition food on the menu. Stood looking over the rota for the week I peeled back the wrapper of my Wispa and dipped it into my scalding black coffee. When I pulled it out a thick band of melted gooey chocolate clung to the rest of the taut, untainted bar. I put it in my mouth and slowly pulled it out, collecting all of the melted chocolate on the inside of my teeth,

'Urgh, what the fuck are yee deein?' Jonny snapped, standing at the kitchen door watching me.

Startled, I jumped and dropped the Wispa into the bin at my knee. 'Nothing.'

'You're fucking minging. Where's Barry?'

'I haven't seen him yet,' I said, wiping my hands down the front of my apron.

'Well let's get wor prep on then, instead of standing around noshing off Dairy Milks. Ye nar what he's like.'

'It was a Wispa.'

'Whatever, dee the tomatoes.'

'Fucking prick,' I muttered to myself as I lined up the green chopping board, knife and box of tomatoes in front of me.

I'd originally been hired to take orders, make drinks and bag up meal deals on the front counter with another girl called Cheryl, but I was moved to the kitchen after three months. When I first got the job, I had long hair that my auntie would dye a specific Nordic blonde in my mam's living room once a month. I'd saved up for extensions that made men in vans shout things like 'Here Goldilocks, you can come and kip in my bed,' as I walked to the corner shop for milk.

At night after work, I'd watch make-up tutorials and test out various contouring kits that apparently brought structure and definition to my cheeks, nose and chin. Before each shift I'd spend an hour getting ready, layering and blending skin-toned liquids on my face, sticking false eyelashes to my eyelids and applying lip liner precisely two millimetres over my lip line. At work, I'd smile and greet the customers, standing poised, muscles pulled tight, in my thick make-up and perfectly managed hair, ready to take their orders. I'd catch young lads staring at me while they waited for their food quickly averting their eyes if I looked in their direction. Occasionally I'd feel how you're supposed to feel in that situation: validated, happy, pretty. But most of the time it made me feel tired. On a Friday or Saturday night shift, someone with breath that smelt like sick and stale cigarettes might ask me out or make a comment about what they'd like to do to my burger. Then when their order was ready they'd pile back into the minibus they came out of with twelve other lads and head down the A1 to Middlesbrough or Peterlee.

When I stopped wearing make-up Barry the manager asked if I was feeling OK.

'Yeah,' I'd said. 'I feel fine, why?'

'No reason, you just look a bit different. A bit pale. Just wanted to check you're not coming down with something.'

The week I cut off my hair he'd said my new look was daring and was I sure I was feeling OK.

Jonny had shouted, 'Why aye check oot Declan Donnelly,' from the back of the kitchen.

And in the staff room, Cheryl had said, 'I'm not trying to be shan or nowt but like, did you pay someone to do that to your hair?' Her boyfriend Daz let out a guttural 'hor hor hor' and took a large swig of his can of Red Bull.

'This is the staff room Daz. It's for staff. You don't work here,' I'd spat.

'Fuck off ya fuckin loser.'

'At least I don't hang around here when I'm not even being paid.'

Sandy was the only one who didn't seem shocked by my make-under.

'Ah I like this new look pet,' she'd said when I walked into the shop that first day. 'What's brought this on? Did your auntie do it?'

'No, I did it, I just fancied a change.'

'Well nowt wrong with that. Girls these days put loads of

rubbish on their faces and all look a bit deformed, don't
they?'

'Yeah, I suppose.'

'When you're a natural beauty like me, you don't need
nowt do you?' she'd said, flicking an imaginary mane behind
her neck and laughing a belly laugh that made her whole
body bounce in amusement.

Barry knew he couldn't sack me for not wearing make-up
and he couldn't force me to wear it so he'd put me on the
grill in the kitchen with Jonny and worked the counter
shifts himself while he looked for my aesthetically pleasing
replacement.

The kitchen was a mix of stainless-steel worktops, fridges
full of pre-prepared food wrapped in plastic, hotplates,
fryers and laminated hygiene signs. Some of the signs came
from head office but most had been rewritten, redesigned
and laminated by Barry as he felt the originals weren't thorough enough. Stealing glances at the Wispa that lay on top
of the rubbish in the bin next to me, I quietly worked my
way through a pile of plump beef tomatoes, chopping them
into thick slices that I'd later layer on top of grey burger
patties. The juice that escaped from each tomato found its
way into the tiny cuts that lined my fingers, making my
hands ache.

'Good morning my little burger flippers, how are we
both today?' Barry called as he burst through the double
doors of the kitchen.

'Hi Barry,' I said, turning my head but not my body.

'Alreet Baz,' Jonny shouted from the corner where he

tried to hide the newspaper he'd been flicking through. Barry was a small, compact man. He kept a trim and tidy brown moustache which broke up the features that wanted to meet in the middle of his face. He moved with precise, sharp gestures and loved his job. He had worked every station in the place and knew how each section should run for optimum efficiency.

'Yes, yes, I'm good. It's Friday. The sun is shining. The traffic is flowing and I have a feeling we're going to be busy later so I'm happy. Deborah, before things kick off I want to show you the new ordering system in my office. Come up when you've done with the tomatoes. Barry hoped to be area manager one day and had told me I could follow in his footsteps as manager if I applied myself and 'brightened up my appearance'. He felt bad he'd essentially demoted me because of a lack of lip liner and wanted to try to inspire loyalty or at least motivate me to care more about burgers. Pointing at the pile of tomatoes in front of me, Barry continued, 'Actually, Jonny can you finish these?'

Jonny shot me a look that meant I would pay for this later on.

'Aye Baz,' he said moving slowly. 'A can dee that. Nee botha like.'

'Good, come on then Deborah,' Barry said, holding the double doors open with his heavy Slipbuster shoe, which he'd bought through his favourite catering catalogue. I placed the knife down on the dripping chopping board and refused to make eye contact with Jonny.

*

Barry's office was a wood-panelled room at the side of the stairwell which led to the bridge over to the other side of the services. Along one wall hung framed hygiene awards and manager of the month certificates. A grey metal filing cabinet sat stubbornly in the corner next to a coatrack draped in a pink feather and diamante cowboy hat from a past staff night out. On the desk was an industrial-sized bottle of hand sanitiser, and an old black PC screen and keyboard with faded letters.

'Have a seat Deborah.' Barry pulled over an orange plastic chair for me. 'You're looking very sparky today,' he said flittering his fingers in my direction.

'Am I?' I said doubtfully.

Before even opening the new software, Barry ran over the basics of everything I already did on a daily basis: checking stock at the beginning and end of each shift, noting when anything was running low, letting the next team leader know if there'd been a rush on any one product. He then took me through the new ordering system, delving into an unnecessary amount of detail about supply chains and import laws. Sensing my waning interest Barry put down his pen and looked at me directly. 'You live down in the barracks don't you?'

The barracks were a stretch of long streets at the bottom end of town that had gained their name because the rows of terraced houses looked like an army base.

'Yes.'

'Still with your mam?'

I looked at the floor. 'Yes.'

'But you're clever, aren't you? You want to move up to Vigo or one of the new-build estates, don't you?'

Moving up to Vigo was code for anyone who was doing well. You were a success if you moved out of the barracks up to Vigo or up to one of the new Avant estates with their hoardings covered in tag lines that read: *Dare to live differently*. In the red-brick houses of the barracks people worked multiple jobs on zero-hour contracts for low wages. Windows looked out onto concrete yards to the front and back. Along the whole stretch of uniform terraces there were no trees, patches of grass or carefully planted flower beds – there wasn't the space or money for them. Day and night, young kids scrawled their initials onto the road with stones, or rode stolen bikes in packs. The older kids gathered in the darker corners of the terraces to drink and take drugs, some of them already lived on their own in cold council flats where the electricity and gas ran on meters they couldn't afford to top up. In the opposite direction, the wide breezy streets of Vigo were lined with large houses fringed with manicured front gardens. Open garages spewed out bikes, scooters, rollerblades and tennis equipment, and squeals of laughter floated from back gardens as children bounced merrily on trampolines. Dads walked pedigree dogs with their daughters or washed Qashqais on the drive. The streets were named after areas of the Lake District rather than just being numbered like the barracks.

One day on the minibus to work, I'd looked through the large lounge window of an end house in Vigo. A woman reclined on a bed-like sofa in front of *Lorraine* on a wall-mounted TV so big I could read the topic of conversation from the bus: *Lose weight with what's in your cupboard!* On the surface these lives looked calm and comfortable, but underneath the material abundance lay a palpable fear that everything they had acquired could be taken away. A fear that one day, something or someone would come along and disrupt the harmony. Difference became a threat. The odd quirk of any neighbour became a reason to hate them, or at least an excuse to wage a passive-aggressive war about a car parked in the wrong spot, a barking dog, or an unkempt front garden. This would lead to an altercation on a drive-way or via a community Facebook thread until one of the parties moved away or everyone once again adhered to the unwritten rules and order was restored. This is where Barry assumed everyone wanted to end up.

'I'm not sure I want to move up to Vigo or if I'll move anywhere,' I replied. 'My mam needs …'

'I'll tell you what you need to do Deborah. You need to engage that brain of yours. Stick to the processes I've taught you, watch your timings, stay on top of the cleaning, stay smiling and you could make it all the way.'

'But Barry—' I hesitated. 'Do you like going home and smelling of greasy burgers every night?'

His face fell, and in a low quick voice he said, 'When I get in I strip down in the garage and put everything straight in the washing machine then have a shower immediately. No greasy odour gets into my home. Besides, area managers don't work with the food. Now let's crack on.'

In the kitchen after my training Jonny moved mechanically and slowly in a way I'd not seen before. I put it down to his hangover. Cheryl had arrived for her shift and was chatting to a lorry driver who held her hand over the counter like he was making a marriage proposal.

'You allowed to wear these for work like?' he asked, scaling his hammerhead fingers over her pink-tipped acrylic nails.

'Not really but don't tell anyone!' she laughed, covering her mouth with her free hand.

'Smashers those are. Hope they divn't end up in me Whopper!'

One of the benefits of working in the kitchen was being able to snatch better glimpses of Cheryl, something I couldn't do when we worked side by side on the front counter. Watching Cheryl was addictive, even in her Burger King uniform she was mesmerising. She had a deep, year-round tan, which she said she got from her nana who was Portuguese, but Steph who worked the earlies said Cheryl's nana was from South Shields and that her tan came from her auntie's sunbed shop. I didn't care. Her electric jade eyes were catlike, exaggerated with eyeliner, she had plump high cheekbones and a ballet dancer's posture even without any lessons. Her acrylic nails once scratched the back of my hand as I passed her an XL Whopper with bacon and I thought about it for days. Long dark hair extensions fell down her back from the ponytail she gently fed through her cap. Initially, she had refused to wear anything over her head, especially not a hairnet because the human hair she bought cost 'more than three weeks of Barry's wages'. But a mystery shopper had marked Barry down five points on hygiene because of it so they compromised and now she wore a cap in return for an extra ten minutes on every break.

We both lived at the north end of the barracks, we'd attended the same primary school but I had gone to a different secondary school on a scholarship so we hadn't seen much of each other until we worked together. When I first started and still had my long hair, she talked to me about the best hair products she'd been using, the arguments she'd had with Daz, and the girls we both knew who had already had a baby. I laughed in the right places and asked passable questions but we both knew there was something slightly off about me. I was like the counterfeit Nike tracksuits my mam used to get from the market, you could always tell they were fakes but you weren't exactly sure what gave them away. Once I'd cut off my hair and stopped wearing make-up I made sense to everyone. They could align my appearance with what they saw as my odd personality, they knew to avoid me rather than continually try and work out what was going on. Now Cheryl only engaged me in conversation when she absolutely had to.

Seeing Barry coming down the stairs from his office Cheryl pulled her hand back from the lorry driver's grasp and shouted, 'Who's next?' to the group of people who had gathered behind.

'Oh, good to see things are getting busy, I think it's going to be a bumper weekend. Traffic looks bad so people will be curling off for a break,' Barry said replacing an old laminated health and safety notice that I'd never registered before. Barry's love of hygiene was second only to his love of beating Nigel Graham's weekly figures. Nigel was the manager of Burger King at Durham Services, a further fifteen miles down the A1. The two men were embroiled in a never-ending competition that had been raging for years. I didn't understand this competition and the satisfaction that both men took from beating each other's weekly figures. Neither Barry nor Nigel seemed to take into account the extraneous factors that affected how many customers came through the service station door, they just took the numbers as a true reflection of who'd run the cleanest, friendliest and best-managed burger franchise that week.

'What we on this week Baz?' Jonny asked as he shot two Whoppers down the pass to Cheryl waiting on the other side.

'It looks like we're about 4K over Nigel's weekly takings from what I can tell. He's going to be livid. I love it,' Barry chirped, smoothing down his new sign on the white-tiled wall.

'But, I don't get it,' I said, filling a ketchup bottle from a larger industrial urn of sugary red liquid. 'Do you not think that people stop at motorway services because they need the toilet or they're suddenly hungry, or there's a traffic jam coming up, and not because of how clean or friendly a particular service station is?'

Barry let out an exaggerated sigh. 'Deborah you have such potential and then you come out with ludicrous things like this? You know what, you can forget your last break today and you can spend it cleaning out the fridges for an extra thirty minutes.'

Overhearing this, Jonny shouted 'WHAT A DAFTY!' as he threw a new batch of frozen fries into a vat of nuclear oil.

'In fact, you and Cheryl can go on your first breaks now.'

'What? Why do I have to go?' Cheryl called from the front counter. 'Daz is coming in later. I was gonna have me break with him.'

'Cheryl, you know how busy pay-day Fridays are. You and Deborah go. Now.'

'What a load of shit.' She took her apron off and threw it onto the worktop next to me.

I made myself a cheeseburger, fries and another black coffee. Cheryl grilled some chicken, which she put in a burger box with strips of lettuce and gherkins. We walked in silence to the seating area. Passing WH Smith's I caught Sandy's attention as she was serving customers and tried to mime to her that I had to take my break early. She put her hands in the air then gave a thumbs up. Sitting opposite Cheryl at the corner table of the restaurant reserved for staff my breathing slowed. I watched her nibble the grilled meat slowly and precisely. I could see her tongue and realised I was staring.

'You have really white teeth, have you had them done?' I asked as I took a bite out of my burger, trying to act like I wasn't painfully aware of my every move.

Cheryl observed me closely and wiped her fingers on a serviette. 'Aye, I got a load of those whitening strips off our Angie for cheap. You're only supposed to leave them on for fifteen minutes but I do them for thirty. It gives you proper bad headaches but I reckon it's worth it.' She pulled an exaggerated smile to show off the fruits of her labour then yanked my hand towards her face and inspected my nails. Her hands were soft. I thought about the rest of her body and what it would be like to touch her stomach. 'You've actually got nice cuticles. Do you push them back or put any treatment on them?' she asked.

'No, I used to but … well, I can't really be bothered anymore.'

Her hand dropped back to her chicken and she looked at me suspiciously. 'How come you cut your hair off and stopped doing your face, you used to look proper nice y'know?'

I ate a fry in small bites all the way down until my finger pressed against my front tooth. 'I don't know, I just got tired. I had loads of stuff to buy for me mam and it just started to feel like a waste of money.'

'A waste? What's a waste?' she said with her eyes wide open, a flaccid gherkin pointing towards my face. 'You're wasting your looks man.' She smiled at me, this time covering her teeth with her lips.

I felt her hand brush my ear as she inspected my short hair closely.

'I mean you could at least get some colour on this, or it's not too short to get extensions through it. I could ask our Angie if she can get you some for cheap, she'll just need a colour reference.'

'Maybe. I think I'm OK at the minute.'

'Suit yaself.'

She sat back in her chair and started telling me about the beauty treatments she was saving up for: a lash perm, microblading, Botox in her forehead and more filler in her lips, chin and cheeks were next on her list. She asked about my mam and told me about her brother who had just gone to prison for aggravated assault. She said it wasn't his fault, that it was self-defence, but her brother got sent down for eight years and the other guy was still in a coma so I wasn't sure what to make of it all.

Moving the empty burger box to the side she picked up a copy of *The Sun* left on the table by one of the lorry drivers.

'That Prime Minister is proper funny, isn't he? You seen the state of *his* hair?' she said looking over the headlines on the front page.

'I hate him, he's full of shit. Are you gonna vote in the election?' I asked.

'What? Na, why like are you?' she shot me a questioning frown over the top of the newspaper.

'Yeah, I think so.'

'Honestly why bother?'

'Because we might get someone who can do stuff about the state of things around here.'

'Listen man, they don't give a fuck about us. Why would they? They reckon that all poor people do is doss around on benefits and smoke spice. It's been the same for years, it doesn't matter who the prime minister is.'

'It was different when—'

'Nah. Nah it wasn't. All the community centres got shut down, all the jobs are gone, the high street is all bookies, vape shops and charity shops, the schools are like prisons, they just keep the kids locked up all day and it's been like that for years. You wouldn't know though cos you went to that posh school. Mind, that didn't do you any good, you're still working here with us lot.'

I tried to say something but my throat closed around my words and all I could do was swallow down the shame of Cheryl saying the thing I knew everyone was thinking.

'Do you reckon the people we're supposed to vote for ever come round ours and see what it's really like?' she continued. 'None of them give a fuck about us so why should I give a fuck about any of them? There's no point in voting, you've just gotta do a little extra on the side to get by. That's what me da says and I reckon he's right.' She picked up her phone in one hand and tapped her acrylics on the other hand against the plastic table.

I couldn't finish my cheeseburger. I wrapped it up in the greaseproof paper and squeezed it into a ball until a haemorrhoid of burger patty broke through the wet paper. My break time was over but Cheryl still had her extra ten minutes to go.

'I'd better get back before Barry goes off it, see you back round there.'

She didn't look up but let out a loud laugh and showed me a video of a cat falling off a wardrobe.

Back in the kitchen, Johnny's long face was waxy and yellow. He had a thick layer of sweat all over his skin, the heat from the grill punishing him more than usual. Barry pushed through orders from a queue I couldn't see the end of, the kitchen phone rang repeatedly and the volume on the radio was broken so hits from the eighties and nineties like the 'Macarena' burst out at an assaulting frequency. We needed more salad chopping, all of the burger boxes needed to be restocked from the store cupboard and Jonny had sent out the wrong burgers three times in a row. It was a mess.

On a hot shift, we normally wedged the fire exit open with a chair but it was closed. There was no through breeze. I called to Jonny to go and open the back door as he was nearest but he didn't move. I pushed past him to do it myself.

'Watch what you're deein ya daft bitch,' he called after me as he suffocated a Double Whopper in branded greaseproof paper.

Pushing a plastic chair under the handle of the fire exit I checked to make sure the wind wouldn't push it closed. Glancing out over the car park I could see Daz's tiny red Micra parked in the loading bay. Through the steamed-up car windows I saw Cheryl straddling him awkwardly on the back seat, moving up and down, one hand on the seat behind his head and the other where the window met the door. He had her boob in his mouth, then in his whole hand. I stared until Cheryl stopped moving and she sat back in the seat. The buzz of an electric window going down filled the area and Cheryl held my gaze as she blew out a thick, straight line of smoke. I imagined what the inside of the car must have smelled like. The thought of the grease from Cheryl's uniform mixed with semen and nicotine made my stomach churn. I kicked the chair away from the fire exit, slammed the door shut and went back into the kitchen.

Barry moved quickly, bagging up meal deals and assuring customers through a plasticine smile that their orders wouldn't be long. Jonny was at the drinks machine filling up a large cup.

'Can you do me a Fanta when you've done that?' I shouted over the noise of the radio and the agitated queue.

'What?' he shouted back.

'Can you get me a Fan-ta when you've done yours?'

'Who the fuck am I, like? Your little fucking lackey? Dee it yaself.'

'But you're already there, I was only asking ...'

Jonny bent down his head to stretch out the muscles in his neck and looked at me from under his heavy brow.

'Well don't just fucking ask me anything. Right?' he said staring at me with his finger on the Diet Coke button as liquid and ice flowed over the brim of the cup.

'Jonny that's full now …'

As soon as I spoke everything slowed down. I couldn't hear the customers' voices or the radio blaring out B*Witched's 'C'est la vie', I couldn't hear Barry shouting 'COME ON!', Cheryl knocking on the fire-exit door or the alarms from the fryers alerting me that the last batch of fries was ready. All I could make out was the rhythmic beeping of a lorry reversing in the car park and I watched in slow motion as Jonny lifted his overflowing cup of Diet Coke and launched it at my head. The cup sailed silently through the air followed by a wave of brown liquid and escapee ice cubes. Jonny moved behind it throwing whatever he could find in my direction. The cup hit my head first, its weight knocking me off my feet. As I lay half-pressed up against the stainless-steel fridges that lined the kitchen, Jonny pelted me with burger buns, weighty sauce bottles, long sword-like packets of cups, handfuls of fries, a bowl of lettuce, full tomatoes and a large spoon covered with mayonnaise. When he reached where I was lying he stooped over me with his fists clenched and screamed a tirade of abuse down on me. He looked like a demonic figure in a Francis Bacon painting I'd seen in a book at school; his eyes were dark and he was leading with his jaw like he was trying to push through an invisible barrier with his chin. Outside of my own body, I looked down at Jonny screaming. I watched it all happen to someone else.

Barry pushed his body between us and a rush of sound burst back into my ears.

'Jonny get back and get out of this kitchen now!' he shouted, lifting me off the ground as a buffet of food fell onto the floor.

A line of hungry customers stared open-mouthed at the scene that had just unfolded in front of them, the unexpected violence perfectly framed by the walls, counter and menu of the burger franchise they had chosen to stop at. Cheryl stood with the kitchen door open, her hand over her gaping mouth, a nail missing on her left index finger.

'Barry I'm … I'm sorry, the, the numbers … the customers, you'll miss the target,' I stuttered as he helped me up the stairs to his office.

'It's alright, don't worry about that. Come on let's get you cleaned up and dried off.'

Barry put me in his plush leather office chair and mumbled something about going to get Sandy. I sat enveloped by the padded headrest and closed my eyes. A bright orange light sat behind my left eye where the industrial-sized sauce bottle had hit it, I could sense the skin around it inflating, rising on each side to cushion and protect my eyeball from the damage Johnny had inflicted. I tried to assess how messy my hair and face were by feeling around but gave up when I didn't recognise anything by touch. Everything that had been hard was now soft and everything that had been soft was now crusty.

When the door opened again it was Sandy. She waddled in and knelt next to me on the floor of Barry's office.

Speaking softly, she said, 'Ah pet, look at you. What a mess eh?'

I sank from the chair and wrapped myself around her body. Her soft folds cushioned me and I cried into her stomach. I cried for all the times I had tried to play along in the performance but didn't know my part. I cried for all the times I wanted to be more of myself but didn't dare admit what that might look like. I cried mainly because the woman who was comforting me, and the woman I comforted at home, terrified me the most. No part of their lives was their own and I felt guilty for not wanting to be like them.

'Come on pet, you sit on here and have a drink of water,' Sandy said bundling me back up onto the chair. I tried to drink but my erratic breathing made me gulp down too much water and it spewed quickly out of my nose. 'Just try and breathe slowly, OK pet. Just breathe.' She held me for a long time and rocked me back and forward as I sat in a crumpled mess.

Barry stuck his head around the door. 'How are we doing in here?'

'We're doing OK, aren't we pet?' Sandy said.

'Good, good. Listen, Deborah. I've sent Jonny home on an instant dismissal and one of the weekend staff is on their way in now. Once they're in to cover we'll need to get a statement for the incident log, then you can go home, OK? Do you want to wait up here with Sandy and I'll come back with someone who can act as a witness because HR isn't in at the minute?'

I nodded as I blew my nose.

'OK great.' Barry smiled quickly with his eyes and slipped his head back behind the door.

Sandy took my face in both hands and looked me directly in the eyes. 'Now listen. This isn't yours to eat up and push down inside. You tell Barry what happened, you leave here and you let it go. OK? That Jonny is a wrong un, he always has been, his family are a mess but that's not an excuse. You don't listen to whatever it was he said or did. That's his rubbish and he has to deal with it, not you.'

'I know but—'

'No buts! You are not going to carry this around with you. No. You get to choose what you take with you into tomorrow. OK?' Still holding my face, she made my head nod and stroked down the hair that had become spiky with hardened ketchup.

'Ooh me knees are killing, hang on.'

She brought over a plastic chair and sat next to me as we stared out of the large window that overlooked the motor-way below. Brake lights and headlights snaked up and down in opposite directions, moving in a seamless flow. The constant motion of the motorway felt calming, there was a promise of escape as long as the traffic moved north or south away from this point.

'I don't want to move to Vigo.'

'No of course not pet. Why, who's moving to Vigo?' Sandy said, patting my hand gently.

'No one. I don't know, but that's what's supposed to happen, isn't it? Get a job, get married, save for a new-build house with a laundry room and bi-fold doors.'

'It looks boring up there, they spend all their time clip-ping their lawns with hairdressing scissors.'

'I don't think they do that,' I laughed, holding my ribs that were already agony.

'Well, I wouldn't be surprised. Our Janice said they have front rooms they clean and never go in, I mean have you ever? Here, do you want one of these?' Sandy said, offering a warm Werther's Original from the front pouch of her tabard.

'Yes please.'

I smiled. Sucking on the toffee, I put my head on Sandy's shoulder, she held my hand and we watched the wind turbines spinning on the horizon as the motorway rumbled on below.

Lego

Kevin had to recalibrate his brain to enjoy looking at her face on his computer. He'd been conducting one-to-ones with his students all day and the dramatic switch from the hopes and dreams of twenty-one-year-olds to what he was now discussing on the same screen disturbed him.

'So, you're happy for me to use all of the names we've just listed?'

'Yes, I'm happy with those names.'

'Are there any others you'd like to add?'

'No, that all sounds good for now.'

'And the budget, you're happy with the amounts for each item, £300 per call, plus £50 fines for disobedience?'

'Yes, I'm happy with the amounts. Will the fines be added after the calls?'

'Yes, you'll be charged £300 before each call up-front, then the same card will be charged for any fines accrued.'

'OK good.'

'Now to confirm the safe word is "Lego"?'

'Yes, correct.'

'And you understand that you aren't permitted to enquire about my personal life during our sessions or calls will be terminated?'

'Yes.'

'OK, I'll draft the contract and then we can arrange the first call when you've signed it and sent it back.'

'Perfect, thank you Mistress Bee. I'm looking forward to it.'

'Me too, see you soon, Kevin.'

He pressed the red button to end the call and stretched his arms out in front of him. He opened up Mistress Bee's profile to reassess the woman he had chosen to do this with. Clicking through the gallery on her website he examined each shot. Her face was elongated and angular, she wore barbed black eyeliner and exaggerated maroon lipstick that turned her cupid's bow into a sharp pair of scissors, her body was encased in gothic latex, long boots and extreme corsets that contorted her body into a cyber-slut silhouette. He wondered if he could request different outfits, perhaps something more like the women he used to see on the Tube during rush hour. He made a note to email and ask Mistress Bee about this later.

Outside, the light was weak. The clocks had gone back and although it was only 4.30 p.m. the row of gardens below his window were losing detail. The remaining leaves on his neighbour's tree flickered at speed as a vicious wind snapped through the sparse branches. The leaves were a bodily red which drew his hand to the scar of the same colour under the waistline of his faded grey jogging pants. His ex-wife had mocked his pain when the first procedure failed, she wasn't willing or able to allocate any sympathy when his stitches became infected. She treated his extended hospital stay for blood poisoning as a major imposition. On his fifth day in hospital she brought him clean underpants and talked about how busy she was at work. He felt foolish when the man in the bed next to his asked him how long he'd been married. The insanity of the whole arrangement came into full view as he talked about his wife, their kids, where they lived, what they did at the weekends. He couldn't believe he'd banked so much on the emotional whims of another person. It had ended up costing him so much. He tapped the scar, a neat beetle-shaped nodule that ached when it was cold, and pushed his hands down into his underpants. It was too early to masturbate so he decided to FaceTime the twins instead.

'Girls can you stop moving? My signal is terrible, I can't see you very well.' His daughters' faces moved too quickly for his connection to catch up, causing pink blobs to trail across his screen.

'Daaaad, why don't you get a new phone? Urgh it's been like this for ages.'

'It's not the phone, the internet around here is really bad, honey.'

'Whatever. We can see you. What happened to your glasses?'

'Oh nothing, they broke. I need to order a new pair,' he said rearranging the pair sellotaped together on his face.

Momentarily his phone connected with a signal and his daughters' faces came into focus. The daughters that he hadn't seen in the flesh for four months, who he hadn't lived with for five years. Each year the bond between them stretched thinner and thinner until he found himself not daring to disturb the stretched elastic between them, fear-

ing it would never snap back into place. Friends with older
children comforted him with promises that if he just stayed
rooted as a solid point in their lives, they would swing back
around in their own time. He tried to maintain a central
balance, but he worried that he was losing his footing and
they'd wash away from him, unable to hold on to the fragments of their fading relationship.

When he looked at baby pictures of them both, he could
see clues to how they'd develop: their wide mouths, their
green eyes framed by dark circles regardless of how much
sleep they got, even as babies, their Anatolian bone structure and olive skin. It was all there in those early photos
and fleshed out now on his screen. Everyone always said
how funny it was that they looked so much like his wife
and nothing like him, he could never understand what they
found so amusing.

'So, what have you been doing?' he asked his daughters
with an enthusiasm that he hoped wouldn't make them
hate him.

'Nothing.'

'Nothing Dad,' they both agreed, hoping to cut down
the length of conversation.

'Have you finished your latest assignments? Were they
for geography?'

'Yeah I finished mine, it was an art history essay.'

'Rebecca?'

'What?'

'Have you finished your assignments?'

'What assignments?' his youngest daughter asked wearily,
her hand shielding her eyes from the glare of his annoying
line of questions.

'The ones that you were doing the last time we talked.'

'I don't know, I can't remember what they were.'

Silence. The two girls stared out of his screen at him. He was desperate for them to ask him something, anything. He wanted so badly for them to show any interest in his life, but he could see they were both looking at other screens, possibly messaging each other from their separate university halls about how pathetic he was. He opted to ask about their friends, only to be met with a cast of names he'd never heard of. It heightened his sense of being an outsider in their lives. Someone had a place by the coast and they were hoping to go there when everything was back to normal.

'So, nothing else to report then?' he asked. They both shook their heads slowly.

'Well OK girls it was lovely seeing you. I hope you both have a good week.'

'Yeah, bye Dad.'

'OK. Bye bye.'

The room was dark except for the blue light emanating from his laptop over on his desk. He felt himself spiralling into a crashing low, a swirling hysterical place where every mistake and misstep intertwined with a rich revulsion of what and who he had become. He laid his body flat on the bed in preparation for the tsunami of self-loathing to wash over him. He'd take it, he'd lie there in the dark and wait for it to subside. Then he'd have to think about what he was going to eat for dinner.

*

The rest of the week was busy with online tutorials, staff meetings and strained discussions with his ex-wife about tuition fee payments. In between these plugs of activity, he ate soup and drafted an email to Mistress Bee requesting a change in outfit ahead of their first call. An hour later she had replied.

> Yes, this can be arranged. It will be an extra £200. If you order all of these items for me in a size 10–12 and send them to my PO box I'll wear them for our first call on Tuesday 19th at 19.00. Use the link and username/password listed in the contract to connect.
>
> Mistress Bee

The night of their first call Kevin logged on early and was pleasantly surprised to find Mistress Bee already on the call.

'Hi!' he said, not knowing if that was how he should greet her.

'Kevin, I'm not quite ready. I'm going to turn off my camera. I'll be back in five minutes.'

'OK, see you soon. No rush.'

Of course, there was a rush, he didn't want to be left alone pondering the situation he was about to embark on. Left alone with his thoughts, he might abort the whole thing, and he didn't want to contemplate what would happen if he bailed on this. He thought about watching a YouTube tutorial on changing bike chains but he knew this would throw him off, so he just sat and willed Mistress Bee's face to appear back on his screen. Six minutes and forty-five seconds later she reappeared.

There she was, she'd done what he'd asked. She was wearing less make-up than she normally did, her face was broken up with dark-rimmed glasses, her hair had been blow-dried into large waves that fell down to her chest, framing a loose silk blouse tucked into a tight black skirt. She held the black leather handbag with gold chain handles on her knee as requested, she looked just like the woman he used to see on the Tube to work.

'Hello Kevin, welcome to this space we have given ourselves.'

'Thank you, it's great to see you.'

'This outfit isn't what I normally wear but as you arranged for it and paid me extra I'm happy to do this for you.'

'You look perfect, thank you.'

'Do you feel comfortable?'

'I'm nervous but I'm excited I think.'

'Don't be nervous Kevin. You wanted this, you deserve this. Now, for this to work you have to do exactly what I say unless it crosses one of the boundaries you stated in the contract and if that's the case use the safe word and it stops. Understand?'

'Yes, I understand.'

'I will keep going as you requested high levels of punishment, but you have to be mindful of what you're comfortable with and I will respect your wishes if you want to stop.'

'I will be.'

'OK, we'll start. Are you touching yourself?'

'No.'

'Do you want to?'

'No, I don't think so. Can you use the fine threats tonight?'

'Shut your fucking vile mouth. Don't tell me how to speak, you disgusting little mole. I tell you how things are going to be, do you understand?'

Kevin nodded silently.

'Do you understand?' Mistress Bee repeated in a more aggressive tone and threw the leather handbag he'd bought for her against the wall behind her.

'Have we started?'

'Yes, we've fucking started, what do you think this is, you deluded little fuck pig?'

'OK I understand. I am under your control Mistress Bee.'

'Good.'

He felt light-headed, listening to Mistress Bee's words spewing out through his speakers. It unlocked a space in his chest and his breathing flowed flawlessly. His jaw unclenched, his shoulders dropped, his brow softened. He answered her questions and demands in a blissed-out state for the next thirty minutes with his palms facing upwards. When he refused to open his eyes, she added a £50 fine to his bill and he felt his dick turn hard. He clenched his eyes closed as she commanded him to open them again.

'Open your eyes you disgusting piece of shit or it will be a £100 fine.'

He looked down at his penis which had created a circus tent in his loose, grey jogging bottoms and, with his eyes bulging, screamed: 'They're wide open!'

*

Several calls with Mistress Bee followed. Each time he felt the calmest and most relaxed he'd been in years. The abuse was manageable, he wasn't on a perpetual high alert, unsure where the next reproach might come from, he knew exactly where it was coming from. He just had to sit back and enjoy the attention Mistress Bee gave him. Their calls were his number-one luxury. He stopped spending money on alcohol, porn, gadgets, art, clothes. He saved all of his disposable income and splurged it on his time with Mistress Bee. His loyalty was rewarded and she offered to send him some physical punishments.

'It can be anything you want. Something to use against yourself – a whip, a plug, a harness, a hammer. Or one client likes it when I send him things to eat.'

'What like?'

'Whatever you want. I could send you food you don't like or maybe rubbish and you eat it in front of me.'

'Like actual food from a rubbish bin?'

'Yes, if you would like that.'

'I like the sound of that. Can I email you a list of what I want?'

'Yes, make it five things and I'll arrange for them to be delivered before our next call.'

A brown jiffy envelope fell through his letterbox two days before their next call. Inside was a zip-locked bag containing a half-eaten brown apple, two smoked cigarette butts, a snapped-off piece of dark chocolate, a mouldy block of cheddar cheese and an open bag of rotten bistro salad. All of the items had rubbed, leaked and disintegrated all over each other. The cheese smelt of tar and was covered in chocolate, the apple was covered in slimy rocket leaves.

There was a handwritten note at the bottom of the envelope that was wet and crumpled and read:

For my pathetic little pussy moth xx

Kevin's hands shook. He sat on the hard-tiled floor in the hallway and tried to focus on the sound of the cars passing by outside. He tried his deep breathing exercises. He tried to focus on one of the wooden spindles he'd spent weeks sanding. Nothing worked. His breathing was polyphonic and vomit rose up from his stomach. Lying down on his side he pulled the envelope and plastic bag of rubbish up to his chest and let himself start to cry. He lay there heaving until he heard the six o'clock news on the radio next door. He sat up and lifted his T-shirt over his head, wiping all of the mucus and liquid from his face. This was good, he thought, it was good to explore new things, to feel new emotions. He put the plastic bag in the fridge and made himself a cup of tummy time tea.

'Did you receive my gifts?'

'Yes, Mistress Bee.'

'What do you say?'

'Thank you. I say thank you, Mistress Bee. I'm very grateful.'

'Good. Now, what do you have on the plate in front of you?'

'I have the apple and the cheese.'

'Is that all?'

'Yes.'

'This isn't some kind of ploughman's luncheon you vile, stinking Mangalitza PIG. Where are the other things I so kindly sent to you?'

'In the fridge.'

'THEN GET THEM.'

Kevin scrambled to the fridge and brought back everything piled onto one plate.

'Now eat,' Mistress Bee ordered.

He put the chocolate in his mouth first, it was hard and cold from being in the fridge overnight. He closed his eyes and worked the bottom side of the square with his tongue to try and unleash some flavour. A sharp pain pierced his jaw as sugar leaked into his mouth.

'Does that feel good?' Mistress Bee's mechanical voice came though his speakers and he nodded his head slowly. His limbs weightless, his neck loose and long.

He stayed like that until the chocolate had melted, listening only to the sound of Mistress Bee's breathing. In and out, in and out.

'Wake up!' Mistress Bee ordered. 'Now chew the cigarettes.'

'I'm not sure I'd like to …'

'Did you or did you not ask me to send you two cigarette butts to eat?'

'Yes but …'

'Then stop wasting my fucking time, you spineless little amoeba. Eat them.'

'Please can I take a sip of water first?'

'No! No water, that isn't what we agreed. Eat.'

Kevin put the hard cigarette butt into his mouth and closed his eyes. He pictured himself in a circle of friends.

He was sixteen, in Billy's back garden. Billy's parents were on holiday and he'd invited all of their friends around for a party. Kevin had just had sex with the girl he'd been fantasising about for months. He thought maybe she was a virgin but didn't ask. He didn't ask if he could take her top off or if she wanted to have sex. On the peach bedspread of Billy's mother's bed, he put on a condom with trembling hands and pulled down her knickers. She made snuffling noises and he kissed the small breasts hidden within her sports bra. In the garden ten minutes later, he ignored her as he drank cans of super-strength lager and smoked a Benson & Hedges cigarette down past the letters. Billy dared him to eat the butt, he dared him to do it in return for another four cans. Kevin agreed. Stubbing the cigarette out, he took a long swig of lager and threw the butt into his mouth, chewing quickly, trying not to taste it or think about the hard, ashy end, crushing it in between his molars. Everyone in the garden cheered, the neighbour next door spoke into her landline as she looked out of the bedroom window into Billy's back garden. He swallowed the butt to the sound of everyone chanting his name. 'Kev! Kev! Kev!' He opened his eyes and saw Mistress Bee's face on his laptop.

'Did you swallow you naughty worm?'

'I DID IT!' he screamed. 'I FUCKING DID IT!' He opened his mouth and put it up close to the camera on his laptop.

'Good boy, good little cash pig.' Mistress Bee clapped her hands approvingly.

*

The students popped up one by one on his screen, disembodied faces still spotty with excess hormones and sebum. Sitting in their childhood bedrooms they told him about the final projects they wanted to execute before graduation. Some he could muster genuine enthusiasm for, others were so badly pieced together they were barely ideas. Carl was a puppy in Palace streetwear, his energy bounced all over Kevin's screen wearing him out and making him feel depressed about how tired he always was. Carl would graduate, he'd make films for brands, he'd publish books and zines, he might start a collective and they'd put on club nights when all of this was over. He'd have sex with lots of young women, he'd break their hearts and probably have his own broken by someone he'd held tightly on a mattress in his rented room.

Kevin couldn't wait to get him off his screen. He had an online meeting with the rest of the department in twenty minutes, he wanted to masturbate before the call and make a cup of peppermint tea, if Carl didn't stop talking soon he wouldn't have time for either.

'This all sounds great Carl, why don't you have a look at those references I've sent you, go through the edit again and let me know how you get on?'

Wrapping the conversation up, Kevin's mood dipped further when he saw Holli's name enter the chat room. A message popped up on the sidebar.

Hi Kevin, sorry I'm late. Do you have time for a quick chat about my project before the end of the session?

Unable to refuse a student when he was technically still on call, he wrote back:

Of course!

And gave her access to the virtual classroom.

'Hi Holli,' he said as her face replaced Carl's on his screen.

'Hi Kevin, thanks for fitting me in. It's been a nightmare getting everything done remotely and on time.'

'No problem, tell me where you're at with the project and what you're stuck with.'

Holli launched into an in-depth breakdown of her project, an app designed to destigmatise periods for young girls all over the world. Holli shared her screen and talked him through the wireframe, the branding she'd designed and social launch campaign she'd mapped out. She'd used an obvious palette of red, pale pink and beige, something Kevin wanted to pull apart, but he couldn't find the words or an alternative suggestion so he let it slide. Holli would do well after university, she was thorough and had a good eye, she had already adopted a professional way of presenting her work, using language that made her ideas seem bulletproof even if the substance was often lacking. He really couldn't find anything to say about the design work but wanted to give her some feedback so she felt like she was getting value for the £9,000 she was paying in tuition fees.

'How will you make this relatable for boys?' he asked.

'Hmm ... I don't really know, I mean this isn't really for boys.'

'Yes, but if you're trying to destigmatise periods for a younger generation don't you need to get the boys on board, educate them as well so it becomes normalised for everyone?'

'I don't know, they're not really my target audience.'

'Well I think this is where it's lacking so maybe you could add in a section for them or at least think about how you would amplify the messaging to platforms where boys and young men would engage. OK?'

'Fine, I'll think about it,' she said in a way that suggested he would be looking at a final version of the presentation with none of his suggestions actioned.

He closed his laptop. He had nine minutes left until the department meeting, he could either masturbate or make a cup of tea and scan the headlines. Trying to gauge if an orgasm would fit into the allotted time, he gently massaged his penis to see how receptive it would be. He thought about the woman who worked at the local Co-op, about her breasts bursting out of her work shirt, about bending her over the tills and watching them fuck on the CCTV camera but nothing about that scenario aroused him. He thought about Mistress Bee shouting at him in her city woman outfit and felt a mild twinge, but nothing that gave him the confidence that this wouldn't be anything other than frustrating. He decided to make a peppermint tea instead and got back to his desk in time to not be the last person on the call.

In the meeting, colleagues talked over each other, cut in with obvious statements that didn't need to be vocalised or remained silent throughout, not daring to throw themselves into the pixelated fire pit. The agenda item under discussion was a project from last term, Marie and Sondra were praising Kara, who'd developed the brief and had led the project.

'I feel like the students really engaged with the subject matter,' Marie said, to which Kara gave an appreciative thumbs up.

'I agree, it was a great way for them to develop their research skills and think a little more critically about their role as designers,' Sondra smiled, raising her shoulders in a mark of support.

'That's great to hear, I'm so glad they responded well to it,' Kara said with a humility that irritated Kevin.

He used to like Kara, seeking her out for lunch and break-time coffees. When he returned from his yoga retreat in Goa, she seemed distant and uninterested in the progress of his practice. She'd picked up her phone at one point when he was describing a difficult asana that he'd mastered and looked at the main entrance of the cafeteria when he was explaining his chakra work.

'Actually Kara, can I just build on some of the comments?' Kevin interjected.

'Of course, Kevin, go ahead.'

'I just felt that perhaps the planning stage wasn't fully developed, like there could have been some better internal communication.'

'Can you expand on what you mean by that for the evaluation notes?'

'Maybe there could have been more opportunities for others to input on the initial idea stages before everything was decided?'

'But we had five meetings before the brief was finalised.'

'Yeah I'm just not sure the brief was as developed as it could be, some students seemed to struggle getting their head around what we were actually asking them to do.'

'Did anyone else have this problem?' Kara asked the group earnestly.

The grainy heads of his colleagues shook from side to side in synch with one another.

Peter, the course leader, jumped in. 'OK everyone, I think we should move on. Can everyone send their feedback to me over email, I'll collate and circulate. So, next on the agenda is the final year exhibition ...'

Kevin lowered his head, muted his laptop and shouted, 'LEGO!!!!' at the top of his voice.

The shaved band of hair that fringed his skull bristled against his hands as he rubbed them all over his ears, face and head. The top of his bare scalp filled his section of the screen on his colleague's laptops, pink patches of angry eczema catching the eyes of the people he worked with who'd never seen the top of his head before. The call carried on for another fifteen minutes as the options for a digital end-of-year exhibition were tabled, and they all sang happy birthday to Marie who wore a paper hat for the occasion.

Without saying goodbye Kevin clicked out of the meeting. His small game-show square on the team call took over the whole screen and he was faced with his own image. His broken glasses hugged his face too tightly, causing the bridge of his nose to turn purple when he took them off to rub his eyes. He scratched at the eczema around his nose and over his left eyebrow, why wasn't that cream working? He'd have to try and get to the doctors to get a higher-strength prescription. He couldn't stand to look at his face so close up anymore, he tapped out of the app and messaged Mistress Bee:

Can we have a call in an hour? I'll pay double.

She was online and messaged back immediately:

Sure, call me at 7 xx

Can we do blackmail?

Yes.

He breathed deeply and had a shower to get ready for her.

'You know I have those photos and emails. You gave me access to your laptop. I have all of your contacts and all of that material, unless you pay me the money everyone you've ever been in touch with is going to get a very interesting email on Monday morning. Do you understand?' Mistress Bee shouted. She hit the back of the chair she was standing next to with a riding crop.

Blackmail was his particular favourite role play, he saved it for when his stress was crippling. He knew Mistress Bee didn't have access to his laptop. Some subs did this, giving their financial dominatrix control of their bank accounts as part of the total power exchange, but Kevin wasn't in that deep. He knew there weren't any compromising photographs or emails but a part of his brain suspended disbelief and allowed him to suspect there might be. The cognitive dissonance he went through in these calls was the sweetest relief of his week.

There was enough safety to know he wasn't in danger, but the role play was so convincing that while he was in it everything else floated away. He didn't have to think about anything, he was at the mercy of Mistress Bee and her domination over him. He felt safe, he trusted her more than he trusted anyone else. She delivered everything she said she would, she respected his wishes, never overstepped the mark, did everything he asked. Ultimately, he was the one in control and it helped him sleep peacefully at night.

'I don't have that money Mistress Bee, is there anything else I can do?'

'NO! Listen to me, you creepy little pervert, pay me that money tonight by midnight or I'm going to add on £100 for every day you're late and if I still haven't received the money by Monday, I'm sending that photo of you and the plastic fist.'

'No, not that one please, my ex-wife will stop me from seeing my kids.'

'Then you know what to do pig dick ...'

She carried on talking but the sound of her voice was interrupted by Kevin's sister calling through FaceTime on his laptop, he could see Mistress Bee was still in role play but he couldn't hear what she was saying. He thought about declining his sister's call but she'd know that he had cut her off and would continue calling until he picked up, or she'd get their mother to call to test if he cut her off too. He just had to wait it out. After thirty seconds the ringing stopped.

'Sorry I missed what you were saying, my sister called and I had to let it ring out.'

'Oh,' Mistress Bee said, thrown off her stride. 'So, you missed that whole monologue?'

'Yes.'

'Should we pick it up where we left off, where did you hear to?'

Kevin couldn't muster the excitement to retrace their steps, he'd lost all enthusiasm for what they were doing. He wanted it to stop, he wanted it all to stop but he couldn't bring himself to say the word.

'What's your real name?' he asked.

'What? That's no way to speak to Mistress Bee.'

'Just tell me your real name. Please.'

'NO! That's not how this works.'

'What do you like to watch on TV?'

For the first time Kevin saw a flash of the woman behind Mistress Bee, she was tired, she was frustrated. She too wanted this to be over. Who was this woman when she wasn't pretending to be someone else? What was her real name? Natasha? Lindsey? Maria? Who was she in her own clothes, who did she live with? Did she tell her friends about the men she abused online? Did she laugh about him and her other clients and buy bottles of champagne with the money they paid her?

'Don't you ever get tired of pretending?' he asked.

She sat down, rested her elbows on the table in front of her and put her face into her hands.

'Kevin, I'm not the person you should be paying to talk to about this.'

'Please?'

*

She looked at his grainy face on her screen. The light beaming out of his laptop bleached out the centre of his face and darkened the shadows around the edges. His ears were huge handles on each side of his head, his chin blended fluidly into his neck, into his chest: a flaccid slope of neglect. She eyed the clock in the top right hand of her screen, 19.38. Their session was due to end at 19.45. She'd known Kevin would try this at some point, they always did. For her, this was where it got interesting.

'Please talk to me. What's your name? Where do you live?'

'Kevin. That's not how this works.'

He stood up and moved away from his laptop. She could see he didn't have any trousers on, the tip of his penis hung just below his lime-green T-shirt. He paced back and forth across the room until he was off camera and the room was empty apart from a bed in the corner covered in a £5 bedspread she'd seen in IKEA that she was glad she hadn't bought. The front door of her house opened and closed.

'Kevin, you knew the rules. You have a choice now. You can throw this all away or you can come back and sit down.'

She sat back in her chair and checked if her mother had replied to her message about borrowing the car that weekend. She hadn't. A sliver of light from the hallway floor fell across the centre of the empty room on her screen. From beyond Kevin's bedroom she could hear water falling freely from a tap, splashing on porcelain and draining down a plughole, then she saw a shadow move in the corner of the room. Cupboards in her kitchen opened and closed, the radio came on.

'Kevin, this is your last chance,' she said before muting herself so the radio waves from downstairs wouldn't soak through her microphone.

A shadow crossed the room on screen and stood over Kevin's laptop. The kettle began to boil downstairs, footsteps started to come up the stairs in her house.

With her finger poised over the 'End Call' button she said: 'Do you submit Kevin?' A creak came from the hallway outside her room. 'Kevin, do you submit?'

On screen, nothing moved, then a faint but audible 'yes' came through her speakers.

'Good,' Mistress Bee breathed out heavily. 'I'm glad we understand each other. You can book our next meeting through the app,' she said before pressing the red button to end the call.

Paper Dolls

Carmen packed up her computer and notes as the train crawled over the river into the station. Checking her phone, she read a message from her mother saying that she'd be on the other side of the bridge waiting in the usual spot. Her mother didn't like to drive to the train station in the centre of town because the traffic made her nervous. This bothered Carmen. A lot about her mother bothered Carmen: her hypochondria, her severely compromised financial situation, her refusal to engage with any kind of online banking or life management. Then there were her arthritic hands that had started to look like chicken feet, and the fact that her diet consisted of nothing but slices of ham, tinned sweetcorn and dried fruit.

'The traffic isn't even that bad coming to the station and then you just use the slip road to get back onto the motorway,' Carmen had once tried to point out.

'How do you know, you don't even drive?'

*

As the train came to a standstill Carmen stood at her seat with her head bent under the overhead luggage shelf, waiting for the man in the aisle seat to let her out. She said 'Excuse me' four times before he moved without apology. Stepping off the train, Carmen was pleased she'd opted to wear her winter jacket. Even though it was May, the station forecourt was freezing, the temperature on the large station clock read 7 degrees. Her friends had tried to persuade her to go to Portugal with them that week but she'd found herself being coerced into helping her mother move house instead.

'What if I pay for a removal company to come and pack up all of your stuff and move it for you?' Carmen had suggested on the phone whilst giving a silent thumbs up to the Uber Eats driver at her front door.

'I don't want some strange men going through all of my stuff and touching everything. How would I know where anything is?'

Pulling the lid off her katsu curry, with the phone cradled between her head and shoulder, Carmen replied, 'You can tell them where you want everything to go and they'll label all of the boxes. It's just much easier and quicker, they do this all the time.'

'If you're too busy I'll do it on my own.'

The walk over the bridge was biting but it was a clear and bright day, Carmen took in a deep breath of clean air and thought to herself that maybe this week wouldn't be so bad. As she turned the corner she saw her mother's boxy red car, her shrunken head peering through the steering wheel, headlights flashing in Carmen's direction. She couldn't remember her mother ever being this small, she seemed to be retreating into herself with each passing year. She waved as a signal of recognition, but her mother continued to try and attract her attention until she opened the passenger door.

'I saw you Mum, you didn't need to keep flashing the lights.'

'Oh well, hello to you too,' her mother said picking something out of her teeth. 'The boot's open. Put your bags in there, not on the back seat.'

Carmen closed the door, making sure to not slam it so that their first argument couldn't be attributed to her aggressive behaviour. She opened the boot and tried to create space for her suitcase amongst the objects already in there: a large gym bag, a twenty-litre bag of compost, three Christmas puddings, an industrial can of de-icer, a scattering of 'Bags for Life' and four boxes of firelighters.

'There's no room in the boot Mum, can I put some of this stuff on the back seat?'

'What's in there, I thought I'd cleared it out.'

'A load of stuff. Compost, your gym gear, some Christmas puddings.'

'Christmas puddings? Ah, that's where they are. They're for your Auntie Sandra, I was looking for them for weeks at Christmas.'

'Of course you were,' Carmen muttered to herself with one hand on the open car boot and the other on her suitcase. She looked at her mother in the rear-view mirror waiting for the next instruction.

Tapping her hands on the steering wheel to plot a solution her mother called back, 'Put your suitcase in the footwell of the back seat but not on the seat.'

Carmen's mother had passed through her early life in plumes of Rive Gauche perfume and unpredictable mood swings. She'd run the pub on their estate and worked twelve-hour shifts, six days a week. She was often inexplicably absent for long stretches of time but her presence loomed so large that Carmen had to override her memory when it tried to trick her into believing that she'd been a hands-on mother. At unexpected moments she would emerge into Carmen's day dressed like she was out for revenge in tight dresses and silk blazers, her hair a serving of teased candyfloss, set in place with gusts of hairspray. In any situation, her eyes would suspiciously scan the room, calculating where the drama might come from as she unwrapped black bullet sweets from her blazer pocket, popping them into her mouth quickly, never sharing. The distant shrewdness that had defined her mother in the earlier years had now been replaced by a viscous chaos which oozed into every area of her life. This messiness, this emotional detritus, was exactly what Carmen had wanted to avoid. Closing the car boot, she pushed the front seat as far forward as it would go to make enough room for her suitcase in the footwell behind. With everything in place, she got in, reached back to put her seat belt on and sat with her hands on the dashboard, bracing for impact.

*

On the motorway, her mother drove at a steady forty-five miles per hour and they settled into a familiar round-up of gossip about her neighbours and what she'd been watching on the TV. The people two doors down had put their house on the market having only been there for four months; Barbara, her old dog-walking friend, had fallen and broken her hip; and Brian next door was back on the oil rigs so she hadn't had to put up with his drumming.

'I thought he had agreed to soundproof the garage and only play his drums between 12 and 2 p.m.'

'He did.'

'So why does it bother you if you can't hear him playing anymore?'

'Because it just does.' On the subject of garages her mother checked her rear-view mirror and said, 'By the way you've still got all of that crap in the garage and you'll need to decide what you're keeping or it'll all go to the tip.' Since Carmen had moved out twelve years ago, the real estate in her mother's garage had been an ongoing source of friction.

'OK, I'll have a look but I'm sure there's not that much stuff in there now. I sorted it all out the last time I was here.'

'No, you didn't,' her mother said with a breathless exasperation that bubbled up from her throat. 'There's still a load of shoeboxes full of photos and tatty old rubbish piled up.'

'Fine. I'll have a look.' Carmen said squeezing the dashboard.

Her mother lifted up one side of her bottom, 'Ooh I've got some terrible trapped wind. I've been getting this new dried fruit from Morrisons for a change but it doesn't half go through me.'

'That's nice Mum.' Carmen smirked and angled the funnel neck of her coat towards her nose.

'Oh, and I forgot to say. I saw Leanne Jenkins's mam in there last week.'

'Where?'

'Morrisons.'

'Last week?' Carmen said in a raised voice she didn't try and control. 'Why didn't you tell me?'

'I don't know, I'm telling you now.'

'How did she look?'

'Terrible. She was such a good-looking woman before it all happened but it just devastated her.' Carmen stared silently at the road ahead. Changing lanes her mother said, 'Open your window, it's a bit stale in here.'

Carmen met Leanne on their first day of secondary school as they lined up for English.

'Can I ask you a favour?' Leanne said.

'Me?'

'Yes, you. Can you see my fanny pad through my trousers?' Leanne asked, bending over to show Carmen the outline of her bum in some black stirrup ski pants. None of Carmen's friends had started their period at that point so she wasn't sure what she was looking for but wanting to be helpful she said, 'No, I think it's all good.'

'Nice one, I don't want to start my school career with everyone saying I wear nappies.'

Carmen was impressed that anyone would have the foresight to consider their long-term school career, she was still trying to mentally prepare for her first lunchtime, never mind planning how to cultivate a durable reputation.

In the classroom, they sat next to each other and inspected the contents of each other's pencil cases. They discussed what they had each brought for their packed lunches, whether they had older siblings at the school, which teachers they'd heard were perverts and how far they'd each gone with boys. Leanne talked with a confidence Carmen had never seen in girls her own age, she moved her hands when she spoke, she used the word 'procrastinate', she drew attention to herself and enjoyed performing for whoever was watching. Carmen had spent her whole childhood trying to deflect attention, it was disorienting but thrilling to meet someone with the exact opposite approach to life.

They became inseparable from that first meeting. Carmen looked to Leanne for clues on how to be in the world, how to pull out the bits of herself that were important. As a friend, Leanne gave without an agenda. She loved reading Carmen's stories, she made her mixtapes of songs she'd recorded from the radio, she let Carmen borrow her clothes and taught her how to use tampons. Carmen had stayed at Leanne's house for two weeks after she'd fought with her dad and had watched herself scream in the reflection of his glasses. When she couldn't sleep Leanne had stroked her forehead and read Roald Dahl stories aloud until she drifted off. She was her safety net and her springboard. They ran with a wider gang of girls but were each other's central reference point. They spoke in code and intuitively understood every subtle gesture. Their bodies were always connected: linking arms, plaiting hair, lying on each other, holding hands, constantly searching for a physical reassurance that one was within reach of the other. Without Leanne, Carmen wasn't sure who she was or how to be, but when they were together everything flowed. She didn't agonise over what to say next, she just said it. She didn't stumble over her punchlines, all her jokes made Leanne laugh until she couldn't breathe. Even her clothes hung right on her body when she was with Leanne, everything was just … right. She was able to see herself through Leanne's eyes, and for a short time she felt free.

In the car, Carmen's heart rate rose to match the clicking of the indicator as her mother signalled to come off the motorway early. Carmen shifted in her seat, struggling to find any room to accommodate her discomfort. Sensing the heightened anxiety in the car her mother said, 'I know you hate going this way but I might as well call into your Auntie Sandra's on the way through and drop off those Christmas puddings.'

'Why? She's survived without them until May. I really don't think she's going to be desperate to crack into them now, is she?'

'You know what she's like for those Christmas puds. I thought I'd lost them but I bet she could still eat them now. They don't go off, you could take them into a bunker and eat them in five years, they'd still be moist.'

'Why would you want to take Christmas puddings into a bunker?' Carmen asked, bewildered but unexpectedly entertained at the tangent their conversation had taken.

'What?' Her mother took her eyes off the road and turned her head slightly to gauge her daughter's expression. 'I'm not saying I would want to take them into a bunker, I'm just saying you could—'

Carmen interrupted her mother with a heavy sigh.

Taking the hint, she remained silent for a few minutes. 'You could take tins of custard in the bunker as well and have them together,' she continued.

Carmen stared vacantly at her mother.

'Listen it'll only take five minutes otherwise she'll never get them. We're going.'

'Fine, but I'm not getting out of the car.'

'Fine,' her mother repeated with a shortness Carmen refused to acknowledge.

Carmen's Auntie Sandra lived in a small hamlet of houses in between two old mining towns, one where Carmen had grown up. To get there you had to drive down a winding country road and tackle several blind bends. A visitor to the area might delight at the pastoral scenes of rolling fields and working farms. They would admire the quaint church on the left and wonder what had happened to the collapsed dry-stone wall on the right of the intersection, which hadn't been rebuilt since 2001. Carmen focused on her hands splayed out on the dashboard as her mother drove towards the junction they'd take to get to Auntie Sandra's. Wiry tendons rose up causing the eczema-ridden skin that gathered around her knuckles to wrinkle, her brittle nails were splintered and cracked.

Leanne had painted Carmen's nails on the last night they'd seen each other.

'Stop moving your hand man or I'll get it all owa,' Leanne had said as she broke to take a drag from the Regal King Size resting in the ashtray.

They were getting ready for the boxing match organised by her boyfriend Dean's amateur club, they felt sophisticated drinking blue WKD out of Leanne's nana's wine glasses.

'Leanne, you better not be smoking in your room,' a raspy voice from downstairs shouted.

'AM NOT!' Leanne turned her head to shout towards her closed bedroom door. 'Quick, stick your head out the window.' They hung out of Leanne's window and lit another cigarette to share. The window took up the full width of the small bedroom, opening up at the bottom like a cat flap. A blast of cold January air unsettled the flyers and posters arranged on the wall, knocking an After Dark club night flyer onto a pile of Northern Soul vinyl that Leanne had siphoned off from her dad's collection downstairs.

Looking out at the lights of the industrial estate in the distance and the bellows of steam that spewed out of the local factories Leanne said, 'If I had to fuck one of the other lads out of the boxing club, it would be Westy.'

'No, you wouldn't.' Carmen turned her head to see if Leanne was being serious. 'He's proper small, he'd probably only come up to your tits.'

'Aye, and his head's canny big isn't it? Aye maybe not Westy then. Maybe Peebles – if I had to.'

'Westy has got a muckle head hasn't he?' Carmen said as she took the cigarette from Leanne. 'Donna Gibson told Helen that Peebles has got a big dick but weird pubes.'

'Noooo way!' Leanne laughed, allowing the smoke she'd just inhaled to escape from her mouth in short bursts of breath. 'What kind of weird pubes?'

'I dunno, like thick and clumpy and she said they go too high up.' She moved her finger up two-thirds of the cigarette.

'Urgh minging, I'll definitely be sticking with Dean then.' Leanne blew on her nails and checked she hadn't smudged them. 'Has knobhead been around to see your mam again this week?'

'No, not yet, he'll probably be round tonight coz they know I'm out.'

'Do you want to stay here? Or I could stay at yours?' Leanne leant over to pull out the ash that had landed on Carmen's fringe.

'Nah it's alright. I haven't got any of my stuff for tomorrow and you won't want to take a big bag out tonight. It'll be alright.'

'You can use my stuff. It's no bother if you change your mind,' Leanne said before ducking her head back into her bedroom to finish the final coat of nail varnish.

Carmen smiled and blew a smoke ring out into the cold night air.

At 7.30 p.m. Leanne and Carmen burst through the double doors of the community centre into the brightly lit main room. Plastic tables and chairs framed the temporary boxing ring that stood in the centre, a makeshift coliseum. Leanne wore a black asymmetric top she'd saved her Saturday job wages to buy and a short silver skirt she'd borrowed from her sister. Her skin shimmered with bronzer that made her face two shades darker than her neck. Carmen wore the dress she'd shoplifted from Miss Selfridge that had a slight tear in the seam where she'd smashed the security tag with a hammer. It was too short and too tight to be comfortable, but she felt it was worth it when the boys from school tried to catch her eye.

For the first four years of school, the same boys had crushed and ruined her days with savage insults thrown carelessly across the yard or written on tables in various classrooms. Every aspect of her body and personality was up for inspection: too big, too small, too available, too hidden, too much, not enough. Her arms had cradled any part of herself that felt under attack as she walked from lesson to lesson. But in that room, the boys looked like overgrown toddlers as they sat at tables on the outer ring begging people to buy them beer because their embarrassingly underage faces barred them from being served alcohol. Rob, from physics, stared from the other side of the room. He'd once asked if he could finger her under the table during a lesson about gravitational fields. When she'd said no, he had told everyone she'd let him and for months boys had walked past her pretending to sniff their fingers. That night, she wanted him to stare at her. She wanted them all to feel the confused longing and anger of never really knowing what it was like to touch her body.

Carmen and Leanne sat ringside at a table that Dean had saved for them as the compère mumbled names and weights into a microphone which he held too close to his mouth. The girls on Carmen's table let the first four fights go on around them as they gossiped, smoked and drank dark, sweet drinks with no ice. Their attention turned to the ring when Dean took to his corner with his coach and younger brother. His body was lean, a thin covering of pale white skin stretched tight over stringy muscles. His arms made Carmen think of the chicken in the meat aisle of the supermarket that she used to like to push her fingers into as a child. When no one was looking she would slowly push her fingers onto the cool cling film until they burst through and plunged into the cold, wet meat of the chicken. Eventually a shop assistant had caught her, and her mother never took her shopping again. She wanted to push her fingers into Dean's arms to see how deep they would go before his skin split open like the cling film.

As the compère announced each fighter, Dean jumped up and down on the spot beating his gloves together and shaking his head from side to side.

Watching Dean in the ring Leanne put her hand to her mouth and screamed, 'Oh my god Dean's so fit!' On the next table Carmen noticed the girlfriend of Dean's opponent look from Leanne to her friend and mouth, 'What a daft bitch, I wouldn't dare.' Instantly, Carmen lunged towards the girl, flicked her lit cigarette at her head and shouted, 'Shut your fucking mouth.' The cigarette bounced off the girl's arm spraying a Catherine wheel of red hot ash over the plastic table in front of her. Leanne pulled Carmen back into her seat as the girl shouted, 'What's your fucking problem?' Everyone within earshot stared at Carmen and the bell rang out for round one.

The punches in the ring were rapid and wild and didn't always connect but, when they did land, the sound of the leather glove making clean contact with a jaw or a meaty flank made Carmen's mouth water. During the three minutes of each round, the young men exploited each other's weaknesses. Heads ricocheted backwards and sideways, undefended body parts were punished, each punch powered by a feral machismo. At the end of the fifth round, Dean knocked his opponent out with a punch that sent his mouth guard flying through the air. The chewed piece of plastic covered in the blood and saliva of the loser landed next to Carmen's chair and she studied it as applause erupted around her. The young man lying in the middle of the ring had failed at this specific expression of masculinity, she wondered what that shame would do to him. She wondered who he would take it out on. Himself? Weaker boys in the kebab queue? The girlfriend Carmen had just flicked her cigarette at? The compère announced Dean the winner and lifted his arm in the air as his opponent dragged himself to the tiny stool in his corner and let his coach squirt water into his face.

After the roster of fights had finished, the tables were pushed to the side of the room, the lights were lowered and Corona's 'The Rhythm of the Night' hauled all of the girls onto the dancefloor. A charged energy from the violence everyone had cheered on hung in the air. Girls curved and twisted their bodies into suggestive movements and sequences. Dresses rode up and down, limbs became moist with sweat. Girls screamed lyrics at each other and acted out sections of songs that they'd practised in their bedrooms. Boys lined up around the periphery of the dancefloor and watched with mouths open. Bottoms, waists, crotches, boobs, arms and legs were devoured over the tops of pint glasses as if they didn't dare look directly at them. Carmen and Leanne instinctively meshed together throughout each song without thoughts of what their bodies were doing. Years later, Carmen would try to access this part of herself again on dancefloors in various cities around the world, but she was always too self-aware. She'd lost the ability to create pleasing shapes, she'd lost sight of who she was trying to please. No drugs had ever brought her out of her head enough to stop the internal monitoring of every movement she made. The only time Carmen's body had ever overruled her mind as an adult was when she had an involuntary orgasm watching a woman eating ramen at LAX Airport. It happened in under a minute, Carmen wasn't touching herself, she didn't know the woman and she'd never been able to recreate it, no matter how many mukbang YouTube videos she watched.

In an attempt to cater to the older contingent of the crowd, the DJ shifted gear and played 'I'm in the Mood for Dancing' by the Nolan Sisters.

Carmen grabbed Leanne tightly around the neck and shouted into her ear, 'I'm gonna get one more drink then I might head off. Davey's driving back my way and I can get a lift.'

'Ah what, so soon? It's still proper early.'

'I know, but I don't want to have to get the bus on my own, anyway, look who's here.' Carmen signalled with her head over Leanne's shoulder.

Dean had been fixed up after his fight and was walking across the dancefloor towards them. His bruised, swollen eyelids looked like pieces of liver, the white of his right eye was a deep cherry red.

The deep cut down the middle of his bottom lip split open as he shouted, 'Alreet lasses!'

'Oh my god!' Leanne squealed as he took her by the waist and spun her round and round into the centre of the dancefloor.

Carmen gathered her jacket and bag, said goodbye to the other girls and waved to Leanne.

Still clinging to Dean, she cupped her hand to her mouth and shouted, 'I'll ring you tomorrow, careful getting home.'

'You too.' Carmen blew five frantic kisses in Leanne's direction.

Sitting at the roundabout at the bottom of the motorway junction Carmen's mother eyed the passing cars as she waited for her opportunity to pull out. 'This traffic is bloody terrible round here, I'm sure it's getting worse,' she said, turning down the radio to concentrate.

'You should have stayed on the motorway then.'

A gap in the flow of traffic appeared and her mother revved the engine to pull out, the sudden g-force dragging them both back into their seats.

Following the outside lane all the way around the roundabout her mother took the third exit towards Kibblesworth. 'How's work going? Did you get that big order sorted?' She breathed a sigh of relief to be on a quieter road.

'Yeah, it's going good actually. Everything was confirmed and there's been a lot of press. Means more travel but I like being away.' Carmen's body stiffened as she spoke.

'It's good to be busy.' Her mother lightly rubbed Carmen's thigh then changed gear.

The road wound left and right through fields and farm-land. Even though her mother stuck to a solid twenty miles per hour it felt faster. On the slight incline ahead, Carmen could see the church on the left and the intersection coming into view.

'When was the last time you were round here?' her mother asked.

'It's been years. I can't remember,' Carmen answered with a dry mouth.

The day after the boxing match, Carmen woke up hung-over and managed to persuade her mother it wasn't self-inflicted.

Standing in the kitchen pouring herself a glass of full-fat Coke, avoiding any contact with her mother's boyfriend who was hovering in the doorway, she said, 'I didn't even drink last night coz I was starting to feel ill. I think it's the start of a virus or something.'

An audible snigger came from behind which both Carmen and her mother ignored.

'I can't be bothered to argue with you,' her mother said checking in her handbag that she had everything she needed. 'If you're staying home, you can keep off that phone and do the hoovering. I've got to go to work.'

Carmen lay on the large flowery sofa all morning watching MTV. At lunchtime she made a sandwich in the kitchen with the local news playing on the TV in the background: a fundraiser for the swimming pool was taking place that weekend and the planning application for the new estate near her school had been contested. As she took a glass jar of mayonnaise out of the cupboard, she tuned in to a story about a car crash the previous night on the strip of winding country road near her Auntie Sandra's house. She turned to see footage of the wrecked car being hauled onto a truck, men moving bashed-out sections of the dry-stone wall to the side of the road. She sat at the kitchen table, and took a large bite out of her ham sandwich, the sweet creamy mayonnaise oozing onto her tongue.

'The two boys confirmed dead at the scene were named as Dean Allman and Paul Scott and the two girls were named as Leanne Jenkins and Kelly Dean, the families of all involved have been informed.'

She heard the words and then looked up at the screen for confirmation. Carmen spat the bread back out onto her plate and continued to stare at the TV as the news moved on to the next segment. She got up and knocked the jar of mayonnaise off the kitchen bench as she tried to steady her legs, which wanted to give way. The mayonnaise jar smashed on the floor; gold gelatinous splodges of it would still be found months later on the kitchen ceiling. In a trance she walked to the phone on the wall and dialled Leanne's number, her sister answered.

'Simone?' Carmen said slowly, not wanting to hear what she knew was coming next.

'Ah Carm … me dad was just gonna ring ya.'

Outside the church, all of the girls from school gathered together shivering in coats that were too thin for the January frost. Their heavily made-up eyes streaked and leaked through the rough pink toilet roll they'd brought

from the school bathrooms. Filing inside, holding hands like
a line of delicate paper dolls, they jostled on the cold hard
pews unsure what to expect. Some of the kids from school
who didn't like Leanne had turned up to the funeral, it had
fallen on the same day as the French exam and anyone
attending got an instant pass.

Carmen stared at Leanne's coffin lying solidly on a plinth
in the sanctuary of the church. With her head bowed and
mouth open, her eyes fixated on the pale angular box
containing the body of her best friend. As the vicar spoke to
start the service Carmen couldn't calm her mind. Images of
what Leanne's face might look like in the coffin layered and
glitched over each other. Was her face purple? Were her
eyes open? Had scabs formed over the cuts and injuries
from where she'd gone through the windscreen, or were
dead bodies unable to form scabs? When would her skin
begin to rot? Was her hair still curly? What clothes had her
mother dressed her in? What was it like to dress your dead
daughter? Carmen's body closed in around her knees as she
struggled to process the increasingly dark questions and
images that flooded her mind.

In front of her the vicar circled the coffin, wafting a
smoking golden censer as he blessed Leanne with incense.
The billowing sickly scent caught at the back of Carmen's
throat and a nauseous wave rose up in her body. The damp
coming in through the large stone bricks of the church
seeped into her bones, lodging an ache in her hips and
back. As low prayers were called out she became aware of
a noise, a guttural siren calling out again and again; the
arms of the girls sitting next to her broke her trance and
she realised the groans were coming from her. The rest of

the service went on around Carmen in a blur, she sat in a catatonic state as Leanne's sister gave a reading of what, Carmen couldn't be sure, and they played Whitney Houston's 'I Will Always Love You' to mark the end of the service.

Externally life went on after the funeral, but internally time stood still. Carmen sat in a hazy stupor during double maths on a Thursday afternoon after smoking weed in the underpass close to school. Mr Pearson would ask her to repeat what he had just explained about finding the length of the hypotenuse in a right-angled triangle and she'd wonder where she was. Before she was due to take her final exams, she stopped going to school altogether. She spent her days watching TV, sleeping or staring out of the window, amazed that her body was remembering to breathe. Her mother carried on working long shifts at the pub, often only speaking to Carmen if she hadn't finished the list of jobs she'd left for her each morning. 'You're not lying around the house doing naff all, you can make yourself useful,' she'd shouted up the stairs when Carmen had forgotten to take the bins out one day.

Two of the girls from their group got pregnant shortly after Leanne died. Carmen thought about them years later when she planted sunflowers in her own garden. Some had flowered earlier than others, her neighbour mentioned that they must have experienced a trauma at some stage in their growth process. 'If flowers get stressed or feel under threat, they bloom early so that they can secure their future. It's a defence mechanism,' he'd explained over the low fence separating their gardens. Carmen had suddenly wished the fence was higher.

In her relationships as an adult, Carmen was disappointing. She entered into a new friendship in good faith, excited by the possibility of connection, but somewhere along the way she became exhausted by the banality of adult friendships. With her late replies to text messages and emails, cancelled plans and unreturned phone calls, she was trying to communicate what she couldn't say out loud: *I'm not that person, don't rely on me for anything.* Routinely she put physical distance or a barrier of frustration between herself and anyone who tried to form a meaningful bond. She chose not to share stories of Leanne with the friends who had learnt to operate at a comfortable distance. How could she distil her down into an understandable package without flattening out her existence? It was the millions of small details that made her who she was. Who would want to know that she loved pickled onion crisps but couldn't stand real pickled onions? How could someone picture her round, gnawed fingernails, and what it was like to hold her warm, dry hands? Carmen wouldn't be able to describe how she smelt or her deep throaty voice and her high-pitched giggle. They wouldn't be able to visualise her hyperextended knees, or the diamond-shaped pupil in her left eye, or the look on her face when she took acid at fourteen and saw a Care Bear surfing on her kitchen floor. No one would react the way Carmen wanted them to if she described Leanne, so she didn't try.

*   *   *

Carmen thought about all of this as she sat and waited for her mother to finish handing over the Christmas puddings to her Auntie Sandra. The two women spoke in quick, clipped sentences, never laughing or smiling at each other. Her Auntie Sandra, wearing a grey, knee-length woollen skirt and pink checked tabard, dipped her head and waved slowly at the car. Carmen waved back but didn't move from her seat.

'She didn't even want them,' her mother said as she got back in the car and closed the door behind her, shivering without a coat on. 'Bloody freezing isn't it, you wouldn't think it was May.'

'Can we go?' Carmen pleaded, pulling her coat tight, also feeling the unseasonal chill from outside.

Driving down her street at a crawl her mother gasped, 'Oh look there's Juan, the new neighbour. He's Spanish you know.' Putting Carmen's window down from the button on her door handle she leant over and shouted 'Hola!' waving eagerly at the man unpacking his car.

The man held his hand up nervously before quickly turning his attention back to the ALDI bags in his boot. Pulling onto the drive her mother eased the car slowly up to the garage until there was a one-inch gap between the door and her car bonnet.

'We're going to need to open that soon to move all of the stuff out,' Carmen said nodding at the garage door.

'Well, I'll move the car then.'

'Why don't you just move it back now since we're in the car?'

Her mother twisted to get out of the car and repeated Carmen's words in an excruciating baby voice.

Inside the house, Carmen dumped her suitcase in the hallway and went straight into the garage through the door in the utility room. A stack of shoeboxes leant sideways next to old toys, board games, photo albums and tins of paint. The bottom shoebox sat crushed from taking the weight of the memories above it. Taking each box in order she found flyers from nightclubs she'd gone to underage, notes passed back and forth between friends in class making plans to sleep at boys' houses or outlining which STD clinic was nearest to them and which one was quickest. There was a He-Man ring that used to glow in the dark, the knickers she'd worn the night she lost her virginity and a ticket stub from Disney World the year she'd gone to Florida with her dad and his new family.

Each box was an instant window back into her life as a thirteen-, fourteen-, fifteen-year-old. The crumpled box on the bottom was from her sixteenth year. It was empty except for one photograph of her and Leanne taken at the tree where they used to meet every morning to smoke a cigarette before school. She couldn't remember the photo being taken or having ever seen it before. They weren't posing, it captured a rare and random moment in time. Leanne was holding an unlit cigarette in the centre of her lips, letting laughter seep out of the sides of her mouth, her eyes squinting with amusement. Her tiny chewed fingernails, painted a bright pink, were clutching the box of matches she was about to strike. Carmen was leaning on her, laughing into her blonde permed hair. Leanne's school tie was precisely styled into a tiny knot with the skinny end coming down to her second shirt button. Her huge gold earrings catching the flash that someone had used even though the picture was taken in bright sunlight.

Carmen wondered what they would have talked about as they shared that cigarette. The day that would have followed, the things they would have laughed about and what their teachers would have tried to teach them. Leanne and Carmen weren't friends, they were an extension of each other. They lived inside of each other. Carmen looked at Leanne's stomach in the photograph and crawled inside. She lay down and felt Leanne's fingers stroking her forehead, lightly counting the freckles across her nose. She could hear her asking if she was going to ring her mam to ask if she could sleep over for the night. Carmen could hear her talking about what she wanted to eat for her tea and how much she loved the new TLC video. She was planning to put all of the duvets on her bedroom floor so that they could make a camp and watch horror films all night. She was debating whether she would get a flat with Dean when they left school and what kind of dog they might get. She was telling Carmen not to worry about her mam, to give her a break because she had her own stuff going on and to forget about her dad. She was flicking through a magazine and humming the song from a TV advert. Carmen felt Leanne's fingers playing with her hair and felt loved.

'Have you sorted that stuff out or what?' Her mother appeared in the doorway of the utility room, wringing her hands. 'You haven't got time to read every bloody note you ever wrote in chemistry when you should have been learning something.' Carmen held her breath, stood up and put everything back in the boxes except for the photo of her and Leanne.

'What's that?' her mother asked.

Carmen looked at the photo lying flat in her palms. 'It's me and Leanne.'

Without moving her mother cocked her head to get a better look. 'You were inseparable,' she said in a small whisper.

Carmen nodded her head slowly, allowing the nod to develop into a rocking motion that took over her whole torso as she tried to propel herself from the spot where she stood. Her mother took a step back, breaking the trapped energy, and Carmen put the photograph into the top pocket of her shirt.

Pointing at the remaining pile of shoeboxes Carmen said, 'I'm done with all that. There's nothing else I want to keep.' She turned and put her arm around her mother's small hunched shoulders. 'Should we start in the kitchen and get this place packed up then?' Her mother nodded slowly and quietly shut the door to the garage behind them.

Next Gen

Jameela placed a Danish pastry into her mouth, icing side down, and held it there as the sticky sweetness dissolved on her tongue. She took a bite and let the excess crumbs fall onto the thick meeting room carpet as she watched a tourist couple take selfies on the South Bank. With their heads pressed together in conjoined reverie they posed and laughed, pouted and kissed each other in front of an outstretched iPhone. On the snap of the last shot their expressions fell back into neutral as they reviewed the photographs, presumably reams of their own smiling faces flying past on the small screen. Jameela wondered where they'd come from, why they were up so early (making the most of the day?) and what they had planned for their mid-week city break. Had they put on their out of office to eat at the Angus Steakhouse in Leicester Square and pose with celebrity waxworks at Madame Tussauds? Or did they see themselves as a little more discerning? Maybe they weren't hop on, hop off kind of people. Had they read blogs and searched Instagram hashtags for the best new places to eat which served natural wine? Did they have a list of 'cool places' in their phone notes from a friend who used to work in London? Jameela's colleagues complained about the number of tourists in the area surrounding the office, their slow walking blocking access to a speedy lunchtime sandwich, but she liked that they caused accidental delays to the schedules of her self-important co-workers.

The meeting-room door opened and she was momentarily glad to be distracted from thinking about Ed Sheeran's Madame Tussauds waxwork until she realised it was Andy.

'Jameela, can you clear that rubbish out of here,' he said pointing to the trays of half-eaten pastries from the 8 a.m. meeting. 'We've got the casting agency in at 10 a.m. and Lucy's running late.'

She continued to chew her pastry, watching Andy plug in every lead he could find before he pointed all of the remote controls at a huge screen mounted on the wall. He put everything down, rested both hands on the oval table and stared at her. Jameela focused her attention on the buttons straining to keep his shirt fastened across his stomach.

'Please?' he said witheringly.

She blinked hard to hide her eye roll, picked up the trays that needed clearing and pushed the glass door open with her bum.

'And get Carrie in here, we need to review everything before 9.45,' he called after her.

*

Andy was a relic from ad-land's late nineties, early nough-ties heyday, when budgets were in the millions, drugs at lunchtime were commonplace and white men from art college were given icon status for making Guinness adverts that you could no longer find on YouTube. This was pre-internet, when all you had to think about was how an idea would run across TV, print and out-of-home. A sticker campaign was seen as anarchic, and projecting naked women onto the Houses of Parliament without their permission was revolutionary. Now everything was different. Now there were new social platforms every six months, nobody watched programmed TV anymore, everyone was a content creator – and there was Andy, out of his depth, but still in charge. Supposedly bringing maturity, wisdom and guidance to a younger team whose ideas he passed off as his own.

As Jameela carried the leftover trays through the office, random hands grabbed croissants and Kløben buns without saying please or thank you. In the kitchen Carrie stood at the Nespresso machine waiting for her coffee to flow smoothly into her Alessi espresso cup. Without turning her head she greeted Jameela with an even but friendly, 'Morning.'

'Morning Carrie, you good?'

'We're good. How are you? You ready for this casting meeting at 10 a.m.? Did you manage to get together some good names?'

'Yeah, I've been speaking to some decent people and pulled a deck together.'

'Perfect, you always come through. Just bring them on your laptop to the meeting, no need to send them over beforehand.'

'Cool. Cool. Oh, Andy's in the meeting room, he was looking for you. Said he wanted to go over something before the agency got here.'

Pausing to tap a teaspoon aggressively on the side of her cup, Carrie said, 'He probably just needs help connecting his laptop.' She put a gentle accomplice's hand on Jameela's shoulder as she turned to leave the kitchen. 'See you in a bit.'

'Yeah see you.'

At her desk Jameela scrolled through briefing notes on the client they were casting talent for – a global retailer who wanted to persuade their customers they were becoming more sustainable by launching a capsule collection made from recycled cotton and a new enzyme that broke down materials in twenty to thirty years so their products would disintegrate in landfill rather than lying stagnant for millennia. There were a lot of environmental buzzwords in the strategy section: community; regenerative action; waste-led design; circular systems. Jameela couldn't yet work out how they were going to use this to distract consumers from the bulk of the client's business as a giant of low-cost fast fashion, let alone persuade anyone with credibility to be part of the campaign. But that was what she'd been hired to do.

She'd finished top of her year at university and had won a D&AD New Blood award for her project designed to encourage young people to vote, which the judges said was 'era-defining'. The agency spotted her when her final major project did the rounds on creative blogs and her Instagram followers went from 894 to 10,899 in under one week. Signing into her own agency email on the first day of her internship she momentarily forgot about the sacrifices her family had made to send her to university, and the £40,000 worth of student debt she owed.

When the agency hired Jameela at the end of her three-month internship Carrie sent her an email saying:

We're going for lunch today, be ready at 12.30.

At 12.28 she arrived at Jameela's desk dressed in a long camel coat that looked like vintage Prada. 'Shall we?'

Travelling down twenty floors in the lift Carrie ignored a cell of project managers discussing a true crime podcast and which Ganni dress one of them was going to send back from the three she'd ordered online. Carrie's gold rings and simple gold band bracelet caught the overhead light as she stood silently tapping out emails on her phone. Jameela thought about checking her phone to appear busy, but couldn't remember what her last Google search had been and didn't want to risk anyone in the packed lift seeing 'Is it normal that my vagina bleaches my knickers?' flash up on her phone. At the ping of the ground floor Carrie pushed through the women waiting and sailed through the revolving front doors without touching a handle.

The area of the South Bank near the office was populated with vapid chain restaurants, punctuated by a Pret or a Costa every hundred metres.

'This place is so depressing. Where do you live?' Carrie asked without making eye contact.

'Peckham,' Jameela replied, bracing herself for the follow-up question about where her family was from.

'So, you don't have too far to travel into the office, that's good.'

Jameela auto-responded with, 'Where do you live?'

But Carrie had already walked ahead with no intention of answering. 'Let's go here,' she shouted, pointing at the minimalist Italian restaurant, empty apart from two men in suits sat at a long family-sized table.

Carrie walked to a table for two by the window without waiting to be seated by the host. An overly friendly waiter tried to make small talk while he filled up their water glasses and reeled off the specials. Jameela was too nervous to engage with him and Carrie had no interest in what he was saying. They scanned the menus in silence, Carrie ordered a burrata salad and sparking mineral water, Jameela ordered lasagne with fries and a Coke, which she instantly regretted.

'Sorry, do you think that will take too long?' she asked.

'Who cares?' Carrie said still tapping out emails on her phone. 'Enjoy your lasagne.'

With the arrival of their drinks Carrie put her phone away and interrogated Jameela about which college she had attended, what part of the course she had enjoyed the most, her favourite artists, who she lived with and what they did. She felt she was in an interview that she hadn't prepared for, but Carrie's face seemed warm and she laughed easily at the jokes Jameela slid in. After they'd eaten Jameela felt sick, the Coke curdling with the melted cheese and rich béchamel sauce of the lasagne. She wasn't sure whether to leave some so as to not seem greedy, or whether to eat every last mouthful so she didn't seem ungrateful. She opted for greedy but grateful. Carrie ordered an espresso and Jameela sipped some iced water, trying to find a comfortable position that meant her lungs weren't so restricted. She distracted herself by asking Carrie about her career, she told her she loved some of the campaigns she'd worked on, that she found her creativity and approach really inspiring. Carrie put her coffee cup down and gave Jameela a rigid look.

'Try not to be so impressed by other people in this industry. Do you understand?' Jameela nodded her head and looked down at the table, unsure she did.

'Advertising is full of people clinging on trying to stay relevant but we're going to change that. You're the future, you're the only person you need to impress. Got that?'

'OK,' Jameela replied, clearing the crumbs that lay in front of her.

In the three years since that first lunch Carrie had mentored Jameela closely. She'd guided her ideas, her thinking, put her on the best projects, taken her to the Cannes festival where they'd lived like 'rich white men' for a week. At work events Carrie had introduced her to other industry figures and press, proudly presenting her as the 'next generation', always pointing out it was under her tutelage, of course. Jameela had repaid Carrie by staying late, working weekends, putting forward every part of herself, her network, her own culture. She had observed how Carrie operated, emulating elements of how she crafted the kernel of an idea into a fully fledged campaign, how she dealt with difficult clients, and she'd mirrored her love of Studio Nicholson clothes – although Jameela had to settle for the cheaper high street replicas. As a result, Jameela was considered the young star of the agency, a resounding success; she had the industry awards and the envy of the other junior creatives to prove it.

That morning the casting agency bounded through the office like unleashed puppy dogs. They worked from a leaky arch in Hackney so were easily impressed by the perks and quirks of large agency life. They had come to present the talent they thought the client should be working with: a collection of people connected to sustainability who had a large following on social media which they could attach to the project.

Jameela knew the script, she'd seen it happen time and time before. They'd present a deck of people to piggyback on, using their cultural cachet to tap into a difficult-to-reach demographic at a fraction of the cost it would take to reach their audiences via traditional methods. In the past she'd put forward people from her own community; people she'd met at club nights, art galleries and friends' birthday parties. People she'd grown up with or those she followed online who spoke on the right social issues and had a palatable aesthetic. She'd promised them good fees and an interview on lifestyle platforms as part of the package. At first, she'd been excited to be in the position to connect people from her world to the world of commercial fees, free clothes and exposure. But as she watched the people she'd brought in post pictures of themselves on advertising hoardings, wearing trainers or jeans made by factories with inhumane working conditions, she came to realise that it

was the brands who were benefitting from the exposure at
a discount price.

She'd sat in countless meetings and calls where it was
clear the clients wanted to be seen to be supporting the
right issues, happy to align with whatever cause the major-
ity of their customers stood for. Jameela found it funny
when a client talked about 'supporting the culture and
giving a voice to marginalised communities'. Because to
her, the people they apparently elevated had always had a
voice, the only difference now was that it was financially
beneficial to listen to them. In emails to activists and artists
on behalf of brands, the agency talent department wrote
gushing lines that read:

> We'd love to give a platform to your community and
> amplify your message.

Which translated in real terms as:

> We'd love to use you to make more money and if that
> means destroying the planet as a by-product, well,
> our bad — here's some gifted products. P.S. don't
> forget to tag us on your socials as per our watertight
> contract.

The brands measured the success of social media campaigns
on metrics such as 'reach' and 'engagement' that everyone
knew meant nothing. Jameela would watch it all play out as
she waited for her 10 p.m. Uber Eats to arrive, scrolling and
wondering where it would all end whilst not having the
energy to think too deeply about it because she was so tired

from working until 1 a.m. the night before on a deck that didn't make it into the final presentation.

After finishing the client-briefing document at her desk Jameela went through her emails and got her slides ready for the casting meeting. Oli slid quietly into the seat beside her, put his sage green Bottega Veneta bag on its own chair and turned on his monitor.

'Do you think anyone has noticed I'm late?' The loading boom of his Mac made his face cringe. 'Shhhut up you snitch!'

'It's only quarter past nine, you're alright.'

'I know but even Andy's here,' Oli whispered.

'Only because Carrie's started scheduling their shared meetings first thing to fuck him up.'

'Oh, that's cold,' he said widening then narrowing his eyes. 'Look at her in there.'

They both lowered their heads behind Jameela's monitor to get a better glimpse of Carrie without being spotted.

'Who is she today? She's giving me Berlin gallerist vibes in those leather culottes and black bondage shirt. She's giving me "I'm going to my friend's avant-garde performance art piece in an old ammunitions works, then maybe to an orgy." It's very Rick Owens,' he said, snapping his head to face Jameela. 'Do you think it's Rick Owens?'

'I don't know who Rick Owens is,' Jameela said absently, still eyeing up what was happening in the meeting room. 'It sounds like the name of a Sunday school teacher.'

'Honestly,' Oli said, quickly typing in his password. 'I'm wasted here.'

Other than what she presented on a daily basis, Carrie gave up very few insights into her life outside the agency. She didn't want anything in her private life affecting how she was viewed in the agency, but with Jameela she had opened up a little over the course of their three years working together – at lunch when they were having their mentoring check-ins, late at night in the office when they were finessing ideas accompanied by Korean takeaways. She talked about certain pockets of her personal life – the ex-partner who split his time between London and Antwerp and had broken her heart, the illness she'd suffered as a teenager, and once in the airport when they were flying to a shoot in Miami, she'd talked about how she used to want children. She'd had her eggs frozen but hadn't found the time to make it happen and now her career wouldn't withstand the break it would take to raise a family on her own. 'Have you noticed how few women there are at the top in our industry? Kids and exec positions in advertising don't mix,' she'd said. At first Jameela felt these insights into Carrie's personal life were a sign that she could be trusted but as time progressed these apparent secrets had begun to feel like perfectly managed PR leaks.

In preparation for plugging her laptop into the meeting-room screen, Jameela tidied her desktop and began closing all of the interiors tabs she had open in Google Chrome. 'Look, before I get rid of these. What do you think of these ideas for my room?' Jameela asked, angling her screen towards Oli. 'I want to do something to brighten it up but I don't want to spend a load of coin, I'm saving y'know.'

Oli put a hand over his eyes. 'Oh my god, if this is a carousel of pink and peach velvet interiors with some mushroom lamps and a rattan bedhead I'm going to kill myself.'

'How did you know? How did you know?' Jameela repeated at a higher pitch. 'Why are you reading me for filth today?!'

Uncovering his eyes Oli said, 'Because honey, you and your little millennial nesting plans are tragic. I can't take it. This weekend clear your diary, we're going to go to the auction house and vintage markets and we'll see what we can do with that messy little room of yours.'

'Thank you,' Jameela said, her head tipped to the side in appreciation and mock embarrassment. 'What would I do without my very own interior stylist?'

Oli gave a quick smile and got back to acting like he hadn't just arrived.

An email dropped into Jameela and Oli's inboxes from Carrie, who was still pretending to pay attention to Andy and the casting agency in the meeting room.

SUBJECT: REFS

Everyone on the Orbit account we're refining the concept and execution ideas after the casting meeting. If you have any Y2K, Jeremy Deller or Ryan McGinley references take them out, same goes for any lo-fi VHS effects for any film ideas. TAKE THEM OUT.

'Watch this,' Oli said, nodding towards the creative team Andy managed who were sat at a bank of desks opposite. A relay of whispers erupted around the shared table as each of the creatives pulled up their InDesign files and started to delete pages. This job had to go well for them. Their last big project for an insurance company had been a disaster on all levels. In a bid to persuade more young women to buy life insurance, the team – made up of four white men with Thames Estuary accents (one of whom wore a T-shirt that read *Yoots* in the style of the Boots logo) – had come up with an interactive campaign that asked women to post selfies on Instagram in their underwear accompanied with the hashtag #iknowmyworth.

Jameela had watched it come together from the side-lines, offering input and pushback that was ignored. After the shoot for the main campaign she watched as the boys gathered around Andy's screen and focused on the crotch of one of the models. There had been a collective gasp and someone pretended to be sick as they zoomed in on what they thought was a tampon string hanging from the side of her knickers.

'Jameela come and look at this. Is this what we think it is?' Andy called over.

'You're alright, that's really not OK.'

'I know, it's clapped,' one of the creatives said from among the scrum of art directors.

'No. I mean, you lot are not OK, you're all creeps,' Jameela said.

'You need to lighten up, Jameela. Jesus.' Andy shot a look back in her direction.

At the wrap party for the #iknowmyworth campaign, lap dances were paid for with £20 notes from petty cash, which were reconciled with blank taxi receipts. No one ever questioned why the team had taken so many black cabs that night when they all had company Uber accounts. The next morning Andy gave a big speech about how the campaign was award-winning work as they all mopped up their hangovers with bacon naans from Dishoom, which they expensed to the client account. The first week after the launch the client sacked the agency following record complaints and a public trashing of the campaign. Memes were posted in their thousands mocking the visuals and #iknowmyworth messaging. When the agency couldn't avoid the controversy anymore it was Carrie who spoke to the press and gave pacifying quotes even though she hadn't worked on the account.

'Why did you have to be the spokeswoman for that mess?' Jameela had asked at one of their mentoring sessions.

'Because as an agency, we can't have those lot – an all-male team – go on record about the stink they caused. The optics of that would look terrible.'

'But it is terrible, the whole thing. Why were they the team working on it anyway?'

'Listen, it's all about the long game. This industry is falling apart at the seams but out of the ruins something better will come. I'm happy to show my support for the agency as a whole, I don't mind being the one to mop up after those idiots because their time is limited, but mine isn't. Andy thinks he's going to be head of agency in a year but that's my job.' Carrie had been resolute.

With five minutes left until the rest of the teams were due in the casting meeting, Jameela used the downtime to work out how much her flatmate owed her for bills and how much she'd have left for the rest of the month. 'Fuck's sake,' she said tapping the end of her pen against the sums on her pad.

'What's wrong Mensa? What you trying to work out?' Oli leant over, looking at the pad upside down.

'Huda still owes me for three months of bills and it's like,' she paused to check the amount, 'over £300. I'm really skint this month. I'm sick of working all the time just to be skint.'

'You should steal some of the Aesop hand wash from the storage cupboard and sell it on eBay.'

'Right! They should put more money into paying decent wages rather than kitting the place out with all this shit.' Jameela pointed at the row of glass fronted fridges full of free beer, champagne and kombucha that lined their side of the office.

'Honey. That's the scam. You're working on the big brand campaigns with the big budgets and decent catering on set. You've made it. Your name is etched onto a wooden pencil award that you paid £315 of your own money to claim. It doesn't matter that your wages still mean you have to sleep on a lumpy IKEA mattress in a tiny flatshare in south London and you can't afford to save for a house deposit.'

'It's mad innit. I've been stockpiling the free CBD tampons though. I'm gonna ask for another pay review at the end of this quarter.'

'Do it,' Oli said scanning the briefing doc for the meeting, which Jameela had just read through. 'What do I need to know for this meeting, I can't be arsed to read this whole deck.'

'They basically want us to roll their landfill shit in eco-friendly glitter and pretend they're doing everyone a massive favour. Listen to this quote from the client, hang on I'll dig it out …'

Jameela scrolled down through an email exchange with Carrie about the project, looking for the exact quote about the brand purpose. Towards the bottom of the thread, original emails between Andy and Carrie appeared; accidently shared when she'd forwarded on a PDF of image references Andy had created. In their emails they were discussing the teams to put on the account, a plan for the scope of work and early ideas for the creative direction, then Jameela spotted her name:

> > > > > > > > > > > > > > > On 11/09/2019, 16:27,
'Carrie Hall' <carrie@wpkg.com> wrote:

> > > > > > > > > > > > > >
> > > > > > > > > > > > > >
> > > > > > > > > > > > > >
> > > > > > > > > > > > > >
> > > > > > > > > > > > > >
> > > > > > > > > > > > > >
> > > > > > > > > > > > > > Andy,
> > > > > > > > > > > > > >
> > > > > > > > > > > > > >
> > > > > > > > > > > > > > I don't know about those
first two routes but I like the third. Let's chat in
person tomorrow.
> > > > > > > > > > > > > >
> > > > > > > > > > > > > >
> > > > > > > > > > > > > >
> > > > > > > > > > > > > >

> > > > > > > > > > > > > >

> > > > > > > > > > > > > > > > I think there's a way around recruiting talent for something as problematic as this account. I've been working on Jameela for ages, she owes me so let's lean on her for this and get decent names through her connections. I'll make her think it's her idea :)

> > > > > > > > > > > > > >

> > > > > > > > > > > > > >

> > > > > > > > > > > > > >

> > > > > > > > > > > > > >

> > > > > > > > > > > > > >

> > > > > > > > > > > > > > > Dates-wise for the Paris shoot it's looking like 15–18, again let's chat with production tomorrow to confirm. I'll give you the address for Louvreuse to collect my bag order, thanks for doing that!

> > > > > > > > > > > > > >

> > > > > > > > > > > > > > .

> > > > > > > > > > > > > >

> > > > > > > > > > > > > >

> > > > > > > > > > > > > >

> > > > > > > > > > > > > >

> > > > > > > > > > > > > > Carrie Hall | Executive Creative Director

> > > > > > > > > > > > >

> > > > > > > > > > > > > > WPKG Worldwide

> > > > > > > > > > > > > >

'Come on then, this better be good. Have you found it?'
Oli sat with his hand propping up his face on the armrest
of his multi-move Herman Miller office chair.

Jameela closed her laptop and shook her head, 'I can't
find it.' Blood drained from her face.

Carrie's voice boomed across the office: 'Everyone in the
Orbit casting meeting can you come over now?'

Lucy, the studio manager flustered in and out of the meeting room bringing in new bottles of water, plates of fruit
and bowls of unsalted nuts. Oli showed Jameela some
1930s French lamps he was already watching for her on
eBay, and two of Andy's creative team were discussing a
techno night one of them had been to at the weekend while
Carrie applied Elizabeth Arden Eight Hour Cream to her
perpetually dry lips.

Sat at the head of the large boardroom table, Carrie
kicked off the meeting. 'OK. So, as we all know sustainability is a huge driver at the minute and our client wants to be
working with the right people, supporting them, giving
them a wider platform, et cetera, et cetera. Anne-Marie
from the casting agency is going to take us through some of
the influencer, sorry, collaborator options – the client
doesn't want us to use the word influencer – which we can
then present with the concepts later today. We'll go through
the first round of names and Jameela has some extra people
to add to the mix.'

'Thanks, Carrie,' Anne-Marie said shuffling in her seat,
adjusting her comfort levels now that she was the focus of
everyone's attention. 'Yes,' she coughed. 'So, we have pulled

together some of the names we think are really driving forward change in innovative ways. They're the real "Ones to Watch" in the world of sustainability.'

Jameela tuned out as names, profiles and follower numbers were rattled through and everyone rated each suggestion from one to ten on suitability. The words *I'll make her think it's her idea* floated around her head in colourful bubble letters crashing into the sides of her brain, like a psychedelic screensaver.

'This is Charli Aboah,' Anne-Marie continued, 'she has created an online community that campaigns for garment workers' rights and she runs online lectures around tackling the climate crisis.'

Andy interrupted, 'Anne-Marie can I stop you right there. Firstly, can we erase any mention of a climate crisis, the client doesn't want to use alarmist language, and secondly, I'd prefer not to include Charli, she's too radical and I've heard she's very difficult to work with.'

'Difficult to work with' was a well-used phrase with many meanings in the office. When the agency cast a friend of Jameela's in a campaign for a sports brand she was called difficult when she complained that her face was being used on global hoardings but her agreed fee and contract only covered an Instagram campaign. Past interns were labelled difficult when they complained about Andy massaging their shoulders at their desks, and Jameela heard she'd been called difficult by a production company that wouldn't action her feedback on a photoshoot.

'But Charli has a strong following,' Anne-Marie said with an exasperation that Jameela knew would only irritate Andy further. 'People really engage with her messaging. It would look great if she was involved. I'd really recommend we at least meet with her.'

Andy sat back in his chair, letting his stomach expand into the space around him. 'No, no. I think she's too political for the client and she'll bring a lot of extra issues.'

Anne-Marie turned to Carrie with a pleading lift to the right-hand side of her face.

Carrie paused then said, 'I agree with Andy, we don't want any extra complications around this campaign or talent causing trouble.' Carrie switched focus quickly: 'Jameela do you want to share your slides, you said you had some extra suggestions?'

Jameela rested her hands on top of her closed laptop and looked squarely at Andy and Carrie.

'No, actually I didn't bring anything. I haven't got any extra suggestions on this.'

'Are you sure? In the kitchen earlier you said you had some good names?'

'Yeah … no. I went through them and it's not right. I don't want to put them in the mix.'

'It's not right? What, the project isn't right or they're not right for the project?'

'The project isn't right,' Jameela said.

Oli coughed and set off a Mexican wave of fidgeting motions through everyone around the table. Jameela bit down on the inside of her cheek.

'OK. Very well,' Carrie said. 'Let's move on. Anne-Marie who else do we have?'

'OK so next we have …' Anne-Marie continued to take the group through the rest of the deck and they agreed on a list of people including two white men, three white women, one Black woman and a woman from Sri Lanka.

As the meeting wrapped up Oli took his attention straight back to eBay, Andy tried to joke with Anne-Marie about an unintentional double entendre in her presentation and Carrie eyed Jameela as she quietly left the meeting room and walked heavily to the gender-neutral bathroom in the furthest corner of the office.

Standing at the mirror with her hands steadying her on the sink Jameela pressed her nose up to the glass and stared into her own eyes. Her breath fogged up the mirror until she almost couldn't see herself anymore.

'Fuck this place,' she said in a low, weighted whisper, creating a wider circle of condensation with her hot breath. Stepping away from the mirror she drew a smiley face in the mist and matched her own expression to the cartoon she'd just drawn. Carrie walked in and their eyes met in the mirror before she focused on the fading smiley.

'Thanks for your input today,' she said, and Jameela nodded without smiling. 'You OK?'

Jameela nodded again, straightened her shirt and turned on the tap without putting her hands under the water.

'You know, you've got to keep that bigger picture in mind,' Carrie said. 'There are always going to be small sacrifices along the way, we've talked about this.'

'Right, it's all about the optics isn't it. It has to look a certain way even if it isn't.'

'We just have to make it work with what we've got until things move on. Listen, we have a new intern starting tomorrow. She's from your old uni, maybe you could take her for lunch, show her the ropes, get her into our way of thinking?'

'I've got a busy week.'

Carrie arched a perfectly laminated eyebrow.

'Maybe.'

'Good,' Carrie said resting a hand on Jameela's arm, which sent a shiver down her left side until her big toe curled into a cramp.

'That's a nice bag,' Jameela pointed at the Memphis-inspired circular bag slung over Carrie's shoulder. 'Is that the one Andy picked up for you in Paris?'

Carrie smiled, 'Yes he got it …' She fell silent. 'It's from …'

'Louvreuse, yeah it's nice.' Jameela ran water over her hands and turned her back to Carrie who walked slowly to one of the empty cubicles.

Jameela stood perfectly still at the sink and listened to Carrie piss in the cubicle two metres away from her. The stream of urine sounded faint, like she had lined the toilet with paper first to blot the impact. Jameela turned to face the cubicle and thought about what it would be like to take a step back, lunge forward and kick open the toilet door with her large winter boots. Would there be enough space on the other side for the door to burst open and snap back without hitting Carrie, or would her body or face bear the full force?

Behind the toilet door Carrie sat with her knickers and vegan leather culottes held around her knees so as not to touch the floor. She was aware of Jameela standing on the other side of the door, she could see the tips of her boots facing her cubicle. Why wasn't she moving? Was she in the middle of sending an email on her phone? There was stillness throughout the whole bathroom. A silent stand-off. Neither women washing nor wiping.

The automatic flush suddenly gushed underneath Carrie's bare bum, nearly making her jump, but she remained seated until she saw Jameela's shadow on the floor moving back towards the sink. As the last of the water drained away from under her, Carrie heard the quiet but very definite thud of the door closing, and she let out the breath she didn't realise she had been holding.

Look at Me Mummy

The girls are dancing. Their small podgy arms jerk open and closed, open and closed, pretending to hug an invisible snowman. A Black girl stands next to a brown girl stands next to a white girl. Delicate piano chords with a regular beat reverberate around the draughty church hall. Their tummies, round and relaxed in their sugar-pink leotards, curve to meet the waistband of their tutus. As Miss Sophie counts them on the beat, 'One, two, three, one, two, three,' their knees bend and bodies bob up and down out of time with each other. Some of the girls struggle to combine the bobbing with the snowman-hugging, so prioritise one over the other. Collectively it's chaos, but the audience fixate only on their own children so don't notice the overall carnage. Over the top of my phone, I direct the biggest, widest smile towards my daughter as I record every awkwardly executed plié, arabesque and sauté and even though my eyes are locked in her direction my daughter calls out.

'Look at me Mummy!'

Her face is flushed with excitement, eager for me to witness every voluntary and involuntary movement. One girl in the line-up impresses me by maintaining eye contact while pulling out the knickers that are wedged up her bum. I would rather suffer a burning thrush itch than ever touch myself in public, but these girls call to be looked at. They call for eyes to absorb their every move, calling, calling, calling: *Have you seen what I can do?* They jump and prance and randomly convulse without any worry over getting it right. There's so much excitement at simply existing in their bodies. Movement for them is still a novelty, the opportunity to discover that their body can do something new: rhythm, shape, form, precision, it isn't important to them. They're not old enough to have felt the weight of expectation. They don't yet know that to be considered good is to conform to a set of rules. It's too early to have realised that their bodies are supposed to look and function in a certain way. All they know is the burning adoration staring back at them.

At five and six they haven't internalised the limits put on them by others, or registered their body as a battleground.

I registered this at the age of eight. 'You wanna watch her,' was the sentence that brought it all crashing down. I was unashamedly sticking my fingers deep into the pink icing and whipped cream of a peach melba, searching for the fruity treasure nestled inside the folds of the thick pastry base. It was heaven. Lying on the sofa, watching cartoons and licking my fingers my stepdad eyed me with disgust through the serving hatch that linked the kitchen to the living room. He didn't mean for me to hear, or maybe he did. He was warning my mother that a girl like me needed to be kept in check. After that I wasn't allowed any more peach melbas. After that I was made aware that the tummy fat and back fat I'd never noticed before was a problem. After that peach melba I was never again free to be unconsciously fat. I could be fat, but I could never again not care about it. The starving and purging soon replaced any uncomplicated enjoyment of food, maintaining control over my body became my new playtime. My new bodily obsession insulated me from registering the looks of disapproval or hurtful comments and for a while I was thankful for the distraction.

I cradle my tummy protectively and watch as more parents of the ballet dancers – mainly mothers – line up along the side of the large, wood-panelled hall on plastic chairs, and proudly film or photograph their daughters. The music stops and Miss Sophie gives directions for the next ballet routine the girls will perform. My daughter and her friend giggle and paw each other in their momentary downtime. They wriggle in and out of each other and shield their gap-toothed mouths as they laugh. My daughter lost her first tooth last week. She proudly showed me the open wound in her mouth where a small snowball tooth had once been. 'I'm a big girl now,' she announced with blood running into the ravines of her smile.

My little girl waves at me as she takes her position for the next dance and I think of all the netball games my dad came to watch, they're etched onto my brain. He took time out of his life to watch all of the goals, throw-ins, passes and blocks. We conducted deep post-match analyses on the drive back to my mum's house and for a while the memory of this dedication protected me from the terrible things other men did to me in my life. I see all of those men lined up like dominoes: the man with the bare bulging penis who stopped me on the way home from the shop when I was nine; the teenage boy who pulled my knickers down while I was asleep at a party and wouldn't admit what he'd done to make my vagina sore; the man who grabbed me on the way home from the bus stop at night and held a knife to my throat when I was twenty-seven; the man who fired a gun at me and my baby and shouted 'I'm going to fucking kill you'; the man who wrestled me to the ground for the phone in my hand and the purse in my bag; the many men who broke my heart again and again. All of these men would topple one by one in their domino formation when I thought of my dad watching me play netball.

The girls make-believe. They line up along the far wall of the hall and move towards us pretending to spot, chase and capture butterflies. They act out their ideas and fantasies to make them real and tangible. They imagine those butterflies and they appear. They open their hands carefully and show them to each other, before jumping back in surprise as the butterflies flutter away to a branch just out of reach. I used to make-believe that the memory of my dad at the side of the netball court would sustain me, that those memories would always protect me. But make-believe only works if you have something to believe in.

*

It had been the day after my dad's funeral. I was sat in the conservatory of the house he shared with his wife, the woman he left my mother for. She was in the chair nearest the window, her chair. We looked out onto her garden, as she told me about the clematis, peonies and other flowers she wanted to plant in honour of my dad. The conservatory stretched the whole back end of the house that they'd shared for twenty years. The house that had always been spotless, never holding any evidence of children staying there longer than an afternoon or a single overnight visit. She pointed at a black and white photograph of my dad in a frame. Holding up a football trophy, he looked young, his curly hair thick and shiny, not wiry and frizzy like it had been the day before, when we'd incinerated his body.

'He always loved his sports, didn't he?'

'He did,' I agreed. 'I used to love it when he came to watch me play netball. It was nice to have something to bond over.'

'I used to make him go and watch, you know,' my dad's wife smiled, and with her well-moisturised fingers, she gently propped up a sagging leaf on the Chinese money plant on the window sill. 'He was always glad that he'd gone but it was a struggle to get him out of the door some days.'

Behind her on a fence I saw a magpie hopping and squawking manically like a child with a box of matches. I felt saliva flood my mouth, the light from outside became blinding. My senses crashed and failed, but I sat perfectly still and asked if there was any tea left in the pot.

*

The music ends and the girls take a collective bow. Everyone claps. My daughter comes to me, I open my legs and she folds into my body; her homeland, the warm rolls of my stomach her safety blankets. I've known this little girl every minute of her life. I've watched her body acquire new marks and bruises, I've brushed the hair on her head from an acorn cap to the long glassy mane that now tucks itself into the crease of her bottom when it's wet. I've smoothed the fur on her lower back at the end of each day, watched her teeth fall out and grow anew. I can almost feel her growing as she stands at the centre of my body.

With her head tilted back into the nape of my neck she asks, 'Did you like it Mummy?'

'Yes sweetheart, I liked it. No, I loved it.'

We stay like that. I hold her tight and slip my fingers under her hot silky armpits as the other mothers and their children gather up their belongings and start to move around us. I want to remember this moment. I want her to remember it. I want her to remember how for a time we slotted together perfectly like flat-pack furniture.

The Cat

I needed something to pull me out of whatever it was I was in. Nothing held my attention on a micro or macro level. I was seemingly numb. Disturbing news stories barely punctured the flatline buzz in my head. I watched footage of destructive wildfires blankly, protests marched by my face on Instagram stories without raising an emotion anywhere in my body and when politicians told blatant lies I wasn't surprised. Environmental, social and political catastrophes played out on my TV or phone screen and the most I felt was the urge to go to the toilet. My friends and family went through personal dramas and I looked on like their lives were episodes of *EastEnders* playing on the TV in the background of a Chinese takeaway. I needed to feel something. With a dearth of new ideas or any imagination to pool from, I went back to what I knew. I downloaded the dating app.

This new focus quickly piqued my interest. I had a purpose and a distraction. A match led to a chat, then a potential meet up, which could lead to a second date, or sex with another human being – each step would be a quanti-fiable way to measure the success of my new project, of my life. I was almost disappointed at how easy I was to please. I'd used dating apps before but my earlier experiments hadn't yielded many successful results. Maybe I wasn't doing it right. This time I'd do it properly.

To begin with, I went deep into research mode, starting with the data on which photographs performed best for hetero women. According to the top searches, I needed a good heroine portrait. A clear shot of my face smiling but not laughing, looking to the side, in minimal make-up with good lighting – apparently men don't like it if you wear too much make-up, smile too much, or fall under bad lighting. For the main profile shot I uploaded a photo of myself at a wedding in Sicily I'd been at three years ago. The light was golden-hour perfect, the sun had highlighted my hair natu-rally and the camera was far enough away to soften out the imperfections that were showing through my make-up. I looked fun, I looked like I had friends, I looked like the kind of girl you'd swipe right on. I didn't look like that anymore but I didn't think that was the point.

To accompany this main photograph, I also needed a series of supporting shots that would showcase the differ-ent sides of my personality. Images that captured the fun, outgoing yet approachable young woman I wanted people to believe I was. The type of young woman you would take home for the weekend and the girls you grew up with would be jealous of. I found a selection of photos from the same year I went to Sicily, I photoshopped them to make my skin clearer, my lips bigger, the overall atmosphere brighter, and then I uploaded them. I was in a beer garden,

I was walking in the lakes, I was on a beach, I was at a work event looking smart. I was bait.

Next, I researched what made a good profile description. Nothing too earnest, wacky or offensive was the advice. I wrote an appealing middle-of-the-road version of the girl I thought would attract the most men, and made up some bands and music that I said I was *obsessed* with. I found this part the most degrading because really what is the point in trying to define yourself by your music choices over the age of eighteen? What are you hoping someone else thinks of you when you tell them you're into Little Simz, Sonic Youth or some obscure jazz four-piece from south London? What does it mean that you found a teenage techno producer from Belgium before anyone else or that you've just bought some rare Sun Ra cut because you only listen to vinyl? It all seemed so youth club. I asked Ted, who I sat next to at work, if he ever read any of the profiles of the girls he matched with.

'No, why?' he said incredulously, as if I'd just asked him if he washed his towels.

'To find out what they're into. If you like the same stuff. If you'll get on.'

'Who cares about that on a dating site. Are they fit: yes, or no? That's literally all I'm bothered about. Why would I care what you like to eat or where you like to go on holiday? Am I your Auntie Maureen? No. I just want a fuck.'

I deleted the bulk of what I'd written and kept the info to a minimum.

*

Profile complete, I went searching for dates. The initial plan of matching with as many men as raised my interest to spread out my bets was quashed the minute I saw the array of delinquents and subpar men that existed on the first dating app, who thought nothing of sending a barrage of unsolicited dick-on-hand, dick-in-mirror, dick-against-remote-control photographs. The breaking point was a decidedly average-looking man called Darren whose opening line was:

It looks like you've got tiny titties. Do you like anal?

I swapped to an app which put women in control and seemed less about furious purple-headed sex and more about drinks and dinner, albeit in busy, well-lit places like Vapiano and All Bar One.

Regardless of who felt more in control, the apps reflected the worst of human behaviour. After a few weeks of scrolling and chatting to various avatar men I started to feel like I was sale shopping, where you're better to go with the options at the top of the screen because the further down you go, the less attention you pay, and before you know it your basket is full of tatty sequined bodycon items that you're never going to wear. The whole process of choosing a mate online encourages a delusional godlike complex. As you scroll through reams of faces judging someone's earnest love of Fleet Foxes and their decision to wear a faded Hollister hoodie in their profile photo, you forget that someone, somewhere is doing exactly the same to you. Day and night, fingers around the world are scrolling, driven by a subconscious bias that reaffirms what and who we find attractive and desirable, never stopping to think too deeply about what our desires say about us.

In week three of the project, Robert appeared at the top of my screen. He attracted me the most on account of how he didn't remind me of anyone else. His features, hair and body were all completely his own, I wouldn't be able to project anything onto him that he didn't already own. He was an interior architect (which I had to google), he was into cycling, he liked getting out of London and he loved ramen. These details seemed completely unnecessary, maybe Ted was right, what did any of these words really mean to me? Was I supposed to refer back to them during the date like an employer clutching the CV of an interviewee?

I swiped right on him; he swiped right on me. Over the next few days we fell into a rhythm of chatting online, which switched to WhatsApp when we exchanged real phone numbers. The first week was fuelled by the flurries of energy I was hoping for. What would he reveal about himself next? What blanks could I fill with my own fantasy version of him? What could I then say to make him fall in love with his fantasy version of me? Every day I got up early, the smug dad next door didn't bother me, my flatmate didn't bother me, the damp in our bathroom didn't bother me, a potential pervert's groin in my bum on the Tube didn't even bother me. I didn't have time to dwell on the minor irritations and indignities of life, they swept past unnoticed as my brain moved on to composing the next reply. In messages I was funny, charming, and my references were perfect. Delays in responding weren't taken as being boring or unwitty. I was busy. I'd been doing something important (not trying to find an image of Diana Ross in face tape to perfectly illustrate my point about how windy it was that day). I was feeling so good that I forgot the natural progression from this stage was to meet in person and so I felt shocked, almost appalled, when he suggested that we go for a drink.

We met at a place near his office. He arrived early and was sitting at the bar drinking a bottle of Japanese beer when I got there. He was clean-cut and sharp like a high street mannequin. I was wearing a dress I'd bought from COS on my lunch break which I thought pegged me as having an eye for design, something with a directional detail that was actually just a wonky hemline. I had washed and dried my hair into a side parting, and put in a large acetate slide to keep it in place, another directional piece of styling on my part. I wore the new underwear I'd ordered in preparation for this season of dates, had shaved my legs and lightly clipped my pubic hair. I never shaped my bikini line after a woman at work got an infected ingrown hair from being waxed and had to have the wound packed every week by a nurse until it healed. When the dressing came off, she said it smelt of cumin and mature cheddar cheese. I just didn't hate my pubic hair enough to risk going through that.

'Robert?' I said, standing too close to his chair so he had to back it up when he stood to greet me.

'Yes, hi. How are you?'

'I'm good, how are you?'

'Good. Thanks.'

I sat down, ordered a mid-range glass of red wine which instantly dulled my teeth, and noticed that, like me, he didn't look anything like his profile pictures. He looked like he was the stunt double for his online persona, weirdly similar whilst also nothing alike; however, I thought it rude to bring it up given my own digital disguise work. For the next fifteen minutes we repeated what the other said. He liked this area of town, I said I did too. He said he'd had a good day but was busy with work, I said I was too. I said I liked this time in spring when you could feel the heat of summer on its way, he said he did too. When this became too tedious for either of us to pretend we were enjoying it, I asked if he was hungry. He was. We went to a meat place he said he'd taken some clients to recently, you could order off the menu and he knew the chef. I said, 'Sounds cool,' but I wasn't sure it would be.

Over dinner I found myself boring. I was afraid this would happen. Something in his personality locked mine up. I was rationing my words, only allowing them to formulate around stiff sentences on topics such as the areas of London that felt like you weren't in a big city, the differences between my favourite Tube lines, and a man I'd once worked with who said *brought* when he meant to say *bought*. He seemed as bored as me by my stale conversation and the rigid questions I fired at him but we kissed on the street outside the restaurant and he messaged me as soon as I got home saying he'd like to see me again. I said I'd like that too.

We met the following week outside a restaurant that served kohlrabi, decked out with wooden walls and floors and large sharing tables. I was nervous about sitting next to strangers, having conversations they'd overhear. The other diners would listen to what I was saying and roll their eyes at each other, they'd go home and tell their flatmates about the annoying woman they'd had to sit next to at dinner. 'Oh my god,' their flatmates would say, 'that is so funny, can you imagine actually saying that out loud? I can't stand people like that.' Walking towards the restaurant I tried to block out this train of thought by practising how to pronounce kohlrabi.

Robert was already there, his huge hands resting in the small pockets of his jacket, a relaxed smile on his face. I waved and did a quick jog across the road even though there was no traffic coming my way.

We hugged and in my left ear he said, 'So, should we go over your favourite Tube lines again?'

'Oh my god, I'm so sorry for being so boring!' I pushed him and let out a stifled scream through my hands.

'Don't worry about it,' he laughed. 'First dates are always pretty rough. I once told a girl about my new personal finance regime.'

'To be fair, that sounds like it might be pretty helpful! Much better than going into the pros and cons of the Victoria versus the Piccadilly line. Fuck's sake.'

'Come on. Let's get some drinks.'

'Yes!'

The rest of the date was perfect. We laughed, we got drunk, we shared amazing food. He told me about the family members he was close to and described some of the best bits of his job. We found out that we both hated coriander, we had both grown up on similar housing estates but had moved to London as soon as we could, and as children we both chose spicy Nik Naks as a post-swimming snack. I dropped my guard, I didn't worry about the people sitting next to us, I didn't hold my body in any particular way, I let him in and I let a bit of myself reach out to him. It felt like all versions of me had signed a treaty and got their best people on the job, I felt seamless.

At the end of the meal, I gathered up my coat and bag, he fished through his pockets for his wallet as the waitress organised our bill. We were in the limbo part of the night where if you knew each other well you'd just sit and ride it out. You'd have smelt each other's morning breath, you wouldn't need to worry about this slice of silence. But as a couple on an early date, these dips hold great weight. If you can't find something pithy and funny to say to each other in these early moments, what does that say about your chance of a future together? Too aware of the silence my mind went blank so I got my phone out to pretend I was checking an email. Sitting close to my left on a bulky bench, he put his hand over mine.

'This has been really nice,' he said.

I put my phone face down on the table. 'It has. I've had a really good time.'

'Do you want to get a drink somewhere else?'

'Definitely,' I said with a palpable relief I hoped he didn't notice.

When it was all over, I sometimes went back to this moment and thought about how I'd let it veer so far from my control. In that kohlrabi place I was *the* girl. I couldn't believe I played it so wrong.

*

A couple of days after our second date the cat arrived. You might've read something into this if you were that kind of person, but I'm not. Waiting for the kettle to boil, I spotted her lying in the back garden, basking in a hexagon of sunlight that moved across the lawn as the sun bent around the houses on my street. She wasn't a cute and cuddly cat, she looked expensive. Her coat was a glorious mix of emerald greens, browns, whites and blacks perfectly woven together to create an imposing all-over look. Her symmetrical face was framed by a thick blonde regal ruff of fur. Her ears twitched as she registered life going on around her, but nothing disturbed her rest. I unlocked the back door and she opened her eyes. Accepting my interest with good humour, she entertained my smothering strokes and high-pitched greetings of 'Hello you' and 'Where have you come from?'. I'd never had a cat in my life and I was excited to recreate the closeness I'd had as a child with my dogs. Only cats aren't the same as dogs.

She blinked slowly into the sun as I tickled around the back of her ears, she stood up and stretched as I put down a saucer of milk at the back door. Once she'd very slowly and precisely licked up the milk I'd served her, she came over to curl her silky body around my legs. As I went down to reaffirm our bond as new friends, she very quickly (but very intentionally) bit me on the back of my hand. Unprepared for the outburst of violence my breath caught at the back of my throat. My hand bled in four perfect puncture marks where her teeth had punished me for getting too close. I looked around, embarrassed at how stunned I was. She didn't run or cower away after her outburst, she sat quietly on the grass eyeing me with her lime-green eyes. She wasn't going to be first to divert her unbroken gaze.

Over the next few weeks, the confusion that the cat brought to my life fogged my brain. Together we went through a daily cycle of violence and realignment. At first, I tried not opening the door so she'd move on to another house for her snacks. But she meowed and scratched at the window and I eventually felt guilty for my neglectful behaviour. I tried to give her milk while maintaining a healthy distance, I thought it wise to be stand-offish, but she wrapped herself around my legs and cried for touch and attention. When I relented and gave her the strokes I thought she wanted, she'd purr luxuriously. She'd nudge my hand with the back of her head for more touch before lashing out again, leaving me bleeding and bewildered. I could never gauge how much affection was too much. Throughout late spring and early summer this pattern became normal and I stopped registering such shock when she bit, scratched or hissed at me. It became just another quirk in our relationship. Her saucer of milk progressed to a two-course milk-and-tuna-fish set meal and she showed her appreciation by licking each saucer clean. I felt special that she'd chosen me to come and visit each day; it was enough for me, to feel special.

During that time my dates with Robert went from once a week to twice a week to the peak of a whole weekend at his place, and then descended down slowly to a trickle of sporadic overnight stays. It happened imperceptibly at first. After the weekend together, his replies to my messages took slightly longer and longer to come through. A few minutes at first, stretching out to hours then sometimes days. In between waiting for responses and chances to see him, I turned up to work and typed things on a screen. I lifted eight-kilogram weights at the gym, scrolled on my phone until my head flatlined, I binged TV series in twelve-hour stints and spoke on the phone to my parents in a monotone voice, all the while carrying a physical yearning that added an extra ten stone to my body mass. I started to miss the boredom of my life before this project. I knew that wasn't a true emotion but at least I was in control of my misery before this. I looked at other men on dating sites, searching for a distraction from my distraction. I matched with a few but I couldn't bring myself to go through what I was currently experiencing with a wider selection of disappointing men.

When I did see Robert, the orgasms I had with him were intense, but they gave me the same disassociated sensation I had when I watched porn. I climaxed almost in spite of myself. I wasn't consciously turned on; there was another part of me pulling the strings. Move here, touch that, make this noise, get in that position, come now. Done. I was always left confused, suspicious of him and myself, but the heavy pulsating sensation in my vagina told me I'd had a good time.

The morning after the last time he stayed over at my place, I got up, put a retinol serum all over my face, brushed my hair, brushed my teeth, put on a tinted lip balm and lit the Le Labo candle I'd warned my flatmate not to use. When he still wasn't up as I came out of the bathroom I wondered about going back to bed for a cuddle, but he didn't like touching like that in the morning. I thought about taking him breakfast in bed but that seemed too over the top. Instead I decided to set the table and wait for him to get up. After an hour the front room smelt like a disrespectful shop assistant. The Nina Simone playlist I'd put on was down to her more experimental live performances and I was wired from a full pot of coffee that was making me desperate for a poo I most definitely would not be having with him still in the flat. I heard him laughing on his phone as I poured out a plateful of fishy biscuits for the cat. She was curling around my feet and meowing in her perfect pitch. She let her tail trail around my legs, her fine hairs tickling and caressing the skin on my calves. I bent down to stroke her and she closed her eyes at my intrepid touch.

'There there, little one. Here's your breakfast.'

Robert's laughter continued, he was really enjoying himself. The sound of his good mood made me momentarily forget about needing the toilet, about the caffeine overdose I was experiencing and the £43 I'd spent on the breakfast spread. The cat finished her biscuits and weaved her soft body in and out of my legs meowing for her saucer to be ladled with milk for the second course. I filled the sink with water and put in some clean dishes that I pretended to be washing when he came into the kitchen.

'I didn't know you had a cat,' he said standing in the kitchen doorway fully clothed.

'Oh shit, I didn't see you there,' genuine shock raising my already soaring heart rate. 'Do you want some coffee? Some eggs?'

'No, I haven't got time for breakfast. I've got to go,' he said, staring at the cat in the garden who had exited the kitchen on his arrival. 'Is that your cat?'

'No, no. She just comes around for food and sometimes lets me stroke her. I told you about her. I think she lives in one of the houses at the bottom of the street.'

'I can't remember you saying anything about it. Why do you let a stray cat into your house?'

'She's not a stray. It's what cats do apparently, they have a few houses they go to for food and stuff.'

'That's weird,' he said throwing a handful of blueberries into his mouth and drinking orange juice straight from the carton. 'Are you trying to steal it?'

'What? No. Of course I'm not trying to steal the cat, she comes and goes as she pleases. Who would steal a cat?' I asked back, defensively.

'I don't know, I'm just saying it's weird to let strange cats into your house when you don't know where they've come from. It might have fleas or something.'

I picked one of his hairs from my pyjama top and felt my stomach drop – I still needed the toilet.

'Are you sure you don't want some breakfast? I can make pancakes. It'll be nice.'

'No, I've got to go. My brother's in town so I'm gonna go and meet him. You have a nice breakfast with your cat friend.'

'Oh, is that who you were talking to?'

'What?'

'Just now, on the phone.'

'Oh right, yeah. Yeah. It was my brother.'

'Are you going now?' I asked, struggling to untangle the medium-sized rubber glove from my large left hand.

'Yeah I'll message you next week or something. I can let myself out,' he said, kissing me flatly on the cheek without touching any other part of my body.

It crossed my mind to bite his cheek or throw the knife block at him, anything to make him see what a cunt he was. But then he wouldn't be the cunt in that scenario, I would be. So, I just stood there and said 'Bye,' to his back as he walked out the kitchen, out of the flat, down the street and onto the Tube to get on with his Saturday. I went back to bed.

I hadn't planned to sleep so long. When I woke up the Le Labo candle had burned down to the bottom of the glass jar. A friend once told me about a glass candle holder that had exploded when the flame hit air pockets in the glass. I felt disappointed the same hadn't happened in my living room. My empty stomach pulled tight but the pancakes, smoked salmon, eggs, hollandaise and soft fruits still laid out on the kitchen table taunted me. I put it all in the fridge out of sight and got out a single tin of tuna. I drained the tinned fish in the sink, put it in a bowl and spooned an obese blob of mayonnaise all over it. I mixed it like I was whisking eggs and sat alone to eat. On cue the cat arrived at the window, licking the glass and walking backwards and forwards like a confused prisoner who couldn't handle life on the outside. She was free, so why did she come here every day? Why when cats have the freedom to roam anywhere do they stick to the same routine, retracing their steps in self-imposed purgatory?

Settling into a poised sitting position she watched me eat the bowl of tuna with her head nudged slightly forward. I held out a large scoop of creamy fish on my fork in her direction and shouted: 'Do you want some?'

She returned the gesture by pawing wildly at the glass until I put the whole pile into my mouth. I moved over to the window, face to face with the cat, our eyes locked.

'Who the fuck do you think you are?' I whispered, the smell of my fishy breath hitting close against the glass.

She swiped the pane with a thud and a screech. I didn't flinch. We stared at each other through the glass until she lowered her head and looked away. I put the empty bowl and fork in the sink and went back to bed.

*   *   *

The clock flicked to 18.00 as the busy train pulled out of Liverpool Street station. Facing the doors so I didn't have to look at anyone I wrote out and sent the message I'd been mentally composing all day. It had been seventy-two hours since he left my house, I was within a reasonable time frame to appear casual and unbothered by his absence.

> Hey, how was your weekend with your brother? Do
> you want to get a drink this weekend?

No kiss, to match his lack of digital affection, always end on a question. I stared at the screen, waiting for any change, any evidence of life on the other side. My phone went into power save and I clicked back to the message. Two blue ticks appeared in the bottom right-hand corner of the sent message but no reply came back.

I stayed facing the corner of the doors and scrolled through Instagram at a pace that made my eyes hurt. I stared at reams of adverts for bedding and candles – my latest online searches had alerted the algorithm that I was now into interiors and it served up a batch of similar-looking accounts and products. There were girls in sports bras and shorts at festivals, someone was eating swordfish in Italy, there were memes stolen from Twitter and a batch of wannabe social justice warriors announcing the latest cause they were getting behind, calling out their followers to do better. My errant thumb glitched and accidently swiped screens to Instagram stories where I was greeted with my own frowning face, and there looking over my shoulder was the man behind me who had watched my every move. Every like, every comment, every image I'd paused on and zoomed in on, every time I'd gone back to my message to Robert, he had quietly observed it all, and now here we were face to face on my screen. For a fleeting second, we locked eyes before he flinched from his position and I, with my neck now scorched red with embarrassment, put my phone back in my bag.

I looked out through the windows of the train, the tracks were lined with new blocks of flats built to resemble the warehouses they had just replaced. Tiny cubes with floor to ceiling windows and balconies that looked out onto the train lines. I enjoyed focusing my eyes to take in as much detail as possible as the train passed by each snapshot of someone else's life. I tried to spot what the people inside these boxes were watching on TV, where their furniture was from, were they exercising, eating, arguing? Most of the time the flats were empty, a modern Hitchcock set-up where everyone had already gone to work or hadn't yet returned. That morning on the way in to Liverpool Street a couple were making their bed together, he was topless wafting a peach duvet to get rid of their stale, overnight air, his belly protruding out further with each lift and waft. She pulled a jumper down over her black bra and fluffed the pillows, a small child sat in a high chair in the open-plan kitchen and living room watching a brightly coloured cartoon on the TV. I held my breath. Thinking about that scene caused a deep treacly hatred for myself to spread out from a hard boulder that had coagulated in the pit of my stomach. I hated myself for falling into the trap of wanting something so basic. I hated myself because even though I knew didn't want what that scene represented, I was so far away from it, it wasn't mine to reject. But most of all I hated myself because I didn't have the guts to work out what I really desired and instead let myself be depressed for failing to achieve the train-track life that everyone else was clamouring for.

When I reached the front door of my flat, I looked at my phone. No messages. It was a perfect late summer evening, the kind of weather you soak up at 7 p.m. because the dark nights are right around the corner. Rossi's ice cream van rolled down the street, its tinny song luring kids out of their houses, palms sweaty with their parents' loose change. I dropped everything in the hallway and went straight out to the back garden. The old couple next door had their TV tuned to a Romanian channel, the smell from their cigarettes and the loud Romanian game-show music made me feel like I was on a school exchange where everything was brand new and I had no reference for anything in front of me.

The cat was in the shade cleaning herself. I sat on the rusty grey chair that had been in the garden since I moved into the house four years ago and watched her wipe the damp side of her paw over her ears, licking her back, leaving slick trails of saliva down her coat. She gnawed into her fur at something that was consuming her then extended her right back leg and licked her own anus. Dirty bitch. She continued to tend to her puckered bumhole, smoothing it down with her tongue. Once she was pleased with her level of hygiene, she resumed her own position of judgement and stared back at me.

The physical urge to turn over my phone and check the screen again depressed me more than I dared acknowledge. The lead in my core pulled down my shoulders and lower back, cutting my body into the uncomfortable rusted chair. The old couple next door laughed and sang along to the TV theme tune, smoke from their cigarettes floated over the fence, carrying a faint whiff of cinnamon.

The cat changed her position. Crouching on the grass she flicked her tail like a camp villain, her ears twitched side to side like mini-antennae, her eyes focused intensely on one spot of the lawn. There was something in the grass. Something was trying to conceal itself, backing up through the longer patches that had sprouted where my flatmate had spilled a box of grass seeds. The cat trailed the trembling grass with narrow eyes. She lowered her body, pulled back slightly and pounced. Face down in the grass her jaw held something in place while her paws blocked any possible escape route. After a few seconds she stood proudly throwing her head back, back, back to get a tighter grip on the mouse that hung from either side of her mouth. Unsure what to do with her triumphant catch and instantly bored of carrying it she placed the stunned animal down. Watching it, she allowed the mouse to limp away a few paces then pounced again. This grotesque game played out in front of me for the duration of a Romanian commercial break and my mind drifted off.

The algorithm in my brain had fine-tuned itself until the only thoughts it offered up linked back to that last weekend with Robert. The adrenaline that surged through my stomach when I thought of him was sickeningly addictive. I had wanted this; I had wanted to feel something and now I couldn't stand it. What was it that he had found so repulsive that weekend? What had I said? What had I done? What could I do to pull it back around? Was it the fact that I'd suggested going to an improv comedy night that weekend, or that I'd sent him holiday suggestions for later in the summer? Was it because I hadn't been on any protest marches that year and didn't know anything about the situation in Burma? Ted at work once admitted to ghosting a girl because he'd seen her with wet hair.

'What do you mean? She got caught in the rain or something? I don't get it,' I'd asked him in between calls at work.

'No, she came out the shower one morning when I was staying at hers and she had wet hair. She looked weird, like her nose was much bigger and her eyes looked really small. Couldn't do it after that.'

'What, so she washed her hair and you never saw her again?'

'Yeah.'

'Did you ever tell her why?'

'No. Of course not.' His phone had rung then and he'd put a finger to his lips before launching into his speech.

It was nothing. I had done nothing. I had become nothing to him and there was nothing I could do about it. I had been so consumed with trying to mould myself into the winning formula that I forgot to check if he was worth the effort. Up until that point it had been a given that I would have to impress and prove myself a hot and interesting match. I had become so lost in the distraction he offered, lost in my desire to be good enough, that I forgot to check if he was.

From my decrepit chair I watched the cat lick the mouse, holding it in her paws, delicately nursing the injuries she had so enjoyed inflicting. I got up to inspect the condition of the mouse, instinctively the cat curled her paws around the small animal and they both looked up as if I was interrupting a tender moment. The mouse breathed steadily as the cat licked its back, both parties enjoying a sinister symbiosis.

The ice cream van pulled out of the front street, its ghoulish music whirring into gear, announcing its departure and a missed opportunity. I thought about what to make for dinner and messaged my flatmate to see if she'd be home soon, even though I knew she'd be staying at her boyfriend's again. The knives and forks of the couple next door tinkled satisfyingly against their china plates as they ate dinner in the garden with the TV now turned down.

Their chatter, a constant low hum accompanying all of their movements, always caught my attention. The old man had once told me they'd been married for fifty-two years when we were both taking our bins out, and for days after I wondered what they still had to talk about. As a child my mother used to warn me that we only had a certain amount of words we could use in a lifetime, and that I was running the risk of using all of mine before I turned ten. She revealed this was all a hilarious ruse at my cousin's twelfth birthday, but it still alarmed me to this day that other people weren't just a little worried that they'd run out of words. The couple next door definitely didn't share my concerns about their own word count allocation.

The sun started to burn the side of my face as I looked around the garden I'd tended to that summer. I didn't notice the cat move. The once vibrant borders that I'd planned out and planted had descended into an orgy of life on the turn, brown-tinged dahlias fell languidly into foxgloves, faded peach gladioli leant forward, stretching out to meet the long grass, cosmos wrapped around the asters and zinnias and spent peonies lay sprawled, offering themselves wide open to fat bees which buzzed around in the viscous air, their backs covered in balls of pollen, their tummies full of nectar.

Swirls of flies congregated around something on the ground, creating a grotesque emerald blob as the sun caught their writhing bodies. The cat lay with her paws splayed out, looking at me through long blinks. I flapped my foot, causing an exodus of flies that revealed the perfectly still body of the small grey mouse. The cat's eyes remained pinpointed on me, her tail flicking violently from side to side. Reaching towards my phone I picked up the pair of secateurs next to it. Flicking open the safety clasp I bent down in front of the cat. We stared at each other, my head moving closer to hers as I steadied myself with my free hand. I leant down until we were a blade apart, and stopped at the sound of her purring. A deep, rhythmic rattle emanated from some unreachable place deep inside of her. Putting down the secateurs I reached out my hand and stroked her head. She lifted up her chin to let me in, gently licking my knuckles. I bowed my head down, she pushed hers against my forehead and trailed her whole vibrating body along the top of my crown. A shriek of laughter from the couple next door drew her underneath me where she cowered and let me pick her up for the first time since the day she'd slunk into the garden. I sat with her on my lap as the flies devoured the mouse carcass behind us.

Later that night, after I'd deadheaded the decaying flowers and shovelled the remains of the mouse into a small hole at the back of the garden, the screen of my phone illuminated with the first lines of a message.

Hi, mad week but all good. Do you wanna ...

I read the rest of the message through shallow, even breaths before deleting it. I deleted his number and the app that had kick-started the whole charade. I locked the back door and made a bed for the cat out of the jumper Robert wore on our third date. She's slept on it in my kitchen ever since.

Women of Pret

'Yara, can you watch Archie while I take this outside?'
Camila motioned two fingers from her eyes to her son, and
then to Yara. She didn't wait for an answer before shouting
'ALEK!' into her phone and ushering a stray drooling child
out of the way of the door with her knee.

Yara watched through the safety glass door as Camila
paced backwards and forwards, talking loudly into her
phone with her palm pressed against her forehead.

Before motherhood, Camila ran TV and film productions
– she'd been responsible for huge crews and million-pound
budgets. Recently the spells in between jobs had begun to
stretch out longer and longer and she'd been told more
than once that her availability was an issue now that she
couldn't work 24/7 on productions because of what were
described as 'her childcare issues'. Without work to soak up
her frenetic energy she directed it into managing the builders who were extending her house up and out.

The base of Camila's clenched fist pushed her heavy
fringe away from her forehead revealing more of her

features. Yara was always surprised by the details of Camila's face, the reality of what she looked like never matched the mental image Yara had in her head, no matter how many times she recalibrated it. In the flesh Camila's eyes were always a little closer together than Yara remembered, her mouth a little wider and thinner, her forehead a little higher.

A little girl in a grubby *Frozen* dress pushed open the door with sticky hands, bringing in with her an agitated waft of Camila's voice.

'Alek, I know what they've told you but honestly, it's just not good enough and we need it on the original ...'

The door closed softly to make sure little fingers weren't squashed, blotting out the rest of Camila's complaint. As her face became redder and her voice continued to climb through the glass, Yara turned to check on Archie. He was wrestling a plastic dinosaur out of the hands of another boy. She thought about intervening but she'd have to take off her shoes to get over the crash mat and she didn't have the energy to do that for someone else's child – besides, Megan was on her way back with their coffees so she let the two boys battle it out amongst themselves.

Megan walked towards her with the soft footing of a nurse doing her rounds in padded shoes, her hair fell in waves around her perpetually smiling face in a way that made Yara think of light entertainment TV presenters from the nineties. Since having her twins she'd left her job as head of finance at a frozen food distributor and had started a business as a professional organiser; decluttering the homes of people who didn't have enough time to use or sort through the excess *stuff* they'd bought. As far as Yara could tell it was an occupation that involved throwing away a lot of H&M clothes, broken plastic toys and decanting breakfast cereals and pasta into clear containers – although Yara did appreciate that the before and after client videos on Megan's business Instagram account had a relaxing and pleasing quality about them. Megan stopped briefly to check in on her twins, who were decorating each other in ribbons like tiny Morris dancers, and continued on with the drinks.

'Here you go, you didn't want sugar, did you?'

'No this is great, thanks.' Yara took the mug of anaemic instant coffee and remembered not to take a sip straight away or she'd skin the roof of her mouth like she had the week before.

They were at an under 3s messy play session at their local community centre. It was a hotbed of germs and anxiety. All of the children looked like they'd been rescued from a sinking ship and were now drying out. Their hair was matted and crusty, their clothes were ripped, covered in glue and paint or hanging off their small bodies. Their faces were red, their eyes wild with excitement. The pitch of their screams caused Yara to wince at regular intervals. They were on their own psychedelic journey bouncing from one area to the next looking for their next battle or victory, their next playmate or potential nemesis. A loud squeal followed by a pained cry came from Archie's direction.

'Ooh dear,' Megan grimaced. 'It looks like Archie's playing a bit rough again, where's Camila?'

'She's on the phone outside,' Yara said distracted, looking for somewhere safe to put down her nuclear mug of coffee.

Unable to find anywhere to put the cup out of the way of small hands, she held it awkwardly with the tips of her fingers.

'Oh, she's getting herself stressed with all that building work, isn't she? I know when we did ours it was all-consuming and I think she's managing it all on her own.'

'I'm sure she's got a project manager on the job.'

'Yes, but they're always on the side of the builders so you still have to watch their every move and check on costs and deliveries yourself, plus if you get one of the Eastern Europeans you have to be even more careful,' Megan said, half-whispering the words 'Eastern European' like they were catching.

'We had the same guy Camila's using, I thought he was alright.'

'Oh, you bought your place? For some reason, I thought you rented,' Megan exclaimed with raised eyebrows that she left suspended in the middle of her forehead.

'Yeah, I grew up round here so we bought about ten years ago. Where are you from again?'

'I grew up in a little village in Suffolk. It was very boring when I was younger but I love it now. Lots of fresh air, large back gardens, friendly people. I think we'll sell up and move back there eventually,' Megan said, with a jolliness that only comes from being born into money and then marrying into more.

'OK. That makes sense,' Yara said taking a sip of her coffee, which instantly scalded her top lip. *I fucking knew that would happen*, she thought holding the back of her hand against her raw mouth.

*

Camila burst back through the door then, her fringe verti-
cal from where she'd repeatedly driven her sweaty palm
over it.

'Was that Archie I heard screaming?' she barked towards
Yara and Megan.

'No, it was that other kid over there,' Yara pointed to a
small boy being nursed by his mother, who was frantically
trying to work out who Archie's mother was so she could
demand an apology. Unaware of his trail of terror, Archie
crashed the stolen dinosaur into a pile of stickle bricks that
two girls had laboured over at the opposite end of the
room.

'Oh well, it all looks under control now,' Camila said
unbothered. 'Is there any coffee left?'

'I think there's some left in the pot, but you have to put
your 50p in the little bowl this time,' Megan said pointing
repeatedly to the glass jar filled with dirty coins, an anxious
spasm taking over her mouth.

'Honestly even 50p is too much for that watery shit.
Who even carries cash these days? It's not much better, but
should we go to Pret after this?'

'Oh yes! I love their new matcha lattes, can't have too
many though,' Megan said making a spinning motion with
her fingers at her temples.

'Yara?'

'Yeah sure, I think we'll have time before the doctor's,'
Yara said checking the time on her phone.

'Where's Sally?'

'She's outside pushing Martha on the swings.'

'That woman. Why does she bother playing with her
own child at one of these things? Just get them in and let

them go!' Camila shook her head ferociously as she opened the door and shouted, 'Sally we're going to Pret after this, you in?'

Sally nodded and put her thumb up, but didn't say anything. A mother who was trying to get her child to sleep in the corner of the garden glared at the space where Camila had just been as the door closed on a slow release.

Inside the community centre, the three women stood in a row and watched the carnage unfolding in front of them. The children acted on pure instinct. They hadn't yet been conditioned to suppress their self-serving urges into socially acceptable behaviour; they snatched toys from each other on a whim, walked off in the middle of a game if boredom struck. They thought nothing of slapping a playmate's face if the impulse grabbed them, they hoarded as many crackers and grapes as they could fit on their plates at snack time, without concern for whether there were enough to go around, and ripped out toy after toy from various boxes with no intention of tidying up after themselves. Some parents hovered like helicopters, ready to guide or scold any perceived misdemeanour for fear it would reflect badly on their own character; others stood back and relished the fact it wasn't their house that was being annihilated.

Yara scanned the room for her daughter, Maya, and located her through the Wendy house window stockpiling plastic food with a boy in a Ziggy Stardust T-shirt. She made a mental note to tell her husband Anjwar about the boy's T-shirt. He felt sorry for the kids who were never allowed to embrace the tackiest recesses of their personalities, who were kitted out in tasteful black and cream outfits with bedrooms full of wooden toys and alphabet posters set in bespoke typefaces. Yara was just pleased Maya was out of the mess and that she wouldn't have to wrestle the 'washable' paint out of her clothes when they got home.

When Yara first gave birth, Veronica, her health visitor, had told her about all of the local playgroups she could go to. Veronica had visited regularly until Maya was twelve weeks to give Yara the extra support she'd requested. She carried a large musical arrangement of keys, which jangled in sharp contrast to her soft voice and slow, considerate movements. She wore her hair in the same tight coils as Yara's favourite neighbour from when she was a little girl and she often thought about the moments of raw tenderness they shared in those early visits when she wasn't sure she'd make it through the next hour.

'These groups yeah, they're good for making new friends if you don't know a lot of other parents. Is your mum nearby?' Veronica had asked as she showed Yara how to swaddle Maya after their first breastfeeding session.

'No, she's not around.'

'Any other family who live in the area? Just tuck in that bit of the blanket ...' She'd mimed the action for Yara to follow. 'There you go.'

'No, they're all outside of London,' Yara had said as she picked Maya up gently like Veronica had shown her and kissed her lightly on the forehead.

'OK well done. Ve-ry good. You're getting the hang of this.' Veronica had smiled and put her hand gently on Yara's shoulder. 'Do you have friends with kids?'

Yara shook her head and looked down at Maya swaddled tightly like a chrysalis.

'OK well look,' Veronica said standing up from the sofa, smoothing down the creases that had gathered at the front of her black trousers. 'Get out to some of these playgroups, just do the coffee mornings at first. They'll be good for meeting people, good for getting out the house. You'll find some support there, OK?'

Yara had looked up at her with wet eyes wishing she wouldn't go. 'OK.'

'You're doing just fine OK baby girl?' Veronica said, cradling the side of her cheek.

'Thank you.'

Yara discovered that finding support at these groups was a tricky balance of working out who could offer real advice without judgement, whilst opening herself up to the anxious projections of equally vulnerable women. The pressure of keeping a small person alive while carving out a new identity under the watchful eyes of others did something strange to a woman's psyche. Sat in a small group of mothers with wet-faced children on their knees, Yara had listened as they shared blow-by-blow descriptions of their child's routine. They rattled through each stage of the day from the moment they woke up to the moment they went to bed, cataloguing the number of times their child did or didn't wake up during the night. These personalised timetables didn't seem to offer much support to the mothers who were struggling, if anything it only increased a heightened sense of anxiety that their child wasn't as good a sleeper/eater/walker/shitter as they were supposed to be at that age. But Yara came to realise these performances of togetherness weren't meant to comfort anyone other than the main protagonist. That woman, veiled in a sheen of routine perfection, was looking to her audience to reassure her that *she* was doing it right, that her way was the right way. That's all any of them were looking for.

Amongst the round-robin exercises of one-up-womanship were rare moments of genuine care between relative strangers, and it was these slivers of support that Yara initially saw in Megan, Sally and Camila. Between them, they'd helped her with weaning Maya onto solids, the best approach to sleep-training, and how to handle irrational toddler meltdowns – although no one seemed to have a solid grip on this eternal conundrum. In return, Yara had offered her own support; listening to Sally as she went through her divorce, advising Camila on finding freelance work and helping Megan secure a strategy for dealing with her mother-in-law. Their relationships were supportive, functional and bound by proximity.

Alongside the women chatting, fussing and wiping bums at the playgroup was the occasional solitary dad who always cut an awkward figure, no matter how much they tried to blend in. That week Tim, tall as a lamp post with thinning tight hair and black office socks on his feet, was building a camp with his daughter out of large stuffed triangles and squares. Handing out homemade gingerbread men covered in the cack-handed icing of her five-year-old Megan eyed Tim suspiciously. 'I'm not sure about the blokes who come to these groups. Like, what are they trying to prove?'

'Ah mind yersel. And what do you mean by that?' Sally said, joining them inside and waving away the Tupperware of biscuits. 'I'm not sure they're trying to *prove* anythin'.' Sally's soft Irish accent, fine features and flyaway hair disguised a much steelier core; as a single parent she had little time for sentimentality around the traditional nuclear family. She wore walking boots all year round and stood in a rooted stance, as if steadying herself in preparation for the next thing coming her way.

'I don't know. Do you not think it kind of muddies the roles a little? Like, where does his role end and the woman's start?' Megan said, mouthing *take one* silently to Yara, who shook her head at the biscuits and carried on scanning the noticeboard for other groups and sessions she could take Maya to.

'Everyone works it out for themselves,' Sally continued. 'I was chatting to Steve, you know your man with the wee goatee thing, the one who always gets the kids playing those mental games? Well see, he said he liked the break from work, gives him the chance to be with the kids otherwise he'd hardly see them.'

'He's a bit much though isn't he?' Camila said covering her mouth as she bit into the arms of her gingerbread man. 'He's like an overenthusiastic kids' entertainer or something.'

Sally heaved up Martha who was letting out low tired groans by her feet and said, 'Well, we have to come here, why shouldn't they? It's not just our job, is it?'

'You wouldn't know that to look around this place though, would you?' Camila balked, gesturing at the room full of women, children, and Tim who was now quietly reading a book to his daughter in the corner, trying not to attract attention.

'Camila, I meant to ask, was that the builder on the phone before?' Megan said pulling at the black tights covering her thick thighs and rearranging the gusset under her wide jersey dress. 'What's the latest with the house?'

Sally and Yara looked at each other with a common desperation in anticipation of what they were about to experience. Neither shared Megan's interest in Camila's house build, nor did they have the stomach for the level of detail and drama that was about to unfold. Camila normally spoke at a scattergun rate but when the subject of her house extension came up the pace and pitch hit a warp speed. As Camila dived into details about the builders' delays, their substitution of the Danish wood she'd ordered for a cheaper timber and how the marble sink from Italy for the downstairs toilet was still stuck in customs, Yara gathered together some flyers for yoga classes and toddler gymnastics from the noticeboard and Sally excused herself to find Martha's shoes.

'But you know what the fucking worst thing is?'

'Camila, honestly your language,' Megan chuckled with blushing cheeks.

'Sorry, do-you-know-what-the-worst-thing-is?' Camila said slowly feigning atonement before resuming her optimum speed. 'It's that they have that Makita radio on full blast. All I can hear, all bloody day, sorry Megan, is that idiot Nick Ferrari on LBC or Capital FM banging out that shitty chart music all day. I can't tolerate it anymore.'

*

Yara thought then about the things that she had tolerated in the past: the crunching IBS that strangled her stomach, coriander on her dinner when she'd asked for none, the mother-in-law who hated her, the supposedly good intentions of others, her family being priced out of the area she'd grown up in, being scared that no one would take her pain seriously when she was in labour, being followed around the boutique shops that now populated her local high street, being told she was very articulate by patronising white managers. A foul smell broke her train of thought, she looked down to see Maya nursing a full nappy and took her to the baby change room.

Anjwar couldn't understand why she kept going to the playgroup.

'Why do you hang out with them if you don't like them?' he'd asked one night as he was preparing Yara's favourite chilli dish for dinner.

'Because every few weeks there's a new stage and I've got no idea what I'm doing. Who else is going to show me how to do all this mum stuff?' Yara had replied hazily, pulling the tight curls along her hairline straight then letting them spring back into place.

'Nobody knows what they're doing though. Why don't you ask my mum, or my sisters? Or like, the whole of the internet?'

'Stuff online just makes me more anxious and as if I'm going to roll up and be like, "Mumsy, you know how you hate me and think I'm incompetent and not good enough for your son, well what do I do if my daughter won't eat vegetables or sleep through the night?" Imagine!'

'Yeah fair, I can see how that wouldn't go down well. But like, are there no *other* women with kids at these things that you can hang out with? I see loads of women hanging around with buggies chatting shit.' Taking a taste of chilli from the pot on the stove he lifted his knee sharply and snapped his fingers, 'Oh shit, that's good. Taste that.'

Yara leant over the table to meet the spoon he held out for her, 'Yeah that's good, you know you should put some dark chocolate in that, it'll lift it.' Anjwar pulled his face and side-eyed her.

'Swear.' She mirrored his exaggerated expression. 'Anyway yeah, mums and shit. It's not that easy. They're all the same. I can hear the conversations all over the place. I don't have the energy to start again and go through all that getting to know you bullshit. It's boring. At least with these three I know what the levels are and I can just get into it when I need their help. Anyway, Sally's OK.'

'The Irish one?'

'Yeah,' Yara sighed, scraping sleep out of her eye. 'I just wanna feel settled y'know? Like I'm on top of things for a bit.'

'Babe,' he said, moving to her side of the kitchen table, pulling her up by both hands as her body tried to stay rooted in the chair. 'You're doing the thing yeah. Give yourself a break.'

'But it's never-ending,' she pressed her face into his neck. 'The other mums ...'

Anjwar pushed her straight out in front of him and dipped his head to look her in the eyes.

'Fuck those other oat-milk-flat-white-in-a-bamboo-keep-cup mums. Yeah? Look she's gonna be in nursery from next month, then you can go full-time at work again, get back to you a bit.'

Yara lightly banged her forehead against Anjwar's chest and closed her eyes, trying to work out whether now was the time to get into why going back to work full-time wasn't going to make it all better.

'You're not your mum, or those other mums.'

'Babe,' she said, holding his face in her hands.

'Yeah?'

'Your breath stinks.'

'Nooo, you did not play me like that,' Anjwar howled, playfully grabbing her in a headlock as a screaming Maya ran down the hallway into the kitchen, eager to join in on the play-fight.

'Should we go then?' Camila shouted above the heads of the other mothers who were trying to squeeze small chubby feet into overpriced children's shoes.

Everyone agreed, gathering up their children and bags full of milk, wet wipes, snacks, crumbs and rotten banana skins. There was a tailback of buggies jostling to get out of the playgroup gate as women with fixed smiles tried to pretend they weren't desperate to barge everyone else out of the way. Yara saw Camila with Archie and Megan with her twins making their escape at the front of the queue. They had a favourite corner in Pret and raced there every week before any of the other mothers arrived. The corner they preferred housed two hard sofas and was nearest the toilet; the proximity to a changing facility was viewed as a benefit, but Yara thought it stank of stale vagina and the pink disinfectant they used so didn't see the appeal.

Walking down towards the café Yara and Sally pushed buggies that cradled their sleeping children past the park where they'd first met. Huddled under a nearby tree, an embarrassed flock of identical Bugaboos faced different ways, unwilling to look at each other. Children sped down slides, a mother pushed a small fleshy blob on a swing while scrolling through her phone, larger boys who should have been in school blasted a football against a wall, and a little girl sat alone at the top of the climbing frame talking to herself. Yara looked at the far corner of the park where she'd first met Sally.

That October morning Yara hadn't seen Sally approaching from where she'd sat on the cold concrete. She hadn't noticed anything around her, all she could focus on was blocking out the noise of Maya's red-hot screams. Strapped into her buggy Maya had thrashed from side to side, stiffening her back into a rigid position of rebellion, pushing away sleep, pushing away anything Yara offered her. In defeat Yara had retreated and collapsed onto the ground with no next step in mind. Sally had been trying to calm Maya down for several minutes before Yara had realised she was there.

'What's going on here little one? Ay? What's all this noise about?' A red-faced Maya squirmed to avoid any direct contact with Sally, writhing more violently than she had before, but Yara didn't move.

'There, there,' Sally repeated, offering a small purple box of raisins at arm's length. 'You're just testing out your lungs, so you are? Testing that everything is working OK?' Maya stopped screaming and looked at the box through glassy eyes, blowing condensed whimpers that shook her small body. 'Here you go, you hold on to this now.' Sally motioned the box closer and Maya took it slowly. 'There we go,' Sally said, and looked towards Yara. 'I hope it's OK to give her raisins?'

Yara nodded but didn't say anything.

'Are you OK?' Sally asked offering a packet of wet wipes. Yara nodded again and remained silent, her hand automatically plucking out wet wipe after wet wipe.

'Do you want some water?'

Yara shook her head. Without realising how many wet wipes she'd gathered she rubbed the clump of damp cloths over and over her face until it stung.

'She just wouldn't stop crying,' she said dropping the sodden mass to the ground, not blinking. 'I couldn't stop her crying.'

'Ach, you're grand. It gets like that sometimes,' Sally said picking up the discarded wipes, shoving them into the bottom shelf of Martha's pushchair. Making sure the breaks were on both buggies and giving the children a satellite-sized rice cake each, she sat down on the pavement next to Yara.

They didn't compare routines, Sally didn't ask Yara how the feeding was going or if the nights were OK now, if she was getting enough time to herself or if she needed help. They both knew the horrors she'd been through to get to the point of sitting in the middle of a pavement in October. The horrors that from one minute to the next can crush and dissipate until you can't remember what you did with your day and if you're doing OK or not. They just sat side by side watching random children enact games that made no sense. They simply breathed into the space between them and shared the last box of raisins, selecting individual wizened grapes from the allocation in their palms. Parents walked around them without comment and after some time Yara said she had to get back for the boiler man. They stood up together, wiping away small pebbles from their jeans, which left indentations in the flesh of their buttocks. They never talked about that day again and Yara was always grateful to Sally for that.

Walking towards Pret, Yara and Sally's phones beeped simultaneously then Sally read out the message from their WhatsApp group.

'We got the seats,' she said flatly.

'Oh my days, those fucking seats!' Yara blurted out. She thought about not going, about cutting off onto the path that led straight home but as Sally talked about the weird couple from the dating show they both liked who only spoke in baby voices, Yara found that her feet followed Sally's voice until suddenly, without realising it, Pret was in front of them.

The favoured corner had already been completely commandeered by the time Yara and Sally arrived. Buggies strapped with bags, cups, scooters and a large pack of nappies took up any spare space around them. Other customers rose onto their tiptoes to squeeze through any available gaps.

'Which way did you two walk? We would have missed the seats if we'd waited for you,' Camila said, a buffering hostility in her tone.

'We walked down past the park and along Clissold Avenue,' Yara responded casually, peering into the buggy to check that Maya was still asleep.

'What? That's miles out of the way. It's down the dodgy streets as well.'

'Do you two want a coffee?' Megan shouted over from the counter.

'Yes please, can I just get a normal tea?' Yara said quietly, hoping Megan would match her volume.

Megan's whole face smiled back before she directed it to the barista and shouted her order straight at him.

The children who were awake squealed loudly. Open, uneaten sandwiches spilled out onto the sofas, a discarded macaroni serving sat face down on the table and a carton of orange juice slowly leaked its contents onto the floor under the sofa. Yara felt sick at the mess. Sally took Martha to the toilet as Megan shuffled through the buggies with a tray of hot drinks.

'Here we go. Honestly, it's just coffee, coffee, coffee until it's an acceptable time to drink alcohol, isn't it?' She giggled into her pillowy breasts, accidentally sitting on a packet of Pom-Bears which crunched mercifully underneath her.

'Yara, are you going to the doctor's near Grove Road?' Camila asked blowing the froth on her coffee.

'Yeah, I'm just a bit worried about Maya's chest again.'

'Poor thing,' Megan said. 'It's that time of year when the bugs are going around isn't it? Good you're going to the Grove Road doctors, I can't stand the surgery at the other end of the market, it's always full of scruffy people and it's so much rougher down that end.'

'Yeah, but you can get cheap veg on the market. I love looking through some of the tat they sell on the stalls,' Camila grinned, distracted by the stream of limited-edition rugs she was scrolling through on her phone.

'Actually yes,' Megan said brightly. 'I do like to go to Poundland or Lidl every now and then to see what offers they've got on and some of the characters round the market are quite entertaining. I'll give you that, but it's so dirty.'

Yara looked at the children eating their snacks on the floor, she looked at the rubbish that surrounded them, the dirty buggies strewn around the café and for a second thought about what it must be like to believe that everything existed for your own personal entertainment or consumption. She realised that for Megan and Camila, the market with its makeshift stalls selling fruit and veg by the bowl, manned by sellers shouting 'Pound a bowl, pound a big bowl. Biggy, biggy big bowl,' offered them the chance to dip in and convince themselves they weren't a hundred per cent middle class if they still bought the odd item from a traditional working-class market, even if that odd item was a bag of Hass avocados.

Chatter from the surrounding customers distracted Yara. The Turkish men opposite laughed at a phone they all huddled around, a woman in a blue hairnet carried out a tray of fresh baguettes from the kitchen whilst a Deliveroo driver flirted with the blonde barista with the thick eyeliner. A young man typed heavily on a small black laptop, and dotted all around were small pods of women feeding and wiping wriggling toddlers and babies. Maya stirred in her buggy, a foot rose up followed by a splayed hand struggling to grasp on to anything to pull herself out of the horizontal position she found herself in. A dummy fell out of the buggy, followed by a confused groan.

'Hello MyMy. You must be hungry? Are you hungry?' Yara spoke softly to her daughter who smiled, revealing a mouth filled with small white Tic-Tac teeth. She squashed the back of her chubby paw into her eye and rotated it, willing herself to wake up. Yara sat Maya up gently, pushing back the curls from her face, giving her water from a sippy cup and mixing up the lunch of rice and sweet potato she'd made earlier that morning. Fully awake, Maya said 'I do it,' pulling the spoon and bowl of food towards her as Megan and Camila planned what they were going to make for dinner that night; what they would order online during nap time that afternoon; where they were going with their big group of uni friends at the weekend and what kind of mirror they were going to get installed in the second bathroom.

'If you're walking up to the doctor's, you'll go past that lovely photography exhibition on the wall at the top of Grove Road. It's nice to have a look at as you walk past,' Megan said, running her finger along the inside of her son's chocolate pudding pot and licking it off greedily.

The outdoor exhibition was a series of thirty-two photographs pasted up onto a wall on the street where Yara's old friend Jade and her family had once lived. A photographer had recently moved there from Hackney and wanted to 'celebrate the community that welcomed his family to the area'. Jade and her family didn't feature in the exhibition. They'd had to move out when their landlord sold the house to a family with a whippet and Land Rover Destroyer. The new occupants were photographed smiling on the doorstep where Yara had fallen and lost her front tooth when she was six, the doorstep where she and Jade had made face cream out of water and talc and tried to sell it to the passing neighbours, where they'd sat and eaten ice lollies as the summer street parties rumbled by and the sound systems rattled the windows. The original front door had now been replaced, painted in Farrow & Ball French Gray, framed by freshly landscaped pampas grasses and lavender bushes.

'It's such a cute thing to do. It's nice to see all the families who live there, there's a really nice mix of people,' Camila said of the thirty white and two South Asian families. Yara saw a version of the next five minutes where she explained why it wasn't a cute thing to do, why it wasn't a really nice mix of people. She saw Megan and Camila's blank faces, their responses of, 'It's not their fault, they only bought a house for their family,' and the inevitable awkwardness she'd feel responsible for.

'I'm off. I need to get to the doctors,' she said putting down her half-drunk coffee and packing up Maya's lunch Tupperware.

'Yeah I would get there early, you know what they're like if you're late,' Camila sighed without looking up from her phone.

'You going already?' Sally asked, closing the toilet door behind her and standing on the periphery of their area.

'Yes.'

'Do you want me to walk up with you?' she asked as Yara bulldozed Maya's buggy towards the door.

'No, I'm good,' she said, without turning her head back.

'Alright, mind how you go.'

*

Yara pushed Maya and her buggy away from Pret. Away from the conversations still ringing in her ears, the conversations that caused her hands to repeatedly squeeze and release the pushchair handle. She walked for a while feeling the weight of what she wished she'd said, what she wished she'd done. *But where does it end* she thought, *where would I even start?* Maya's sweet voice pulled her attention back. She was singing her version of the nursery rhymes they'd sung that morning. Not fully able to pronounce all of the words, she replaced the difficult sounds with her own repertoire. A formative language only understood by the small pod of her, Yara and Anjwar. Sounds and words that they had to translate for friends, relatives and strangers.

Reaching the end of her nursery rhyme playlist Maya started pointing out the places she recognised on the walk to the doctor's: houses of friends, the park where she played, a favourite tree and the beginning of the alleyway that led to the playgroup. Maya pointed, 'Paygoop, I wanna go paygoop.' Yara stopped walking. She stood very still and stared down the path where more mothers and babies were gathering for the afternoon session, a fog of animated faces, ARKET puffer jackets and white Veja trainers clogged the pathway. She felt a physical sensation rising, which she struggled to translate, a disorienting sickness, a dizziness. She tried to regulate her breathing. In her peripheral vision a woman walked slowly towards her, moving closer. The woman said something that Yara couldn't make out, she flinched and looked, struggling to place the smiling face staring back at her. 'Hello baby girl,' the woman said, 'it's me, Veronica.' Yara burst forward grabbing and hugging her, wiggling them both from side to side in a unified embrace.

'Veronica, oh my god. How you doin'?'

Veronica laughed into the cloud of mango-scented curls tied back at the nape of Yara's neck and patted her body up and down. 'I'm doin' good you know. How is this big girl doing, let me see her ey?' Veronica leant down, resting her hand on her knee to get level with Maya who squealed in delight at all of the noise and attention. 'Well, well. Look at this gorgeous girl, my baby girl and those teeth, she got all her teeth now.' Veronica laughed looking up at Yara.

'I know, she's gonna be moving out soon.'

'Right – she can come and live with me. Look at those cheeks.' She rubbed Maya under the chin wobbling her putty-like face. 'You girls off to the playgroup?'

'No not today. We …' Yara stopped and looked down the alley where the last of the mothers were filing into the gate. 'We don't go there anymore.'

'Ah well, you move on don't you.'

'You do. We move,' Yara said, smoothing down her eyebrows absent-mindedly.

'Anyway. Where you going? We're walking up to the doctor's, you going that way?'

'Yes honey, I've got a couple of appointments at the baby clinic this afternoon. Come, I'll walk with you.' Veronica put an arm around Yara's shoulder as they walked on in synch. 'So how you been? Tell me what's been 'appening? It feels like forever.'

'It's been a lot but we're doing good.' Yara leant forward to caress the glossy wells of Maya's hair. 'We're doing good.'

Single Serve

The toothpaste on Diane's toothbrush that languished on the side of her bathroom sink had hardened by the time she reached the bus stop. In between turning the radio on and off five times, checking the kettle was unplugged and waiting for trails of school children to file past her front door, she had completely forgotten to perform the basic ablutions of her day.

On the top deck of the bus her tongue skated across her teeth, scaling the sludge that coated each incisor, canine and molar. The sensation triggered a memory of the elaborate performance she used to put into not brushing her teeth as a child. Behind the locked door of the bathroom, she would run the tap for the length of time it would take to brush her teeth, deposit a small plop of toothpaste down the plug hole and flick her thumb across the bristles to mimic the noise of the brush against her teeth. It was never clear who this ruse was for. No one was keeping track of her movements, least of all her teeth-brushing regime. At school she would scrape off the yellow build-up on her teeth with her nails and wipe it onto the blazer arm of whoever was sitting next to her.

Smelly breath had never been a thing when she was a kid, she never worried about it. Before leaving the house in the morning she'd sometimes swill down room-temperature milk without a thought of how fermented and fuzzy her breath would be by 9 a.m. Now it was all she could think about. Mentally she mapped out the route from her final bus stop, along Pilgrim Street and down to work. If she took a detour to Eldon Square she could call in to Boots to buy a toothbrush and toothpaste. But, as the bus crawled around the corner to her stop, she saw a line of people already snaking around onto the high street from the alley that housed the cinema where she worked.

'For fuck's sake,' she whispered as she waited to get off the bus, recoiling at the smell of her own breath. Feeling the pressure of the queue she dived into the first newsagent she came to, where she bought two packets of peppermint chewing gum and the fail-safe egg and cress sandwich that she ate every Tuesday and Thursday for her lunch.

Tuesday mornings at the cinema were the Silver Screen Club, a programme slot catering exclusively for the over-65s. Every Tuesday, regardless of the film, the cinema was packed out with baby boomer women and their occasional male companions. This audience always arrived early and complained about everything – the free tea and coffee was either too hot or too cold, the auditorium was too hot or too cold, the film was too loud, it wasn't funny enough, it was too long, the story didn't make sense, someone was talking in the auditorium – it didn't matter if the issue was outside Diane's control, they often weren't interested in what she had to say, they just wanted to vent their frustrations. Over the years she'd learned not to interrupt, she simply listened impassively and gave them whatever they demanded.

A few weeks earlier one of the regulars had complained that the actors in the film she'd watched mumbled too much.

'I missed the bit about where he had taken the girl because of the mumbling. I didn't know what was going on. Why do the actors mumble so much these days?' As the woman spoke Diane had inspected the long tusks she had for teeth. Frightened gums had receded to reveal sensitive roots and ridges where her teeth had once begun. Diane pictured her drinking a hot cup of tea, wincing like an actor in an advert for sensitive toothpaste and wondered if her own lack of brushing would increase or delay gum erosion. Not wanting that thought to escalate she concentrated on tapping each left-hand fingertip against her thumb. The woman pulled out a screwed-up cotton handkerchief from the sleeve of her cardigan and had continued to complain as she blew her nose in short, sharp spurts.

'You know, PSSSSSHHHHH, I come here every week, PSSSSSSSSHHHHHHHH, and I feel it's just not PSSSSSSSSSHHHHH good, PSSSSSSSSHHHHHHHH enough.'

Diane had nodded silently and tried not to fixate on the nasal bacteria multiplying within the cloth that the woman had tucked back into her cuff. Switching her focus, she'd examined the cauliflower hair sprouting up all over the woman's head and the delicate red scalp that lay in between each floret. The vulnerability of these thinning patches made Diane motion her to a quieter section of the foyer away from the crowds spilling out of the stalls. They moved in unison across the mosaic floor, partners in a dance they'd both rehearsed week in, week out. The woman had then complained for another six minutes before Diane could pacify her with a free ticket for the following Silver Screen Club, and a promise that the sound would be turned up significantly for future presentations.

'That would help, thank you,' the woman had said, walking away with a lightness to her step.

That Tuesday morning, Diane felt rushed and rattled. The teeth-brushing situation had thrown off her usual routine. She passed the queue of women in linen trousers and wide-fitting Deichmann shoes, saying quiet hellos to some of the regulars but avoiding any direct eye contact. The doors didn't officially open for another forty minutes and she knew some of them would be angling for an early admittance. Diane made a mental note to turn the sound up in the auditorium as she walked through the office, straightening and tapping her usual touch points as she went: the paper feed on the printer, the framed poster of Marlene Dietrich that refused to stay at a right angle, the empty tin of Quality Street on Val's desk from her birthday six months ago.

In the breathless staff kitchen, she filled large self-serve flasks with tea and coffee in the ordered and very specific way she filled them every week. In the auditorium she pulled two long trestle tables out of the large storage cupboards and laid out one hundred and twenty-four cups and saucers with all the handles and teaspoons facing the screen. There were only a hundred and twenty seats but one hundred and twenty-four was divisible by four; a safe number. Alongside the precise lines of cups and saucers Diane poured out single-serve packets of Biscoff biscuits into four large wicker baskets. She liked to watch for the women who stole handfuls of biscuits. Some acted as if they were taking spares for their friends, only to stash them in the pockets of their TK Maxx handbags the minute they were back in the safety of their seats. Others were more obvious and didn't engage in any subterfuge, unashamedly they plugged handfuls of biscuits into their Regatta jacket pockets and poured milk into their tea unfazed by any onlookers.

Through the tiny window of the projectionist's room at the back of the auditorium, Diane surveyed her work. She turned off the overhead lights and brought up the sconce and screen lights to reveal the auditorium in its full art deco glory. Originally built as a picture house the cinema had screened films since 1937 and still carried most of its original features alongside some bodged attempts at modernisation from the seventies. Diane had worked at the cinema in various roles for twenty-five years, most of it was habitual now but some elements still moved her. Stepping into the building, she was sometimes transported to a different headspace. The way the gold stage lights hit the folds of the deep-red satin curtain that concealed the main screen, it tricked her into thinking she was part of something grander and more glamorous than the reality of her front-of-house job. The intricate mosaic floors, the wide sweeping staircase that delivered you to each floor, the pleasing curves and lines of the design detail in the plaster – the whole thing seduced her. She wasn't in a dusty old cinema, she wasn't just Diane the front-of-house manager, on some days part of her believed that anything could happen in this place because the moving pictures on the screen told her so. Isn't that why we watch films in the first place, she thought, to trick ourselves into believing that a different reality is possible, if only for ninety minutes.

Andrew was late. She knew his excuse would be family-related: his wife had made him go and buy Cumberland sausages and a pound of tripe from the butchers as if it was still the 1950s. Or he'd had to call into his mam's to fix her blocked sink, or his uncle was in hospital. There was always something. Halfway through counting out her float for the fourth time and lining up the coins in equal tower-block piles he bustled in through the side entrance that connected the cinema to the bar next door.

'Woah, they're wild out there today, aren't they?' he said taking his jacket off as he walked over to the box office at the back of the foyer.

'You're late,' Diane said without looking up from the cityscape of coins in front of her.

'I know, sorry …' Andrew started a story that began with a late bus and involved a runaway dog, but Diane zoned him out and continued counting piles of five-, ten- and twenty-pence pieces.

He scanned the noticeboard as he finished his story and ate the Biscoff Diane had saved for him. He'd grown a beard recently; it was his latest attempt to distract attention from the hair loss on top of his head, which he tried to conceal with brown hairspray. This clumsy cover-up intrigued and endeared Diane in equal measure. She considered how sad his hair loss must have made him for this to be his preferred alternative. She pictured his ritual every morning as he brushed wisps of hair into place, angling a hand-held mirror at the back to make sure he hit the right area. Pumping the brown spray in gentle bursts from far enough away so he didn't leave angry brown spots on his bare scalp. She wondered if he stood in the shower at the end of each day until the brown water ran clear, and what he looked like without this industrial brown skullcap? She wanted to ask him so many questions about his hair, or lack of it, but he never mentioned her tapping, counting or checking and she never mentioned his hair.

Float fully counted, Diane logged in and out of the ticketing system twice, cleaned the serving hatch with antibacterial wipes, untied and retied her shoelaces, refreshed her chewing gum, adjusted her seat and called 'Let the silver surfers in!' to Andrew who was braced with the keys at the double doors.

He turned the key announcing, 'Here we go!' as the automatic doors parted slowly and small groups of babbling women in beige clothes shuffled in.

Everyone else refused to work the Tuesday morning shifts but Diane didn't mind, she could understand why the women of the Silver Screen Club had such bad attitudes. They'd had a lifetime of annoyances and they weren't prepared to be agreeable anymore. Why shouldn't they complain to Diane about the lukewarm tea in their cup? She represented the collective history of every cup of tea that had gone cold because other things demanded their attention, and she was going to hear about it. They had put up with years of unappreciated child-rearing, errant husbands, low-paid jobs or no jobs at all. Now they operated under the radar of society, no one expected anything from them and that lack of interest freed them from the constraints of being nice. They were role models for Diane. She couldn't unleash her inner crone. For now she had a job to keep that entailed managing staff, keeping customers happy and being amiable to her boss, but these women and their freedoms gave her hope.

With everyone in their seats, Biscoffs secured in bags and film projected on the screen, Andrew announced his return to the box office with a heavy sigh. Diane answered a phone call about that night's screening times.

'If you go onto our website all of the times are updated each day, they're on the homepage … Yes, the first page you come to … No problem, you have a good day too. Bye.'

Andrew sighed again as Diane put the phone down. 'Have you finished the rota for next week?' he asked.

'No, I'm doing it now,' Diane answered without taking her eyes from the screen. Sensing Diane's concentration, he busied himself behind her: picking up and putting down old newspapers, piling up popcorn cartons and tidying packets of M&M's before finally deciding to reorganise the noticeboard directly to the left of Diane.

There wasn't enough room for him to do this without encroaching on her personal space. With anyone else she would have moved her seat sharply under the desk to physically communicate her annoyance at this invasion, but with Andrew she let the wheels on the office chair nudge back imperceptibly. Aware of his body beside her she could feel the warmth of his stomach near her head as he took down A4 notices about eating smelly food in the box office and paper printouts of the rota for last week. People drifted in and out of the automatic doors going up to the tea room or into the bar next door, bringing in with them notes from the panpipe performers at the Monument.

'Did you see this?' Andrew handed Diane an A4 sheet she had put up on the noticeboard two weeks ago announcing that the cinema was looking for a head of special programming and inviting internal applications.

'Yeah, what about it?' she said, still looking ahead at the computer screen.

'Well you should go for it.'

'Why?' Diane replied, her fingers hovering over the keyboard.

'Because you'd be perfect for it. You love all the obscure stuff. You could put together amazing new seasons and stuff.'

'I wouldn't get it.'

'How do you know?'

'Because of course I wouldn't get it,' Diane said turning to face him, looking up at his whole body. 'I haven't got a degree in film or whatever they're asking for. Anyway, I'm happy as I am, I couldn't be doing with the extra hassle.'

'Well I think you should at least apply. I'd rather you got it than any of those poncy film studies students.'

Looking up at Andrew's soft tummy rising and falling rhythmically in front of her she said, 'Maybe.' Then, worried Andrew could smell her breath, she swung her chair back to face the computer screen.

She looked at him tidying papers in the reflection of her screen, lining the unused pins along the top of the notice-board behind her. She had the urge to ask him if he wanted to go for a drink after their shift like the younger ushers did with each other but they'd never done that before and she wasn't sure if it would be weird. Weird in the way work friends are weird when you see them outside of the physical place that binds you to each other. Within the walls of the cinema their shared love of film and fantasy fiction created a closeness, but outside the cinema their relation-ship was untethered. Diane had once bumped into Andrew, his wife and their two daughters at the supermarket, she'd thought about pretending she hadn't seen them but they were walking towards each other on the same aisle, there was no escape.

'Hi!' Andrew had called over to her from the other side of the pasta section.

His wife eyed Diane suspiciously as if she was a charity fundraiser knocking at their door on a Sunday evening.

'Andrew!' Diane had called back, trying to match his tone and enthusiasm, her foot kicking the back wheel of her trolley.

'Fancy seeing you here. Marianne, this is Diane from work. Diane, this is Marianne and the kids,' he'd said, push-ing two bored-looking tweens towards Diane.

His wife wore UGG boots that had collapsed at the inner ankle, giving her the look of a depressed camel, her leopard-print top revealed flushed pink cleavage that started at the base of her neck.

'Marianne so nice to finally meet you. I've heard a lot about you and the girls,' Diane had smiled, hoping her forced effort wasn't too obvious.

Marianne had pursed her lips and tightened her eyes, but she didn't say anything. The girls shuffled, trying to escape Andrew's grip on their neck. The smallest one pointed at the aubergine in Diane's hand.

'What's that?' she'd asked.

'This?' Diane said holding up the vegetable she hadn't realised she was carrying. 'It's an aubergine. I make curries with them.'

'Urgh, that's minging.'

Diane wasn't sure whether she was referring to the vege-table, if she knew what an aubergine was, or if it was the mention of a curry that had offended her.

'Chantal, don't be rude. Diane makes great curries, she brought one into work once. You'd like them.'

'No, I wouldn't. How do you even know if I'd like her curries?' the youngest daughter had said, wriggling to free herself from Andrew's hand.

'Remember that curry Diane, it was a belter.'

Diane smiled and nodded, fuming that she'd had to live through the exact experience she'd hoped to avoid.

'Well, I better get on,' she had said then, pushing her trolley past Andrew, her eyes had locked on the dirty tiled floor in front of her.

'You're on with Jan tonight, aren't you?'

'Yes, you in tomorrow?'

'Yes, see you then. Say bye girls.'

The girls had smiled at her sarcastically before turning to join their mother who had already walked away towards the butcher's counter.

'See you Andrew.'

Diane decided not to mention a drink outside of work. Instead, she uploaded the rota to the staff portal, checked it had loaded three times, wiped down the keyboard and pushed her seat backwards.

'I'm going to take my break now; can you check that the rota has uploaded properly while I'm gone?'

'Yep, will do. What have you got for lunch today?'

'Just an egg sandwich. I was running late this morning, plus it's Tuesday so ...'

'Come on, on your birthday?' Andrew stood flush to the noticeboard to let Diane out, not wanting to make a big deal of the day he knew she was trying to avoid. 'No, no no. At least treat yourself today of all days. Go and have a hot chocolate or a bloody brownie or something in the tea room.'

Diane looked down at the sweaty egg mayonnaise sandwich in her hand, the wilted sprigs of cress that pressed against the cellophane like stray pubes. She tapped the bottom of the wrapper ten times. 'I'll see what cakes they've got on,' she said.

'Good!' Andrew smiled.

*

On the way up the wide staircase, past the gold cornicing, Diane counted each step as she thought about her bad breath mixing with Andrew's bad breath to make a super massive black hole of bad breath, then flinched away the thought with ten taps on her forehead.

In the tea room on the second floor, a palace of film memorabilia, red velvet seats and black Formica tables, she chose to sit tucked away in the left-hand corner behind the door. Seeing her enter Pat came straight over from behind the bar.

'Hi Diane, nice to see you in here.'

'Hiya, how you doing?'

'I'm doing good, nice and quiet this morning before the Silver Screen rush.'

'Yeah, brace yourself,' Diane said, sitting very still and upright.

Collecting an empty cup and saucer on the next table Pat asked, 'What can I get you?'

'Can I get a Darjeeling tea and what flapjacks have you got on today?'

'No flapjacks today I'm afraid, we've got a jam and coconut slice or a lovely gooey brownie that our Davey made himself this morning.'

'A brownie?' Diane said tapping her chin quickly with her middle finger. 'A brownie?' she repeated.

Pat smiled at the second mention of a brownie. 'Do you want me to get you your tea and I can come back?'

'No, I can decide. Can I get the jam and coconut slice?' Diane said slowly.

'You sure?'

'Yes.' Diane paused momentarily. 'No, can I get the brownie? And can I get a knife and a fork with it?'

'Course you can.'

Diane fidgeted, pulling at a colony of bobbles that had formed around the elbow of the green woollen cardigan she'd bought in a charity shop for £3.50. Rapidly tapping her fingers against her thumbs Diane looked around the room at the other customers to see if she recognised anyone. Some of the younger office staff from the cinema were having a meeting in the corner, repeating the words 'convergence commission' and 'disadvantaged youth groups'. A member of the Silver Screen brigade who mustn't have fancied the film but wanted to get out of the house sat quietly with a pot of tea, working her way through a Sudoku book whilst Pat and her husband Davey answered questions to a radio quiz that was blaring loudly from the kitchen.

In the mirrored film picture of *Cleopatra* that hung to her left Diane looked at herself in between the inked outlines of Elizabeth Taylor and Richard Burton in a deep embrace. Her skin was pale, her lips were thin and cracked, a copse of nasal hair stuck out of her left nostril. She rubbed her small, naked eyes and pulled her hands down her face, dragging her jaw down into her neck to create as many chins as she could. She inspected whether her teeth had discoloured since not brushing them that morning. Were they more or less yellow than yesterday? She couldn't tell for sure, but she thought they were probably more discoloured as a result of her neglect. Aware that the

Sudoku woman was watching her, Diane smiled weakly and picked up her phone. The time read 13.35, after her shift finished at 5 p.m. she had two and a half days off. With no one at home to reflect her behaviour back to her or comment on what she was doing, Diane had developed the domestic quirks of someone who had lived their entire adult life on their own. Alongside the unwavering tics that had established themselves into the core of her daily routine, her sporadic impulses were the subtle ones that she indulged on a whim, the things that you might suppress if you lived with other people because they'd be difficult to explain. She sometimes read in the corner of the landing because the carpet there was thicker, she once wondered what the skirting board would feel like pressed against her cheek, so she tried it – cool and smooth as suspected. She lined her plants up when she watched a film so that they could all see the screen equally. She watched ASMR videos of a woman called Maria folding plastic bags whilst eating cold custard from a tin and arranged her books in the order she imagined Anne Frank would like to read them. She cherished the small pockets of freedom she allowed herself in the privacy of her own home. It was comforting to have a release from surveying the outside world for affirmations that she was indeed disgusting, but lately she had started to wonder if these eccentricities could sustain her. These routines and rituals she'd created to reassure herself that she existed weren't working like they used to. Her head was becoming fuzzier, her attention waning, the anxiety was always rising inside of her to a higher water mark no matter which compulsion she indulged in.

*

Seeing Pat making her way over with her order, she began to count from a hundred to zero. As she hit sixty-five, Pat said, 'Here we go, one Darjeeling tea and one of our Davey's famous brownies.'

'Lovely thanks Pat.'

'No ...' she said pausing to place the teapot down and turn its handle towards Diane, 'bother.'

Moving her hands from the table to the red velvet seat that ran the length of the tea room wall Diane steadied herself then drummed her fingers on the plump rich material. She lowered her head and eyed the brownie on the faded pink tea plate in front of her. Unwrapping the knife and fork from their napkin blanket she cut the brownie in half. A heavy goo stuck to the knife and bulged slightly into the free space between the two halves. Diane thought about wiping the knife with her napkin as she usually would but that day she licked each side clean until she could see her warped reflection. The armpits of her staff T-shirt flushed damp with sweat. Poised with her licked-clean knife she cut the two halves into quarters then into eighths until the brownie was dissected into small square sections that reminded her of the film poster for *Hellraiser*. Lancing one of the pieces with her fork she raised the brown square with glass-like sides up to her mouth and placed it on her tongue. A piercing sensation instantly shot her in the head, it ricocheted through her jaw, down her spine and into her groin. The frenzied feeling sparked a projection of images in her mind: she was with her grandma in the café where they used to go each week until she was eight, they were eating cake, it was her seventh birthday, her grandma was telling her that she was a good girl, that she'd take her to the park after they'd shared the cake. As her grandma smiled a light flashed, a projector bulb burned through the film images in her mind and her grandma's face disappeared. Diane turned back to the mirrored film poster next to her and in between the negative space of Elizabeth Taylor's body, with chocolate smeared all over her teeth, she gave herself the widest shit-eating grin she could manage as the Sudoku woman looked on.

A bustle of energy and the overpowering scent of Anaïs Anaïs by Cacharel burst through the doors of the tea room. The Silver Screen film had finished and its patrons were on the hunt for tea and scones. The woman who had complained about the mumbling a few weeks earlier moved as a pod with four other women to a table near Diane. They settled themselves with a lot of huff and puff, moving seats and closing the open window nearby to stop the breeze that Diane had been enjoying.

They all agreed they'd get the soup and a sandwich with all but one deciding on a glass of red wine to accompany. 'Why not, it's a Tuesday,' the anti-mumble woman said to the table before creasing her face up in laughter and grabbing the arm of her friend to steady her wheezy hysterics. Diane was entertained by the good time the women shared together in their small brigade. She ate her brownie slowly and listened to them shrieking with laughter as they shared stories about accidently farting in garden centre queues, unbothered that everyone outside their circle could hear their conversations. Around the flatulence-induced amusement, they passed on helpful gardening tips, talked about their grandchildren and their latest trip to Valencia, the Lakes or Cuba on an all-inclusive cruise. They helped diagnose each other's medical ailments: 'That sounds like piles to me, but I'd still get it checked.' They were confused by technology: 'I don't use Google Maps, I can't work out which way it's telling you to go.' They shared experimental recipes: 'So I mix the sausages in with the pearl barley and then at the end I pour mango chutney on top.' And they all had unpleasant things to say about women called Eileen or Dorothy, women who were married to controlling men who wouldn't let them drive on their own or go to the cinema on a Tuesday 'because he wants her to go to the big Tesco with him'. They all agreed they wouldn't put up with it.

As Diane stood up to leave the anti-mumble woman spotted her. 'Diane,' she called.

Surprised she knew her name Diane looked over and waved. The whole table beamed back at her, craning their necks or holding on to the backs of their chairs to swivel around and see her properly. Unsure whether to go over Diane hovered awkwardly between the tea room doors and the table she'd been sat at, but bolstered by a large glass of red wine the anti-mumble woman beckoned her over. 'I just wanted to say thank you for making sure the sound was turned up this week, it was much clearer.'

'Much clearer,' the other women agreed like a small but enthusiastic congregation.

'Good, I'm really glad it helped.' Diane smiled. She asked if they had enjoyed the film, to which they responded with an in-depth and insightful review mentioning tropes and issues she'd not spotted.

'We love our Tuesday cinema trips, don't we girls?'

'We do.' They all nodded. 'Highlight of the week,' one of the women with wine-stained teeth said. On the back of her chair in a large gaping pocket Diane saw a collection of stashed Biscoff biscuits. She smiled broadly and said, 'Have a lovely afternoon ladies, look forward to seeing you next week.'

'Bye Diane,' they chimed together.

On the landing outside the toilets and the tea room, the rest of the Silver Screen contingent were saying their good-byes and brushing their cauliflower hair with pearl-handled combs they'd had for forty years. Slipping quietly up the stairs behind them was a small figure that made Diane's pupils widen. He crept up weightlessly taking two steps at a time, making no noise, sticking to the wall as other customers circled down the wide staircase. Diane had never seen him in the flesh, she'd only ever seen his pixelated CCTV image on email attachments and printed memos. In real life she was surprised at how childlike his frame was, how much he looked like a character from a social history documentary on Liverpool in the 1970s. His navy-blue parka was ripped and shiny with grease, the fur from the hood completely moulted. His Gola trainers were worn on the side where Diane could see some discoloured socks that had once been white. She was also surprised to see him during the day, he normally seemed to strike later in the evening when there were fewer staff members and customers floating around. Struggling through the barricade of Silver Screen clubbers, Diane couldn't reach the men's toilet in time to block his access. Not wanting to draw attention to anything amiss, Diane smiled at the women and headed down the stairs as quickly as he had come up.

Interrupting Andrew flossing his teeth in the box office, Diane shouted, 'Tommy the Shitter just went into the men's toilet.'

'No, no, no, not today,' Andrew replied, struggling to untangle a length of floss from his back molars. 'Why today? Is anyone else due to come in that can deal with him?'

'No, there are no other men in until 6 p.m. tonight. Should I call the police?'

'You can't call the police because someone shits in a urinal.'

'He wiped it all over the walls the last time and flooded the first floor by blocking the sink with paper towels.'

'Fucking hell. I'll go, I'll go ...' Andrew said finally yanking the floss free and rushing to get the mop and bucket from the basement. 'Don't call the police,' he shouted from the stairs at the back of the box office.

'OK, I won't. But you need to properly warn him this time.'

In the box office, Diane pulled at the fraying skin around her fingernails and tried to care about the dilemma a woman on the phone was having. She couldn't decide whether to get her friend an annual ticket for the cinema or take her away for a birthday spa weekend.

'I suppose she'd get more use out of the annual ticket but she'd really remember the spa weekend, wouldn't she?'

'I suppose,' Diane replied with her middle finger in her mouth, trying to stem the bleeding she'd caused by pulling on a ripcord of dry skin.

As the woman on the phone continued to divulge unnecessary facets of her friend's personality that might help in the decision-making process, Diane heard footsteps running down the stairs. Tommy's body hit the tiled floor of the foyer with a thud and bounced out of the open double doors. Pausing in the alleyway he turned back to stare at Diane. The woman on the phone carried on talking but Diane didn't register what she was saying, nor did she move from her position. Tommy corrugated his face to move his glasses further up his mole-like muzzle and stood feet shoulder-width apart, his hands on his hips. Unblinking, even when the automatic doors threatened to close then snapped open on registering his presence. The air in the foyer fell still. No one cut through the alley to catch their bus home, no one came in to wait for their friend in the warmth of the foyer, no one let the glass door of the bar prang shut as they went up to use the cinema toilets. No one moved until Diane slowly raised her bleed-ing hand to wave at him. Mirroring her action Tommy the Shitter lifted his hand smoothly into an open palm and they stayed like that until he abruptly broke his stance and ran away.

'Hello, hello, can you hear me?' a small voice came out of the phone breaking Diane's daze.

'Listen,' Diane said wiping the blood from her fingernail onto the thigh of her jeans, 'it's your decision. Why are you wasting my time with this?' before putting the phone down and switching the ringer volume to silent.

Twenty minutes later Andrew came down with an empty mop and bucket. 'Had he?' Diane asked.

'He had.'

'Was it in the urinal?'

'And on the floor.'

'Oh wow.'

'I suppose everyone's got their thing, haven't they?' Andrew sighed as he shrugged his shoulders and took the mop and bucket down the stairs to the store cupboard.

'Put some bleach on that mop,' Diane shouted after him and thought about what Tommy had done, how he'd manoeuvered himself and how he felt in the aftermath. Whether he'd be high on success and relief or full of remorse? She hoped he was happy.

As the bells from the Northern Goldsmiths clock rang out to mark 4 p.m., Hannah, a Primark goth from the Wirral who had not long been an usher, emerged from the stalls and asked if she could start her break.

'Yes. I'll cover you. I love *Punch-Drunk Love*,' Diane said.

'Really?' Hannah asked without looking up from her phone. 'It's super weird so far and it's got Adam Sandler in it. Why are we showing an Adam Sandler film?'

'Because it's part of the Paul Thomas Anderson season and you would know that if you paid any attention,' Diane snapped back. Andrew looked at her with surprise and admiration but Hannah, who was already halfway up the stairs smiling into her screen, didn't notice.

Diane crept into the end seat on the back aisle of the stalls. The warmth and darkness of the auditorium made her instantly sleepy and relaxed. The film was near the end. Adam Sandler's character had escaped the violence and blackmail of Philip Seymour Hoffman's character. He'd followed Emily Watson to Hawaii and they were in bed together fully clothed. It was her favourite scene. In the frame the two figures are horizontal silhouettes on top of each other, the light from the open door behind them obscuring their features. Stereotypical Hawaiian music soundtracks the scene as they kiss and whisper things into each other's mouths. Adam Sandler apologises for not shaving, Emily Watson's character tells him his face is so fucking cute and that she wants to bite his cheek. His nose is in her eye socket and he tells her he wants to smash her face in, she says she wants to suck his eyeballs out and have them with melted cheese, he whispers: 'OK, this is funny. This is nice.' Diane's eyelids blinked slowly, her mouth turned upwards into a sloth-like smile and she hugged her arms around her own body, her bingo wheel of thoughts quiet for the first time all day.

After covering Hannah's break Diane floated back up the stairs to the box office. Andrew had wiped down the cash desk area in anticipation of her return and sitting in front of the computer was a small, perfectly wrapped gift, bearing a neatly written-out card that read, 'Diane'. She sat down in the padded office chair and handled the small, book-shaped object carefully. She smiled like a gaping envelope, clamping her lips shut when from behind her Andrew said, 'That's for you. I know you don't like a fuss but I was in Waterstones and I had to get you something for your birthday.'

Diane tried to minimise her embarrassment and excitement, pushing down on both emotions, willing them not to show in her face, in the colour of her skin, in the warbling tone of her voice.

'Open it then,' he encouraged, lifting up his hands in his trouser pockets but never fully removing them. Diane relented, bringing the gift to her lap, bobbing her head from side to side as she ripped into the wrapping paper, which gave away easily to reveal a signed copy of the last book in *The Dark Tower* series.

Looking down at the opened gift she said, 'Wow, I don't know what to say.'

'It's nothing. I still can't believe you haven't read it. Let me know what you think when you've finished it.'

'I will. Thanks.' Diane didn't move, she didn't pick up the book to read the blurb on the back or mindlessly flick through the pages. She looked up at Andrew still standing with his hands in his pockets and said, 'Are you doing anything after work?'

'No, Marianne's making lasagne but not got nowt special on.'

'Well, I'm going for a birthday curry with my brother and the kids on Friday but I didn't plan anything tonight. You know what it's like with birthdays, forty-nine isn't really something to celebrate. But … if you're not busy and you have time would you want to get a beer after work?'

Without looking away, Andrew said, 'Every birthday is worth celebrating, let's do it. I'll text Marianne and say I'll be a bit late. I can get the 6.30 bus instead.'

'Great.' Diane smiled.

The autumn daylight had faded outside. Diane could see their reflections in the glass of the automatic doors opposite, the box office lit up like a stage. Behind her Andrew tapped a message to his wife into his phone, 'Babies' by Pulp was playing in the bar next door. She could see her own sloping shoulders in the staff uniform T-shirt, she could see the dark circles under her eyes, her flushed face, and she smiled as she thought: OK. This is funny. This is nice.

Self-Portrait

'Maria just promise me it'll be ready for the show, OK? I think that piece will be the perfect way to close the exhibition.'

'Yes, yes Chloe I try.'

'Can you confirm it will be ready for the show?'

'I can confirm that I try to have it finished for the show. OK now I go. Bye.'

Maria put the phone back into its cream cradle in the corner of her living room and let her breath carry out an extended, 'Stuuuuuupid gallery woman.' Chloe's inane chatter had made her miss eleven minutes of *Jeopardy!*, which would bring down her average score per episode. Settling back into the armchair that held the mould of her body she muttered unfavourable things about Chloe and reached for the remote. Turning up the TV, Maria shouted: 'Who is Ronald McDonald?' and took a sip of her hot lemon and honey.

*

Across town Chloe briskly tapped a message on her iPhone screen. If her face could move it would have registered a great displeasure.

> She said she'd try but honestly, we need that final piece. Jeremy can you or someone from your department go over to her studio and see where we're at ?????

The sharp clacking noise of her nails hitting the glass screen satisfied Chloe that she'd made the urgency of the matter clear.

As the closing credits of *Jeopardy!* rolled up Maria's screen she turned down the volume but left the TV on. Her stomach stirred and she thought about making some dinner. She was staying at her place that night, in the fridge there were left-over herrings and a Middle Eastern salad from yesterday, but no bread. She decided she wasn't hungry, not for herrings and salad anyway. On the small kitchen table, the draft catalogue for her exhibition poked out from underneath a pile of circulars. Bernie often commented that Maria was the only person in the whole Brooklyn borough who actively looked forward to that plastic-wrapped pile of flyers and brochures arriving every week. Poring over the gaudy images of processed food regulated her breathing. She loved examining the price drops on Klondike bars, Ronzoni pasta and racks of ribs. Each week she cut out the special offer coupons and took them to the various participating stores near her apartment. These ad circulars encapsulated what had initially excited her about her new home in America: the choice, the colour, the abundance. Rationally she knew that the deals were never worth it and the products were never as good in your hands as they were on the page, but she was always seduced by the potential. It drove Bernie crazy. She didn't see it as exciting, she saw through the brands expertly designed to feel like old friends. She only saw waste, excess and the annoyance of having piles of paper everywhere. She wouldn't have them in her apartment.

Reading through all of the flyers Maria made her way down to her exhibition catalogue. Printed on the front cover in heavy red pen Chloe's scrawl read: AWAITING MARIA'S COMMENTS. Another thing Chloe had been fluttering about. Maria scrabbled for the reading glasses hanging on a chain around her neck and found a stubby pencil in the kitchen table drawer. Each page of the catalogue pictured various thumbnails of her paintings alongside basic information including the title, the date of the artwork, the medium and which collection the piece belonged to. These details annoyed and amused Maria. She looked at Renata's thumbnail. Renata had chain-smoked in Maria's living room for four days in 1973, she didn't say a lot at first, then on the third day a tidal wave of her sorrows and hardships flowed out. The children she'd lost, the parents overseas, her true love in Chicago, the husband who couldn't find work, the rare moments of joy and tenderness she found in between each unbearable heartache. Renata offloaded it all as Maria painted what she saw in front of her. No one in that white sterile gallery would ever understand Renata's life or the lives of the other people on the walls and in the catalogue. The gallery didn't believe in giving any backstory to the work.

'Viewers should be allowed to bring their own interpretation to the art, allow their own imagination to read what they see,' Chloe had said to Maria with a fixed smile when she'd first asked about this.

'What if the viewers have no imagination?' Maria had replied.

'Oh, you are funny.' Chloe laughed, flaring her nostrils.

Maria hadn't meant it as a joke.

The image of Bernie in the exhibition catalogue was the portrait Maria had painted when they first met. It had been acquired by an influential collector when Maria's work was first discovered. They now owned this version of Bernie, choosing to place her 'in conversation' with one of Georgia O'Keeffe's New York cityscapes on the vast wall of a vapid Miami home where no one ever witnessed the interaction. Bernie's portrait was seen as a pivotal piece in Maria's archive, so the collector – feigning humility and generosity – loaned it for the upcoming show knowing all the while that the visibility from the exhibition would only increase Bernie's value. Since the original sale Maria had tried to buy it back on numerous occasions but Chloe always said: 'It doesn't look good to do that. It's better placed in that collection.'

'But I painted it. It's Bernie's painting.'

'That's not how it works,' Chloe would insist with her eyes suspended mid-blink.

*

Everyone at the gallery spoke to Maria as if she was a child or hard of hearing. They were always fussing over her whenever she saw them. Did she have enough water? Was she warm enough? Could she hear OK?

'I'm not a dog,' she complained over dinner at Bernie's apartment.

'Ah honey, I know they're annoying but they're helping with your career.'

'What do I need a career for? I'm seventy-five years old, I've managed totally well without until now.'

'Oh, get on, imagine you at thirty-five in that crummy apartment in Queens with Pavel breathing down your neck and no money in your purse. You'd die to hear yourself now,' Bernie said, taking a sip of the red wine they'd bought on a trip to an upstate winery.

'They don't give shit about me, they just want money from sales. I'll be worth more to them dead. I bet they can't wait for that. No more silly Russian woman to deal with. You know they still think I'm Russian?' Maria pushed the greens around on her plate and continued muttering.

Bernie started to clear the dishes and kissed the top of her head.

'The other day I was trying to remember my old ZIP codes. You know, the ZIP codes of the old apartments,' Maria said wiping the side of her mouth with a napkin.

'Why? Did you need them for some paperwork?'

'No. I just wanted to see if I could. I don't know, like a test or something, like when you try to remember who your best friend was when you were five.'

'I don't do that.'

'OK but I do and you know what I realised?'

Bernie shook her head as she ate the last piece of bread on the centre plate.

'I never knew them. I never knew my own ZIP codes. The only ones I know back to front are yours and mine.'

Maria reached out and kissed Bernie's hand, letting her pull it away very slowly as she cleared the rest of the table.

Maria had painted Bernie in the lounge of the Queens apartment where she'd lived with her husband and two daughters. This was where she created all of her early work whilst her family was at work or at school, when it was just her and the person she was painting, before the collectors and galleries and museums and studios of her own. She was never nervous when she painted someone's portrait, she loved the intimacy and exchange of stories, but Bernie's presence made her search for the words that usually fought over each other to leave her mouth. To make her sitters feel comfortable she would open with her own tales, sharing anecdotes from her life in Lithuania, Turkey and now Queens. With Bernie she didn't know where to start, everything seemed boring and obvious. Bernie was neither of those things. Maria had watched as Bernie moved her body in the chair, trying to find the most comfortable pose for the duration of the session. Her legs crossed and uncrossed, her long arms draped themselves this way and that, her chest protruded and sank inward, her fingers trailed her neck, her thighs, her lower back. She settled with her legs crossed, one arm slung around the back of the chair, the other across her lap.

'Are you comfortable?' Maria had asked, pretending to prep the canvas she'd already prepped that morning.

'Yes, very.'

That summer had been hot. The traffic outside her third-floor apartment was persistent, no air blew the net curtain that hung limply over the open window. When Maria looked at Bernie to gauge her proportions, she met her gaze in a way that made Maria feel like her skin had fallen off. It was as if Bernie could see the inner workings of her body and mind: the blood hurtling from her heart to her groin, her winded lungs, her stomach lurching, her legs struggling to maintain her position. Avoiding Bernie's gaze, Maria mapped the outline of her body with long elegant lines, then she shaded where the light couldn't fall on the folds of Bernie's clothes, the left side of her face, the inside of her crossed leg. Bernie's collarbone was bare until it met her shoulder and disappeared under her cotton dress. Recreating that part of her body on the canvas confused Maria's senses, she couldn't decide if she was going to sneeze or burst into tears. She could smell the coconut and almond oil on Bernie's hair and blended colours to match her skin: browns, a rich ochre, deep reds. Bernie talked about her new job as a professor of English Literature at the City College of New York, about the books she was excited to introduce her students to and the struggles she'd been through to get to this position. Maria wanted to listen to her forever.

It had been forty years since Maria had painted that portrait. In the painting Bernie wore her hair in dreads that were long gone, now replaced by a closely cropped style and commanding grey colour. She still wore the bright clothes she had always loved, calling attention to herself, demanding to be noticed. 'I dare you to look at me,' her clothes said, 'I exist.' Maria had gone the other way. Once she had left her husband and found an apartment of her own, she started dressing exclusively in white. 'Everything matches!' she explained when anyone ever asked why she dressed that way. She washed and starched everything she'd worn that week on a Friday morning and hung it all out to dry on the fire escape, then pressed it carefully in the evening. Her small apartment was above an old plumbing supply shop that was now her studio. Just like her clothes, Maria had whitewashed the apartment, long before it was fashionable to do so. She'd bought a small sofa and armchair, a kitchen table, three chairs (one for her and one for each of her daughters, never used), a rug from the Persian brothers down the street, a bureau for writing letters to her sister in Prague and three yucca plants.

Now everything was simple and calm. The chaos of her childhood, the dark ocean passages, the oppressive bubble of Queens – they were all in the past, all boxed in a neat compartment that could be taken out and examined with archival gloves but never re-enacted. Now she painted in her studio during the day, ate herrings for lunch in her apartment above, watched *Jeopardy!* at 7 p.m. every evening and stayed at Bernie's place Saturday to Tuesday.

On Sunday mornings Bernie made eggs in the kitchen which looked out over the small yard she tended to. She grew salad leaves and tomatoes in the summer, which climbed up a trellis Maria had helped her build fifteen years earlier. They went on dates to Manhattan to see exhibitions at the Guggenheim or the Met, and ate pastries in Central

Park or drank fresh lemonade if it was warm. Maria linked her arm through Bernie's on those walks and closed her eyes when Bernie kissed her forehead.

On summer evenings Maria made salads like the ones she used to order at the beach in Tel Aviv where she spent one summer in her twenties and they drank rosé listening to jazz through the kitchen window. They lay on Bernie's sofa and watched films one after another. Maria liked old French films and Bernie liked anything with Meryl Streep or Whoopi Goldberg. Sometimes they fell asleep on the sofa, locked onto one another, Bernie would wake Maria in the middle of the night and lead her to the bedroom where they'd remould around each other until morning.

Every other Monday they went to Maria's favourite Japanese restaurant in Midtown. Bernie hated it. She hated Midtown, she hated the tourists, she hated that they had to get there at 5 p.m. to avoid the huge queues. She hated how rude the staff were and she hated that people now stared at their phones when they were eating dinner, but she never complained and went along with it because Maria loved it. She loved the ritual, she loved getting ready to go out with Bernie, putting on a freshly pressed pair of white trousers, a fresh white shirt, a white waistcoat, a white overcoat and her red lipstick. She loved riding the C train from Bernie's neighbourhood in Brooklyn over to Manhattan, in the carriage she read whatever book she was into or people-watched. Tired people, lost people, people in love, people in quiet contemplation. She was always surprised by how many people were willing to risk having their lives torn to shreds by the rat race of New York. The myth of New York had you believe that the city was full of millionaires but they were the minority. The city was powered by people who rode the subway every day, who hustled and haggled trying to formulate their lives into something that resembled the American dream. Just like the circulars, even though Maria knew the myth of New York was a façade, she still believed in it. She still loved coming up from the subway station on to 42nd Street where the energy of the city made her lean forward. It was intoxicating for her and had never lost its charm.

In the restaurant Maria always ordered the same dishes, ebi dashimaki and a salmon tonyu nabe set with extra bonito flakes on the side. Bernie sometimes suggested new options but mostly she'd learned to let it go. She knew that each of the rituals Maria held so dear had brought beauty, meaning and order to her life when it had felt out of control. In return for this understanding Maria went to Bernie's church every week without a murmur of resistance, she cooked her dishes that she didn't eat herself and sat through plays she didn't understand. To Maria this give and take was the greatest expression of love. To let someone show you their most secret selves and not judge them for it – that was real love for her. On the way home with her stomach full, Maria would rest her head on Bernie's shoulder and fall asleep with the bobbing motion of the C train.

Winter tightened its grip on New York as Maria set to work on the last painting of her solo exhibition. Hurtling icy winds from the Atlantic blew straight down the wide avenues into the solar plexus of people scurrying around. The door of Maria's studio was a huge wooden hulk that shrank or expanded depending on the weather. To stop the winds blowing underneath the gap between the door and the concrete floor she put down old blankets and sheets as if she was tucking it up at night. Chloe always made a huge production around the door when she brought potential buyers to the studio.

'This door Maria, it's so classic but so heavy. You should get your assistant to organise a replacement.' Chloe knew Maria didn't have nor want an assistant.

In the studio she installed the prepared canvas on her easel. She turned up the wall-mounted radiators and brought two electric heaters closer to her chair. She tilted the blinds, turned on all of the wall and ceiling lights and took off her robe. She sat very still and looked at her naked body in the large mirror set up opposite the easel. Staring at herself, she let her eyes glaze over until her vision became blurred, until she was just a hazy outline. Then she started to paint.

Quick lines cut across the canvas creating a faint silhouette. With the outline in place, she focused on the sectional detail of her seventy-five-year-old body. Her stomach now hung low over her pubic area like a heavy bag of flour, she exaggerated this dip with a deep navy-blue line on the canvas. Her breasts splayed out to the sides attached to her chest by a length of delicate pancake skin, her nipples resting near where her belly button creased in on itself. The skin on her neck trailed down from her chin to the centre of her clavicle, a length of loose skin that she sometimes teased and wobbled when she watched TV. She mixed blues and greens to shade under her eyes, a pink, white and orange to fill in the swathes of skin over her middle and limbs, shading the folds under her breasts and around her jawline with a purple and light brown. She moved her mouth in the mirror and held it in a defiant position, bringing red and grey around her chin, cheeks and ears. Her paintbrush followed the uniform waves of her silver hair down to a precise line along the bottom of her ears.

Maria looked at her body with wonder, this sturdy frame and collection of soft tissue had brought her so much joy, it had carried and protected her. It had moved her across continents, connected her with the people she loved and it had allowed her to feel the sensation and pleasure of being loved. When Maria turned fifty-five she was momentarily angry with her mother for not having warned her about what happens to the body as it ages. It amused her now that this had ever made her angry – as if her mother had ever had the capacity to prepare her for anything in this world. She swapped brushes to pay careful attention to the smaller details, the moles, the more intense changes in her skin tone, the scars and the pockmarks. She painted it all.

Blending greens and blues on her palette, fragments of landscape from her village in Lithuania came to her mind. She saw small but specific sections of fields that led her to the blueberry forests where she used to play as a child and the Šventoji River where she fished with her grandfather. This sometimes happened when she worked, outdoor vignettes came to her, spliced into everyday thoughts like a glitch, disappearing as quickly as they came. She could never latch on to the images for long enough, they snapped back if she tried to examine them or look directly at them, she had to let them play in the background and steal glances as they flickered by. She thought about how life in the village went on when the crops failed or an animal died or the men went away. She thought about all of this as she brought her sitters to life on the canvases that separated them; the people whose portraits she painted to keep them alive, to keep them with her.

When her daughters were young, she'd painted them in between persuading the neighbours to sit for her. She loved to look at the young girls she was raising, their dark eyes, their full mouths and cheeks that wobbled when they ran. She'd looked for clues in the faces of those little girls. What were they trying to tell her that they couldn't say out loud? Who might they become? But they gave nothing away. Looking at herself now she couldn't see her daughters anywhere in her face, she could only see her grandmother and the other older women in her family: Yuliyah, Lyudmila, Polina, Rimma, Vikusha. The women who had showed her how to cook and clean and sew and iron and mend things. Skills she no longer needed. Now she painted herself naked in her own New York studio.

How strange life is, she thought. How strange it is that now a young woman with bright white teeth and an insistent mouth called her to check up on the status of her naked self-portrait so she could sell it to a stranger. People who Maria would never meet would look at the painting, at her, and say things like: 'Such a powerful piece of work.' And yet, she thought, my daughters and the women who raised me will never see me like that, they'll never see me. What a strange world indeed.

*

A loud knock rattled the studio door.

'Who is it?' she called, struggling into her robe and turning down the radio.

'It's Jeremy ... from the gallery.'

'*Sušiktas* Jeremy,' she said to herself, struggling to cover her naked body. 'Hang on, I'm coming,' she shouted towards the closed door.

Opening up to the blisteringly cold avenue Maria thought she might scream in Jeremy's face but she managed to stifle her howl. Shuffling back in thick socks, slippers and Bernie's puffer jacket, her grey robe hanging limply underneath, failing to cover her bare legs she said, 'Jeremy, let me see. Chloe sent you to check up on me, yes?'

'Ha! No! Of course not, no, no ...' Jeremy stuttered flapping out of his jacket like a defensive pterodactyl. 'I just wanted to call by and see how you were getting on. It's so cold out there, are you keeping warm?'

'Do you want some tea?' Maria asked ignoring Jeremy's questions.

'Erm, do you have any fresh coffee?'

'No. I have hot water and tea bags. You want or not?' Maria said filling the kettle with the plug slung over her shoulder.

'OK yes great, super. I'll have whatever you're making.'

Maria smiled with the top half of her face and turned back to the sink.

'Is this the final piece for the show?' Jeremy asked, walking over to the wet canvas.

'It's the painting Chloe told you to come and chase me about, yes. I'd rather you not see until it's finished, don't touch anything.'

'No problem,' Jeremy said walking towards the easel.

Standing against the makeshift kitchen in the corner hugging a hot-water bottle to her stomach Maria watched Jeremy eyeing the work she'd asked him not to look at. The arrogance of these people still astounded her.

The kettle fizzed and whistled in the corner of the studio kitchen. Maria poured boiling water over a crumpled tea bag in a stained mug and took it over to where Jeremy was standing next to her half-finished painting.

'While you're here Jeremy, you can do something for me?' she said handing him the hot tea.

'Yes, of course,' he replied, adding, 'if I can,' not wanting to commit to anything that might get him into trouble later and struggling to hold the burning mug with its thin inconvenient handle.

'I've seen the proposed layout of the show and I don't like. Can you change the layout to this one that I like?' Maria showed him a hand-drawn plan of the gallery with the names of the portraits next to arrows where she wanted each of them to go. Jeremy looked over the scribbled piece of paper trying not to grimace.

He let out a choked laugh, 'I'll try my best Maria but the show has been curated in a specific way to show—'

'Jeremy,' she cut him off, 'let me make clear for you. If the exhibition of my work that I have painted over the last forty-five years isn't hung like it is on this paper there's no exhibition.'

'I don't know if you can do that.'

Maria stared at him with a mouth so small and purple he had to look away.

'I promise, I'll make sure this happens.'

'Thank you, Jeremy. Now drink your tea, you must be freezing, no?'

The gallery opened its doors at 7 p.m. Maria and Bernie arrived at 5.30 p.m. to have a final look-over of the hang of the work.

'Oh my god Maria, do you love? Are you in love with it?' Chloe gushed as she took large glugs of her champagne and rattled by their side in the first room.

Maria was about to walk away but Bernie held her hand and said, 'Yes, Chloe. We love it. Maria is very overwhelmed. Aren't you?'

Maria smiled and nodded slowly. 'Yes. It's emotional. I haven't seen some of these paintings for a long time.'

'I can totally imagine. The buyers are going to love it! Oh and the sale you wanted me to take care of is all confirmed.'

One of the gallery assistants who had been hovering at the side moved towards Chloe but she held her hand up and said, 'I'll come to you.' Turning to Maria and Bernie, 'Excuse me will you.'

'Of course.' Bernie smiled.

'That woman is idiot, Bernice. Idiot.' Maria whispered sharply.

'Oh be nice, she's just a little wired.'

'And weird.'

'Which ones have sold already?'

'I don't even know what she's talking about.' Maria looked away distracted. 'Come, let's get a drink.'

*

The gallery was still very quiet as the staff glided around silently making final amendments to things that didn't need fixing. Maria and Bernie held hands as they walked around the rest of the rooms. Some of the people in the portraits Bernie knew, others were faces she'd seen on canvases in Maria's studio, a few of the earlier works featured people only Maria knew intimately, people she hadn't seen for years – a meeting of old friends in a starkly lit gallery. She told Bernie stories about George who had ran the tailor's on her block, Carlos who danced in secret, Pappi who ran the bodega on the corner, Damon who worked for Pappi and carried Maria's shopping bags past the men on the corner and Nancy, the woman who lived on the fifth floor of her building with her six children, three of whom she brought to every sitting. Those faces were all gone, the paintings were now worth more money than had passed through all of their lives combined.

'Come on,' Maria said touching Bernie on the elbow, 'let's keep going.'

The walls of the last room were painted a deep burnt orange as Maria had requested. Two portraits hung side by side on the back wall under the glare of perfectly positioned spotlights above. Bernie squeezed Maria's hand as they stood looking at Bernie's portrait from 1977 and Maria's self-portrait from 2017. The two women stared at the illuminated versions of themselves and each other. Bernie moved forward and locked eyes with herself.

'Bernicccccceeee,' she laughed. 'Look at you girl.' Bernie walked towards the painting fanning her face with the exhibition catalogue. She inspected the thick layers of paint that had fixed this version of her in time for forty years, the oscillating brushstrokes that sculpted each curve and directed her eye. Bernie remembered the day in 1977 clearly, she remembered the intimidating woman with the foreign accent who wanted to paint her portrait. She remembered the bright blue eyes expertly reading each section of her being, the quick hands translating her onto the canvas. She remembered the bizarre noises that Maria made and the questions she asked to keep her engaged without needing to. That day they had both unravelled in front of each other, reassembling over time into softer, more tender versions of the people they had been. Eye to eye with her raw edges Bernie smiled and felt an excitement for all that young woman had to look forward to.

Outside of the gallery Bernie hailed a cab to take them across town.

'Up to West 41st Street please.'

'We'll never get in now,' Maria pulled back on Bernie's arm. 'There'll be a queue all the way around the block, let's just go home. I'm tired and I need to lie down.'

'Oh, stop whining, trust me.'

Too tired to argue Maria got in. Resting her head back against the plastic back seat she closed her eyes, aware of the city lights moving across her face as they drove up town. Without queuing Bernie guided Maria through the door of her favourite Japanese restaurant and gave the hostess a hug. The waitress who Bernie normally cursed out on the way home showed them straight through to their usual table where two places were set. The restaurant seemed different at this later hour, the customers weren't the same as the earlier crowd, they were younger, louder. The air had gathered velocity over the course of the service, steam and grill heat mixing with the hot bodies of over seventy covers.

Eyes flitting over the menu Maria couldn't settle on anything, even the thought of her favourite dishes failed to spark her hunger, the nerves and adrenaline from the evening were still making her nauseous, her appetite not able to find its way back yet.

'You probably won't be hungry but you need to eat. Are you going to have your salmon set or do you want to share something small?' Bernie asked still looking over the options through her reading glasses.

Maria's eyes welled up and she hid her face in her napkin. All her life she had wanted to feel understood in the way that Bernie knew her. She couldn't let herself think about the years that had come before. When she watched Bernie cooking or held her hand in the cinema or glanced at her joking with the cashier in the bodega she felt a deep grief for all of the years that had been spent without her. Large blobs of water tipped out from her eyes onto the table as she lowered her napkin.

With her hand on her stomach she quietly said, 'I wish I'd known you all my life.'

Bernie leant across the table and said, 'Honey, you've known me for half of it and I'm here now,' as she lifted Maria's hand to kiss it repeatedly.

'I love you,' Maria said. 'You know that don't you?'

'I know that. I know that.' They each held one another's hand over the table and Maria dried her eyes.

'Should we get the usuals?' Bernie asked.
'Yes, the usuals.'

The following autumn, a month after Maria's funeral, Bernie took delivery of a large pallet. Three men unloaded and unpacked two large canvases that they gently carried up the stoop resting them on wooden blocks in Bernie's apartment. When they'd finished she tipped them $100 over and closed the door. In the lounge she unwrapped the last of the packaging, laid out the two canvases side by side and took a step back. *Bernie*, 1977 and *Maria*, 2017 met her gaze. She sat facing them, matching her own pose until her legs went numb. It was the same feeling she'd had in Maria's apartment, but back then she'd not moved. She'd sat perfectly still, knowing that with each brushstroke her life was moving and morphing into something completely new. Something unknown and terrifying but equally exhilarating. She stood up and went over to Maria's self-portrait, taking in lungsful of air, trying to consume the smell of oil paint that used to follow her around. She put her face up to Maria's and stared into her eyes, those perfect dancing blue eyes, the dashes and lumps of paint applied by Maria's own hands. Bernie smoothed her hand over Maria's hair and kissed her painted mouth.

'I love you Maria Katzen,' she said with her eyes closed. 'You know that, don't you.'

Acknowledgements

The sixteen-year-old me who sat and stared at the train tracks that led out of my hometown, desperate to escape, would die at me now writing acknowledgements in my own book. It would never have happened without Michelle Kane who I am forever indebted to. Thank you, Michelle, for being so open and supportive.

Thank you to Saba Ahmed, Eve Hutchings, Liv Marsden, Nicola Webb and the rest of the team at 4th Estate.

Also, a huge thank you to the brilliant Abigail Bergstrom whose feedback and input really helped craft these stories into what they finally became.

I'm grateful for my family, especially Dan for the laughter, support and endless encouragement and for my mam who has been a constant source of love and light.

Thank you to all the women and girls in my past, present and future. I love you all.

In loving memory of Leanne Soulsby.